TILDA & LÆRKE

Pat Halford

© Pat Halford
Kuopio, Finland, July 2023

done enough international TV interviews and podcasts over the years, and her *LinkedIn* following was almost as big as her bank account. Not that she ever checked either. She was always too busy attacking the next opportunity.

She's heading north now, silently cruising up the spine of Jylland. Her breathing has slowed down and she forces herself to relax her fingers and loosen her grip on the wheel.

Her name is Tilda.

At least that's the name she has used for twenty-three years. She still remembers her given names and she misses them. The thought of her birth first name brings back an assault of memories that she tries to keep locked in a chest, buried deep underground. But when she is alone and driving, the memories dig themselves out and consume her.

She forces herself to lock them back in the box. No time for such distractions over the next few days.

Three cities. Three kills. Four if she's lucky.

Her *iPhone* cheeps and she looks down at it. Her CFO is calling her. She sends it to voicemail and then sees there are another thirteen missed calls from various executives, two investors and one of her biggest suppliers. She made it clear that she was unavailable for a few days. That worked out well.

She lowers her window to let some fresh air in. The silent EV's powertrain interrupted only by the noise of rubber on tarmac, and it serves to bring her back into the present. She looks in the mirror again and runs through her plan for the ten thousandth time.

She knows she can't control every variable. Yet she has built her business empire on precision and control, and that, after all, was how she operated twenty-eight years ago.

In *The Unit*. Precision was her kill-set.

She subconsciously moves her right hand to the old wound on her stomach. You would hardly notice it these days, but it's still a bit tender. She probes it with her index finger and gets the welcoming painful response. It grounds her. It reorientates her back onto her mission. It reminds her of the day they executed her on the Minorcan beach in another time.

She laid low on the big island for five years after Isabella found her in a pool of blood-soaked sand. Eventually, she dared to make her way up to Munich where she got a series of jobs in restaurants. It was there she met the man who would be her real saviour. He would give her shelter and opportunity. And she would grab that opportunity to shape her purpose.

He was long since dead, but he had bequeathed his estate to her, for she had given him as much as he had given her. He had lost his wife and daughter in an accident.

Accident! They were slain by a drunk bastard masquerading as a technology CEO on an autobahn. They were buried, and he got away with it. But not for long. Tilda visited him once.

He was never seen again, and it became one of those cheap TV documentaries where they use C-level actors and voice-overs to try to create a dramatic effect. When Tilda watched the program she wondered who had created such a shitty script. After all, she had ended his life in a totally different way!

Tilda had only known the family for three years, but she had become close. The woman was in her fifties and had given birth to the child quite late. Tilda had babysat for the young girl as the man and woman were central figures on the Bavarian power circuit and dined out many times a week. After their deaths, the man was inconsolable, and he took to the bottle and began to lose his grip on his company.

Tilda, for this was the name she had by now adopted, began to help the man to respond to his emails. As he came to depend on her more and more, so she learnt more and more. Her skills in precision and simulation enabled her to spot when a cabal of executives and activist investors were making a play to oust the man from his position as Chairman of this great enterprise.

He had watched her with awe and then with pride as she reasserted his position in the company through her dramatic actions. He knew he would never return to be the titan of industry that he once was, for his sorrow at the loss of his wife and child was too much to bear, and the alcohol was driving him to an early grave. Yet he resolved to yield Tilda as his industrial sabre, and he spent four more years training her on the known and unknown dark arts of industrial power plays.

He introduced her to all of his global connections across his banking, political and intricate corporate networks. And did she yield it! She transformed *his* business into *her* business, and he was as proud of her on the day he died, as on the day he first met her, when he saw how she told the rude customer to go fuck himself in the Munich restaurant.

He had always known that she carried a heavy burden, and he did not question why she invested so much time and money transforming herself physically. He knew her demons were ever present, and she would tell him about them when she was ready. She never did.

She kissed him on his forehead just after he passed away. Then she buried him in the reserved space next to his beloved wife and daughter.

It rained at the funeral and Tilda stood there in the spring drizzle for some time after the rest of the mourners had departed. Eventually, the Priest returned with an umbrella and put his hand on Tilda's shoulder causing her to jump. The Priest took a step back when he saw the look in her eyes, for it was as if he had seen the depths of something so vengeful. He rushed back to his duties without looking over his shoulder.

Tilda, drenched from the rain, walked back to the BMW limo and climbed into the deep, black leather seat and touched her stomach wound.

She looked icily out of the window across the graveyard. Now she knew what she would do. And now she had the assets to do it.

A breaking car ahead jolts her out of her memories, and she again checks herself in the mirror. She reminds herself that this is now real. It will happen after all these years. She has three stops on her itinerary.

Jylland. Fyn. Sjælland.

And she will kill them all.

His name's Nikolaj and he runs hot and cold, depending on the news cycle.

It's a late Monday lunch, and it's the worst time of the week for him. He spent the whole weekend preparing, then appearing on the usual TV shows, offering his biting commentary, laced with stand-up comedian levels of humour, on the latest political and business scandals. And now on Monday he falls back down to earth.

It's been the same cycle every week for the last ten years. Like withdrawal symptoms. He knows he's addicted. He also knows his addiction has fuelled his success.

And destroyed two marriages, the relationship with his son, and scared off countless potential partners. Well, countless meaning two. One of whom actually sued him. She was an American journalist in Copenhagen. That went south fast, together with his bank balance.

He managed to recover his savings through, the publication of a couple of books, the syndication of his English-speaking podcast, and regular gigs on the weekend talk shows.

To the outside, things might have seemed rosy. But the outside world did not inhabit Nikolaj's inner most workings. Nikolaj's biggest regret, though, was his relationship with his son. He hadn't seen him for a couple of years. He'd turned up at a restaurant with his ex-wife, who still hated him, for a dinner to meet his son and his new wife. You could cut the atmosphere with a knife. And good old Nikolaj was so filled with his own opinions that he failed to understand the importance of the event for his son.

Until the next morning, when he woke up with a blinding hangover. *You fucking bastard*, he said to his dishevelled face in the mirror. That was the last time he'd seen his boy.

Now well into his fifties, Nikolaj could feel himself getting angrier at himself. And everyone else. A self-proclaimed defender of the *kultur eliten*, he was even becoming frustrated with some of his closest friends. And the worst part of it was that he knew it was himself, and not them that had changed. Well, at least he recognised that in himself. He knew of others in his circle who had become increasingly embittered, lashing out at everyone within tweeting distance, and accelerating their path towards an early grave, courtesy of too many long wine-filled lunches and late night dates with over-priced brandy.

He walks out of the *Palæ Bar*, and stands on the pavement, trying to figure out what to do with himself now.

Well, he knows what he has to do, which is to start preparations for the coming weekend's exposé. But he's got serious brain fog. If he can only get past Monday! Once Tuesday rolls in, then he's up and running, honing in on his next corporate or political victim.

Nikolaj prides himself on his humour. He knows that helps him circumnavigate the more accomplished intellectuals that he often finds himself sparring against on the late night shows. His many comebacks have become Nordic memes, often translating well for the international markets, because he often communicates his sharp one-liners in colourful English. In fact, to diffuse his competitors on the highly viewed Danish and Swedish panel discussions, he often resorts to giving counter arguments in English.

It was a neat trick he perfected a few years ago. Once, he had been seriously out of his depth in an argument with a Swedish scholar. He can't even remember the subject of the discussion. It was probably about sex or the rise of social media. But all he, and everyone else remembers, was him sitting there silently, seemingly confused as his Swedish antagonist gloated with the self-satisfaction when landing a mortal argumentative blow.

Then Nikolaj looked up from his notes, and responded in English, "what the fuck are you talking about?"

It was a transformational moment for Nikolaj, and many others, who had been bamboozled by buzzwords that over-complicated simple items for discussion. The reaction was shocking. Even for himself. He soon realised that this was a branding opportunity, and he began to sharpen his sword on the stone of sarcasm. But not nasty sarcasm. No, he used the type that fundamentally exposed the corruption of the opponent's arguments.

His speciality had become taking on film and TV critics. Even those he considered as friends. See, one thing about Nikolaj was, he appreciated hard work. Over his many years, he had visited productions sets, worked with script writers, camera operators, actors, Directors and Producers. And one thing Nikolaj knew was the sheer amount of effort that went into making a show, or movie, by hundreds of people. From the germination of the idea, through to the feeding of the crew, to the sales and marketing efforts required to get the bums on the seats.

So when Nikolaj faced off against critics who were perceived to be the judge, jury and executioner of a production that had taken so much effort by so many, his response was to go full-spectrum-warrior on them.

On live TV.

One particularly distasteful critic who had a fearsome reputation for trashing everything he watched, saw his career go rapidly south after crossing swords with Nikolaj on a Saturday night show a few years ago. After annihilating one new movie debut by an up-and-coming Director, the show moderator turned to Nikolaj for his opinion.

Nikolaj, leaned back in his chair, took a sip of water, then looked directly in the critic's eyes and said in English, "what the fuck have you done lately?"

The Sunday papers had an orgasm, and the movie did great box office, even if it was crap. It emboldened Nikolaj, and sent the shivers down the spines of the *Armchair Generals* who decided what was good and bad.

And Nikolaj was always smart in another way. He never picked a fight that he could not win. And that required a lot of preparation. Usually starting off with a long lunch at the *Palæ Bar* on Mondays.

He feels the satisfaction of the fine food as it settles in his belly. And that reminds him of his belly. He looks down, and again realises he can't see his shoes.

Fuck, I need to get in shape, he says to himself. The same mantra he has been repeating for the last five years. He knows he could lose the *Michelin* tyre if he just put a bit more focus into it.

This week I'll restart my gym membership, he bullshits to himself.

He knows he needs to start getting his shit together for the coming week, so he does the only thing that works. He sets off on a long walk, turning right towards Kongens Nytorv, and the start of his regular hike along the water to Langelinieparken and back. It had been his best source of inspiration for the last few years. And it also helped burn off the three glasses of Valpolicella he has for his breakfast/lunch.

As he crosses over to Nyhavn, he wonders to himself what the angle of his story would be this week. He's been playing with a couple of ideas. His best prospect is a VC run by a Brit who just seems too good to be true.

Nikolaj got the original tip over a liquid lunch at *Address*, down by the marina. His problem is the lack of usable insight. Just a bunch of gossip, really. He was thinking about maybe a two-parter. He's used that trick before, where he splits the story over two weekends. The first Saturday he teases with some mild suggestions about the *target's* business. That then opens the door for new sources to come out from under a stone, to enhance the second part with all the juicy shit.

The biggest problem with this strategy is the timescale remaining for producing a quality second part. Both parts had to be aired within a week of each other or the story would lose steam. He parks the thought, and picks up his pace, wondering if there could be any other stories floating around.

What he doesn't realise is that *his story* will come looking for him.

"OK babe, I'm off." "What do you mean you're off!" yells Rebekka.

"To the office," Simon says picking up the keys and opening the front door.

"It's your turn to drop the kids off, remember? I've got that thing with the Audit Committee," she says running down the stairs, confrontation building.

"Babe, you–" "Don't fucking babe me! It's your turn. I've done the last two weeks," she says, walking right up to his face.

"Look, I can't do this right now, babe. I've got a Board meet, so you'll just have to handle it." Simon goes to peck her on the cheek but she dodges it like a skilled boxer. He rolls his eyes and says, "I'll make it up to you, promise! Later," and with that he walked out into the forecourt to get in his Porsche.

"Fucking asshole," Bekka says a bit too loud.

Her daughter, Cloe, sticks her head over the banister and says "hey, mum I heard that! Is dad taking us?"

"No honey, I'll do it. Go and get ready, we're leaving in five minutes. And tell your brother to get out of bed."

Bekka goes back into the kitchen and looks out across the water towards the Swedish coast. She wishes she was out on their boat right now. Alone. Away from this English prick. The man she married an eon ago.

She pours herself another strong coffee and stares out, watching as a giant *Maersk* ship ambles past.

I wonder where you're going, she thinks. *I wish I was on board, away from all this mediocrity.*

Of course, she loves her family. *Well two of them. And the third? Well he's turned out to be a bit of a wanker.* That's his favourite word that she's hijacked for special purposes.

She should have seen it coming all those years ago. Love affairs that blossom from intense situations are probably doomed. And she counts a gun battle in that category.

She was surprised he fell for her. After all, he had been on and off with that *bitch* from Fyn. But she was *too* crazy for him. And Bekka knew how to win him over.

When she first met him, he was all Mr fancy-pants-British-Officer. Or, more specifically, ex-British officer. He'd departed Her Majesty's armed forces under a bit of a cloud. Basically, he liked getting his gun off a bit too much.

Bekka had joined *The Unit* six months before and she'd rotated back to Denmark after a hairy job in a hot place. They were told that a Brit Special Forces guy was flying in from London to meet them at a Kastrup hotel, and they were to determine if he would compliment the team.

Simon didn't disappoint. He was clearly mission-orientated, in superb condition and handsome enough to get by. The only thing that irritated Bekka was that his posh accent kept slipping. She figured he had a complex about it, and had to lord it up back in the officers mess.

She could see there would be trouble right from the get-go by the way he and Camilla were scoping each other out.

Bekka didn't like Camilla on account of her being a psychopath, but she had to admit that she'd rather have Camilla backing her up in the bad places, than anyone else.

Camilla had the unique ability to kill anyone with anything. If she couldn't go hand-to-hand, then her other speciality was robotics. Drones were big, raw and clumsy in the late nineties, but Camilla could still fly one up a rabbits ass from a long way off. With hindsight, it was obvious that she'd end up helming one of the biggest robotics companies in northern Europe.

Bekka hadn't seen her for twenty-some years, and that hadn't ended well. Mainly because she'd stolen Simon away by offering him something else. Such as love and affection.

She'd heard about Camilla a lot because she was all over the Danish news, promoting her new droids and drones, and sucking up as much capital as she could. But whenever Camilla came on the TV, Bekka would turn it over to reruns of *Mig og min Mor* before Simon had a chance to stare at the screen.

She wasn't sure if Simon had seen Camilla since. She wouldn't bet against it, though if she ever caught him then she would cut his balls off. Literally. She had castrated two men before. It was messy, but essential, because *The Unit* had been on the clock. The bad guys were closing in and they'd needed those codes, so Bekka wasn't prepared to fuck about. The third guy gave her the codes, then Camilla shot him between the eyes.

She's jolted out of her nostalgia trip by Cloe who comes running into the kitchen and pulls a carton of juice out of the fridge, then starts chugging it down.

"For the last time, use a glass," says Bekka, sighing.

"Sorry mom, but we are late. Let's go!" Cloe says, turning on her heels, and heading to the front door.

Bekka follows her, picks up the keys and shouts up to Marky, who is halfway down the stairs looking like he just got out of bed.

"Sorry mom. I just got out of bed!"

"Of course you did!" Bekka says laughing. If Cloe is all about efficiencies, then Marky is all about chaos. But she loves him dearly. Correction, she loves them both dearly.

It's just that wanker husband of mine.

Simon pulls onto Strandvejen to the sound of horns, flooring it to narrowly avoid creating a multi-car pile-up.

Jesus, why did we buy this fucking place, he thinks. *Because your wife wanted a Vedbæk address, you wanker. Well, I am a wanker*, he acknowledges, *for putting up with her shit every day.*

He actually misses the Bekka he fell in love with. That love lasted a long time, but the last couple of years since they moved into this place, well, it's just gone down the shitter. They got the place on the cheap. If you could call a waterfront villa on this stretch of coastline cheap.

Cheap is of course relative to how many millions you have squared away. And Simon only thinks in terms of *Euros*, not *Kroner*. Bekka had talked him into it, and sold him on the lifestyle and the convenience of being near to their health club up the road in *Skodsborg*. The price was pretty good, because the former TV star owner was in a hurry to get rid of it. He'd hoovered up too much coke and it had emptied his pockets.

The place was a dump inside, but fabulous on the outside, and Simon knew that Bekka would transform it. Parking for the two boats that they'd never used was handy, and the nice gated forecourt for their two Porsches was the deciding factor.

Now, as he sits in his German cocoon, snaking its way slowly toward his office in Copenhagen, his mind turns to the preparation for the coming days. And how to handle this German woman who's coming up to meet the Board to discuss a merger next week.

She's a mysterious one, he ponders. *Clearly, she's extremely competent.* He's checked her out of course, and she has a considerable reputation as one of the top German industrialists. But there's something *off* about her. He'd noticed it in a couple of TV spots she'd done. He'd seen her, on a *YouTube* video, walk to a panel discussion in Davos a few years ago, but he couldn't quite put his finger on it. Something about the way she walked. Certainly, he'd never met her before. But she seemed oddly familiar. Or maybe he just thought she was hot. Well she was. Is.

Simon reminds himself that he's got a beautiful wife at home, and that she'd probably cut his balls off if he even thought about another woman. After all, she'd done that before, in a previous life.

The problem with being an alcoholic was the alcohol. Or more specifically, the lack of it. The Professor's mental faculties had been gradually eroded away over the years, and now he even had problems remembering to buy the booze. Not ideal when you are living a lonely existence on a rundown farm just outside Hinge.

He woke up this morning to discover that the place was an even bigger mess than he remembered. During his frenzied mission the night before to find any kind of liquid solace, he had managed to trash the whole downstairs. All of his usual hiding places were booze-vacant, either with empty bottles, *or they had been stolen by someone.*

To make matters worse, he had lost his car keys which meant that he couldn't make it to the nearest watering hole to quench his aggressive thirst. Eventually, he'd passed out, and woke up to the sound of the birds, with a hangover from a lack of alcohol.

He had always been known as The Professor, ever since he'd been in *The Unit*. His meticulous eye for logistics and planning meant that he was the goto guy for ways in, and out of, particularly nasty situations. He was, of course, highly proficient in the art of death and could mix it up with the worst of them. Well, maybe not the other five members of *The Unit*, but most opponents.

He doesn't think about those days anymore. After so many years of being a *real* Professor at the University, his past was just a murky dream that floated in and out of his subconscious.

He'd been warned by the Head of Faculty that his own faculties were being depleted by his self-enforced liquid dependency. While his students flocked to his classes because of his near-messianic presence and ability to inspire, his sloppiness, smell and overall hygiene was offensive to his faculty colleagues.

He looks around at the destruction he wrought upon his own kitchen the night before, as he rubs his eyes. Then he checks his watch.

"Shit," he says out loud, realising he's already missed his first class which started at ten o'clock. He'll have to phone in and get the usual ass-kicking from the department head.

He wonders how long they will keep him on. Or if he will save them the trouble by dying first. He knows he has little time left.

The prognosis from the Doctor was clear. *You are fucked. You committed suicide by diving into that whiskey bottle for ten years. And the two packs a day sped up the clock. Go get your estate in order.*

Jesus, what estate, he thinks. His farm, for that is what it used to be, is a shit hole which would be better off being demolished. He knows the local landowners would give him a reasonable price for the land. If only to get rid of him. But he doesn't need the money. And whats the point? He has no one to leave it to. And he doesn't plan to live out his final days in a fucking hospital prison cell.

No. He will die here. Maybe the kitchen, or just fall asleep in his favourite old chair on the terrace. Looking west as the sun recedes over the lush Jylland horizon. He hopes he will make it to the summer. That's when he would prefer to go. But right now he needs a drink.

If only he can find his car keys.

"Well?" she demands.
"They said no," replies the Legal Counsel, sheepishly.
"Get them on a *Zoom* now," she says waving him away.
"Well, that's not possible at this time. It's gone midnight in Austin."
"I don't care what time it is anywhere. If they want a piece of this action, then they can get out of their fucking beds. Get on it," she says, going back to her *smart wall*.

Camilla's not in the mood for it today. Come to think of it, she's never in the mood for those kind of responses. She has the *Midas touch*, not that anyone gave it to her. She worked her ass off for the last twenty years to get where she is now. And she's nowhere near finished.

She'd ploughed her ill-gotten gains into an early startup venture after exiting from *The Unit*. She'd always been frugal, while the others had pissed and sniffed away their commissions from the various dirty jobs they had pulled over a period of five years during the ass-end of the nineties.

She always knew what she would do. Always had a plan. *Robotics*. But she was way ahead of her time and she needed certain technologies to catch-up with her. She never doubted what she could bring to the world, even as she was carrying out hits. She had the unique ability to compartmentalise all kinds of shit, and that had served her well as she transitioned from the art of killing to the art of business.

She also brought with her the same level of aggression to her business enterprises that she had shown on the battlefield. And it was mightily feared and respected by employees, competitors and investors alike. Over the last sixteen years her company had become, through organic growth and astute acquisitions, the biggest robotics powerhouse in Europe.

Robotics being anything that walked, ran, drove, swam or flew.

She refused to go public because she didn't do transparency, and felt that the *Analysts* wouldn't be able to keep pace with her anyway. In fact they'd probably slow her down. She was way out ahead of all the *Futurists*, mainly because she never communicated her product roadmap strategy. She'd just release new iterations and generations of *droids* and *drones* without any fanfare or announcements. It freaked the fuck out of the markets and the business press, but the clients and partners loved her because of the high quality, and levels of innovation that she consistently reached.

Healthcare, agriculture, construction, utilities, transportation and, of course, military and emergency services, filled her company's coffers with cash and long term maintenance and upgrade contracts, which were the envy of the industrial world.

And she was based in Odense, which also happened to be robot-central for northern Europe. *Partly because of me,* she often mused.

She's scanning the data on the wall and balancing an *iPad Pro* in her hand, when her head of HR comes into her glass-enclosed office.

"Latest stats are in," says the HR guy.

"And?" Camilla asks.

"Well, I'm not sure how to put it—"

"So just put it anyway. Spit it out," Camilla snaps.

"OK, well we are officially at the bottom of the rankings for staff retention in Denmark," he says, lowering his eyes.

"Tell me something I don't know. Is there a silver lining?"

"Well, we are also the highest for re-hiring people," he states, triumphantly.

"And that surprises you? It shouldn't. They might burn themselves out here and need a break, but they always come back, because we offer them opportunities in cutting edge tech that no one else can. How do we stack up against the others on salary and benefits?"

"We're close to the top."

"Good, keep it that way. I'm planning another acquisition in the next three months. Going through the due diligence now. I haven't secured the additional investment needed yet, but I will soon. So I need an organisational integration plan worked up."

She peers at her HR guy over the top of her thick black-rimmed glasses. The HR guy looks up to her but can't hold her stare, and goes back to his own *tablet*.

"Er, OK. When will you get the investment confirmed?"

"When the fucking Americans get out of bed. Don't you worry about that. Just get back to me with a plan by the end of the week. Feel free to pull a few late nights if it will help. I'll get back to you in a day for a progress report. Thank you," she says dismissing him.

She gets a ping. It's from Lucas.

Her pulse races. It always does when she thinks of him. She met Lucas going on for three years ago. He was a young robotics engineer who'd joined one of their advanced prototype teams. She was on a tour of the lab, and he had the misfortune to fall under her gunsights.

The Supervisor was extremely nervous as it was known how much cash Camilla had personally poured into this particular *droid*. The Supervisor had felt her wrath on a number of occasions, and so he chickened out, and delegated the demo to young Lucas.

When Camilla strode into the lab, you could hear a mouse fart. The tension was palpable. She proceeded over to the work bench where the young engineer started to demonstrate the progress they had made on this particular piece of war-fighting tech.

She interrupted him multiple times, and on each occasion he would pause and wait for her to finish, and then proceed to carefully answer her questions, never offering anything more in the form of hyperbole or bullshit.

She remembered looking deep into his brown eyes and thought it remarkable how he met her penetrating gaze with a calm confidence. Camilla never showed it, but her pulse was racing like a jackhammer, and she tried to extend the discussion as long as possible without it being too obvious. Eventually, she was ushered away to her next engagement, but as she walked away, she looked over her shoulder and saw Lucas smiling at her.

Shit.

Over the next few weeks, she kept her distance from him, but she could not stop thinking about him. It was beginning to distract her, and that was not a good thing. Camilla didn't do distractions.

She had discovered that he worked out in a gym not too far from the campus, and then she got her assistant to arrange for a membership. She just happened to bump into him one Friday evening when it was empty.

She walked out from the dressing room and into the weights area, and began stretching, and she saw him in the mirror do a double-take when he recognised her. He wasn't subtle or nervous about it. He just put his dumbbells back on the rack and strode over to where she was stretching her long body.

They ate a hearty dinner that night in *Kok & Vin*, and she had not smiled or laughed so much in a long time. He said goodbye to her outside the restaurant and they agreed that it would be fun to do it again.

She called him the next morning and asked if he was free that night. He said *yes* and he came over to her place. She liked the fact that he was not insecure about, either the size and opulence of her house, or who she was. He was just so easy to be with.

He kissed her lightly on the back of the neck when she was chopping some onions to the sound of *Cantaloop*. It took her breath away, and she spun on him and looked deep into his eyes with her piercing blue gaze. She brought her mouth to his and, gently, feathered his lips with her tongue.

He put his arms around her shoulders and stood up on his tiptoes and laughed, for at one hundred and ninety centimetres, she was a bit taller than him. They both laughed and then brought their mouths together and kissed until the potatoes boiling over rudely interrupted them.

He stayed that night, and Camilla awoke in the morning with Lucas next to her. He was sound asleep. She looked at him under the sheet and bit her lip, uncertain as to what this meant. She had never experienced such tenderness, nor had she given so much in return. She had twenty-one years on him and their paths could not be more different.

Yet, he lit a fire in her that she knew would be impossible to extinguish. *You know when you know*, she told herself.

They saw each other, carefully, over the next two months. Unfortunately, for Lucas, they were spotted in the same restaurant as on their first date. The gossip went round the company like shit through a goose and Lucas was in a bad state.

Camilla had no such qualms, but she had a solution. She would arrange for Lucas to get an opportunity to be head of R&D at a comer that was growing fast in the robotic sensor/actuator space. It also happened to be based in the heart of the Odense robot ecosystem. The company provided parts to Camilla's enterprise, and the Chairman owed her a favour or three.

Lucas started at the new company four weeks later, and he moved in with Camilla later that evening. After two months, they got married. The ceremony was in Antigua because Camilla had no family and Lucas was estranged from his. Both of his parents had plans for him, and they had given him the great disappointment lecture ten years ago when he told them he wanted to build robots.

When they came back, they went for a dinner with his parents once in Copenhagen. It didn't go well. After a couple of months they decided to buy a villa a few kilometres north of Nyborg with a pier for their boat. It was a longer trip for them both to their offices in Odense, but the fresh air and long lazy weekends with barbecues invigorated them.

Camilla would always come home much later, but Lucas would always have rustled up a feast for her, whatever time she got back. She loved the way she could switch off everything, and she loved him with all her heart.

In bed sometimes, as they lay there after making love, he would look into her eyes in a curious way, studying her. While she had never been so open with anyone, she carefully partitioned her thoughts. She had constructed an elaborate back story about her time before her company. She had spent a lot of time travelling and working with various *NGOs*. Lucas had asked to see photos but she blew it off with the pre-*iPhone* excuse.

He seemed satisfied and now, after several happy years together, Camilla is in a different place. Although she still transforms herself the minute she walks through the campus door, or engages on a *Zoom* or call.

She sighs, wondering what time she will be able to get back to him tonight. Hopefully, before eight. But she's got this military deal that she needs to work on to smooth out some ruffled feathers.

She tenses for a second, getting a flashback to another time. It often happens when she gets dragged anywhere near defence contracts. She stands, and slowly walks over to the long window and stares down into the carpark. She can see her own reflection, and something triggers a memory of a team she once worked for.

This was not an ordinary team. They did not build anything. Their only purpose was destruction and murder.

She tried to convince herself it was not murder, for every hit was sanctioned. But murder it was.

They were called *The Unit*, which was bland enough that it attracted no attention in official channels. Not that there were any official channels as far as *The Unit* was concerned. It operated under at least four layers of cut-outs which enforced plausible deniability on all hits that they undertook.

If they got caught, well, then they were terrorists or thieves. And basically fucked. They all bought into those rules, and it had been a long recruitment process. Finally, the make-up of the team was in place and they began to jive.

It was a unique team, and Camilla was the most ruthless of all the operators. Even now she is shocked by how cold and calculating she was in those many missions. But so were all of them.

There was Simon, *the fool. So full of his own shit. And he got what he deserved. That bitch from Copenhagen had always wanted him*. It did not bother Camilla that he had defected to her. She had other priorities.

Then there was The Professor, who was useful, but prone to brooding. She knew that he was buried in a bottle on an old farm on Jylland. Not like Simon and Bekka. They had to flaunt it all over Sjælland.

That left two others.

The other woman.

And she was their last mission. She had called down the thunder upon herself, and they left her on that Minorcan beach to bleed-out. Camilla had insisted they put one in her head for safety, but they were rudely interrupted by a group of locals walking back from their maintenance duties on a fishing boat. When they'd come back later to finish her off, she was gone, but the patch of blood-soaked sand was still there, imprinted with signs of footwear.

They'd searched for her all over the island, and made cautious investigations with the police and local hospitals.

Have you seen our friend? Here is her photo. She went missing on the beach.

They could not find her.

Eventually, The Dutchman called them off and told them to get back to Copenhagen.

Camilla shudders at the thought of him. She hadn't seen him since they had got back to Kastrup after that final mission in Minorca. It had all gone to shit, and they knew they would be shut down. Or even taken off the board, permanently.

She last saw him walking away toward his connecting flight for Amsterdam. And just when he was almost out of sight, he turned and stared at her.

Camilla could handle herself, but she felt nailed to the floor, paralysed with fear. For he was the most evil person she had ever met, woman or man.

She watches as a couple of cars come and go, trying to force him out of her thoughts. But it's useless, and she chastises herself for letting him out after all these years. She always wondered if he was still out there. No, she knew he was. She had tried to track him down over the years, not because she wanted to reach out to him, but because she wanted to get advanced warning if he was coming for her.

He never did. She figured he was either dead, or living out some kind of hermit existence on a remote island.

He's definitely not dead, she tells herself. She shivers again then wraps her arms around herself, and thinks about Lucas, and falling into his arms later tonight.

For a satanist, The Dutchman could be remarkably light-hearted and engaging.

He didn't make it obvious as to his devilish persuasions. It's not like he wore a black cloak with purple lining. However, people who flew into his orbit usually came away with the uncomfortable feeling that their intestines had been examined by him.

He preferred the night but was comfortable in the daylight, indeed, many of his most successful operations had been executed when the sun was up.

He was tall, and in extremely good condition for a man who had reached sixty-four in Earth years. He was a master practitioner of several noble arts from the far east, and as a result of his early years of disciplined training, he was able to rapidly assimilate any new form of martial arts into his repertoire by merely observing it and communicating it to his body.

Not that he needed such skills these days. In fact for the last twenty-three years he had been retired from the wettest of professions. But he had found a much more profitable outlet for *The Dark Lord*'s work, thanks to the insatiable demand from customers the world over.

The Dutchman walks out to his terrace with a big mug of coffee, and stands there, looking out over LockRum Bay as the sun rises over his left shoulder.

Sunrise and sunset, he thinks, *are the only times you feel truly alive. Apart from when you take the life of another. Or direct others to do your dirty work for you.*

He had acquired the land in Anguilla many decades ago, then set about building a lair for himself. He is a private man and has few encounters with anyone on the island, but over the years he has hosted many visitors who are brought across from St Maarten, having arrived at the international airport. They are an eclectic bunch from across the spectrum of political, corporate, philanthropic and military realms.

Some have been connected into the subversive entity known as CORP-ROGUE, woven together by their common interests to influence and profit from the complexities of the world. Others have been individual clients in need of a service to speed-up or slow down policies, competitors or activities that create irritation for their self-important lives.

Few of them have had his same satanic propensities, indeed he has even dealt with the other side. Churchmen, who, through their clumsy contortions, have needed to extricate themselves from unfortunate circumstances. He always charged them triple for his services, and he did have certain principles when accepting purchase orders from them. He refused to help clean-up their messes regarding their employees who had set about the young for their own gratification.

In fact the opposite was true. He had taken a personal interest in certain east coast events, and used his reach to wipe out infestations of these vile creatures who had been protected and shunted round vulnerable communities for so long. The Dutchman, while being in league with the Dark Lord, did have principles.

It was whispered that he had come from extreme poverty, devoid of a father, and raised by a mother riddled by her own addictions. While he became extremely wealthy through his proclivity for evil, he still retained a core set of beliefs, namely, the need to protect the poor and vulnerable. The vast majority of commissions he accepted involved the brokering of power, or the movement of money. He had never been married but he had retained the same ferocious sexual appetite over the last forty years.

Those poor souls unfortunate enough to have visited his bed would never live to see another.

It was an added complexity to disappear so many bodies of his nubile victims over the years, but he saw it as just another part of the mating process, and he had become quite proficient in the art of dissolution.

As the sun begins to warm the side of his angular face, he fires up his *app* and goes through his various secure chats. Nothing out of the ordinary to take note of, apart from a couple of logistical issues with one of his *Units*. It seemed that one operation had been delayed due to two of the operators being double-booked. He reminded himself to pay more attention to his scheduling software in future.

Apart from that, there are also a few obscure requests that he will consider during the day as he processes all of the moving parts of his labyrinthine schemes.

Next he looks at his transactions report, both incoming and outgoing. He long since went past his magic billion mark, but still he counts every penny.

He makes a few moves, swiping a couple of *mil* here and there, and then finishes his coffee.

He gazes down onto the bay and decides that he will cleanse himself in the warm waters later. He will take his *Scarab* far out and drop over the side, away from any prying eyes who would see his heavily scarred body.

He wanders back into his cavernous living room and opens up a side room, secured by a coded lock on the door. Inside, he sits down in front of a bank of monitors and begins scrolling through his *Units*, scattered across the globe. He has three in play at the moment, and two on standby. Each one made up of five highly specialised individuals, who have been nurtured over many years. He personally supervises the final selection process for each new Unit, and there have only been fourteen in the last twenty-six years.

When a *Unit* has run its course, it is terminated and the bodies are disappeared. Only one *Unit* ever lived after its activities had ceased, and that was the original one that he was part of.

Ah, The Unit! He sometimes wonders how they are doing.

Well, thats not quite true. He knows exactly how they are doing as he monitors their activities closely. The four remaining ones anyway.

He doesn't miss them. He never liked any of them, especially Camilla. Unfortunately, he also happened to be in love with her. That was...complex. Especially in combat.

Love and guns, never mix them up, so said the *Dark Lord* to him in one of their more reflective conversations. Occasionally, he would remember the one they murdered, for she was special.

For the last two decades, as he had built up the most effective assassination organisation money could buy, he kept looking out for the *next her*. They were all special in his *Unit*, but she was...*exceptional*.

She had a sixth sense which acted as the team's radar. She was also his most efficient killer. She did not like to make a fuss. It was always in and out as fast as possible, leaving no trace. Whenever the contract called for an *accident*, she was deployed.

However, she was also capable of extreme violence, and she could go from zero to mayhem in seconds.

He recalls that she was a bit of a loner in a team that had a lot of tension flying around. She was probably closest to Rebekka, and that was exposed when Rebekka actually tried to stop them from executing her.

Camilla recommended terminating Rebekka after that, but the Dutchman demurred. *Was it out of charity? No, more like self preservation.*

For this group of resourceful operators had made a pact. If one went down due to the actions of another, then they would all turn on the antagonist. And each of the original operators had stored away all the leverage they needed for self-preservation.

So he knew that, while he was secure out here on his Caribbean island paradise, there was a good chance they would be able to combine forces to take him out, should they feel threatened. It was like an old pirate thing.

How quaint, thought *The Devil*.

He always worked to ensure that any of the subsequent *Units* he created never got such visions of grandeur. That's why he monitored them so closely. Both to ensure they met their customer's demands, and remained vulnerable to his reach.

He sits in his swivel chair and stares at the screens on the walls, and four laptops arrayed on the long table, absorbing the torrent of sensory and other data from drones, first person view cameras and pirated feeds from hacked civilian devices.

He'll spend the first few hours of the morning catching up on *Unit* progress reports, then he will switch modes into pipeline sales opportunities, carefully balancing demand with supply. After lunch he'll take the boat out and go for a long snorkelling session, before returning in the early evening to check the various feeds.

This evening he has a gathering across on St. Maarten, where for desert he has ordered a most particular creature from a very special menu.

Somewhere, out there across the warm waters, a poor unfortunate soul has a date with *The Devil* tonight.

She checks herself into the Airbnb on the outskirts of Århus, about fifteen minutes drive from the centre.

She'd booked a detached house with trees and bushes around it that masked her activities. It had taken her a while to select the right booking because she also wanted a suitable charging point for her Tesla. She had no intention of taking it any further on her journey into Denmark.

Upon entering the house, she runs her usual set of protocols, checking all exits and windows. She shuts down the house's WiFi system, and runs a scan for any devices. Her Israeli-made sniffer is supposed to be the best on the market, but the market moves fast, and her mental clock runs close to paranoid.

Satisfied with her new, temporary private sanctuary, she sits down on the sofa and starts to interrogate her *iPhone*. She responds to all the demands for her attention, then firmly reminds her Assistant that she is down in Spain on personal family business for five days, and is not contactable.

Then she shuts down the phone, removes its SIM and puts both in her backpack. She reaches into a side pocket and pulls out a new phone that she purchased in Hamburg, then spends the next few minutes setting it up with a new SIM, and installs the various apps, new credit card details and security configurations associated with her new identity.

Job done, she goes to the kitchen and makes herself an omelette and a coffee. Next she goes into the bathroom, showers and places her business clothes on the bed in a neat pile. She takes an old pair of jeans, t-shirt and beige sweatshirt out of her backpack, and changes. Then she goes back to the bathroom and stands in front of the mirror, looking at someone else.

Time to say goodbye for a few days, she thinks. *I wonder if I'll see you again? Whoever you are.*

She grabs the black, wavy wig and pulls it over her short, blonde hair, and fluffs it up to create a messy look. Next, she inserts the brown contact lenses and adjusts them, blinking a few times to help them settle. She applies a little foundation but skips the lipstick.

She stands back and messes up her new hair again, then turns round to check all the angles. Satisfied that not even her closest workers would recognise her new killer look, she congratulates herself on her transformation. It's been a long time since she had to call upon these skills, and she's sure she could have done better. However, she had little time to prepare.

She goes back out to the entrance, picks up her new phone and requests a taxi from the app, getting a response saying it will arrive in twelve minutes, so she busies herself rechecking the house before leaving. After the sweep, she puts on her *Timberlands* and an old black leather jacket, and takes one final look in the hall mirror.

Close enough to what a fifty-two-year-old student might look like, she thinks. She sees the taxi pull up out front, and she picks up her backpack and the keys and locks the door behind her. Fifteen minutes later, the taxi drops her off at the Radisson Blu downtown. She goes to the front desk to check-in, and then up to her room. Ten minutes after that, she exits the hotel and walks toward the University campus.

He walks through the campus building, wafting the smell of alcohol like a jet's contrail behind him. His disheveled features are offset by the remarkable clarity from his crystal clear eyes. It was often remarked by students, both female and male alike, that The Professor would be a bit of a looker if he cleaned himself up.

He barely remembers those days, when he was a looker, and how he would deploy his handsome assets to lethal effect. *The Unit* considered his looks a corporate asset, especially when seduction was on the menu for a hit.

Now, his raggedy image carves a hole in the student mass unfolding before him as he walks to the large auditorium.

But while his features have gradually eroded, his mind, when partially sober, works on a different level. And he deploys it to magnificent effect, inspiring even the laziest of the annual intake, to fight for a place on his course.

And that's a big fucking problem for the university's management. He has the highest feedback and pass ratings in the country, let alone this great city. So even as he misses half his classes as a result from his drunken stupor, he more than makes up for it with the energy he releases when he does bother to turn up.

This afternoon he's expecting another full house as it is the culmination of a long series of lectures on how haptics are converging with holographic capabilities, driving a transformative change in human interaction. He doesn't just know this. He believes it, and that belief comes through with some of the most cutting edge insights and practical demos anywhere in northern Europe. He's opened up his seminars to some of the smartest engineers and entrepreneurs to come and preach what he knows to his enthralled students.

And it's had quite an effect. Århus has seen the highest concentration of holographic startups in Denmark over the last couple of years.

Most will fail, he muses, as he nears the room. *And that's how it should be.* He can see the crowd of students talking by the entrance, and almost as one, they turn and watch him approach. It brings the usual infectious smile to his face, and the energy level begins to rise.

He likes his students, for they do not seem to judge him like his older faculty colleagues. For sure the students talk about his eccentricities, and probably his overall hygiene, but they seem to cut him some slack on account of the inspiration and humour he brings into their academic lives.

He fights his way past them and approaches the front bench to get set up, as they stream into the seating positions arrayed high up in front of him.

He does not notice the tall, dark haired older woman who wanders in with the last group, then makes her way up to the back row and sits in the dark corner by the emergency exit.

Tilda's not surprised by the effect The Professor has on his audience.

He always had the ability to mesmerise. And his technical capabilities were off the scale, which was why he always handled comms and advanced weapons.

Unlike the students, she's not that impressed by the technological theory being unveiled. Her labs have been at the forefront of some advanced haptic and holographic design for some years, but they kept it buried under thick layers of the organisation chart, away from the technology media's prying eyes. She knew that her team had actually been monitoring his research, as they did all top institutions, but she made sure she was several layers removed from the findings.

Still, she made discreet enquiries as to the ideas coming out of his research, and privately she monitored his movements. He had not been hard to find. He had grown more careless as he fell deeper into the bottle, but she did not take his condition as a weakness. He was a formidable adversary, and she had witnessed him yield his ruthlessness in the field with a total lack of concern for his own safety.

She sits now, immersed in the darkness as he proceeds with his electrifying seminar, and she considers why she chose him as *the first*.

Certainly it was geography that played a part. When she had located his residence and found that it was such a large, isolated farm, he went to the top of her list. The others were all urban dwellers which added complexity, and required more planning. She was not yet sure how she would deploy her *assets* to murder her way across Denmark. Perhaps she would not even use them. But better to have them than not.

Still, she had decided not to use the *assets* for The Professor. She also needed to test herself. And she considered that a big fucking risk. *Was it ego*? No, she had convinced herself that she must face him alone. It had been a lifetime ago since she had been in a combat situation. Not including the weekly regimen of martial arts training she had put herself through with private instructors for the last fifteen years.

When she first got back on her feet in Munich, she had begun going to open karate classes again. Her movements were still restricted by the slow-healing bullet wound. She found the techniques associated with spinning kicks particularly hard to reacquire. But over time her strength and muscular armour returned.

When she took over the corporation from her *second father*, following his passing, she began paying for private lessons at her gated residence. She had selected the *Lau Gar* form of Kung Fu to be the next discipline to absorb. At the start, she found it difficult to adjust to such a different style of combat, and she burned through a few teachers, blaming them for her lack of accelerated progress.

After a while, she came to the conclusion that they were right all along. Karate had been so ingrained into her consciousness, that her muscle memory refused to adapt to such a demanding new set of instructions. Once she had accepted this, her progress, channeled via a great master from the east, was rapid. She had helped him set up a local practice, and made an agreement that she would be his only private client.

He would visit her three times a week, usually before dawn, and push her beyond the limits of any student he had ever tutored. He was a wise man, and he knew that her core skills were not acquired through hobbyist or sporting activities. Her accelerated approach to attack had been, he considered, lethally honed to solve problems very fast. She did not offer him any explanations, nor did he seek them. He just pushed her harder.

At times she found it hard to keep up the discipline. The early, exhaustive starts always preceded intense business days, full of complex negotiations and corporate ambushes. As a CEO she was considered to be focused, but distant, although she was known for her ability to take the tension out of the air with a light joke or casual remark. It was all the more effective because of her reputation for steely efficiency, and the ramrod posture she adopted in both sitting and standing positions.

It was remarked, by those in the corporate halls of power, and many who found themselves on opposing sides of the conference table, that her knuckles were often raw, and sometimes covered in plasters. The gossip columnists in the company said it was because she had a skin disease. Others said she was under too much stress and it caused blisters on her hands.

No one knew they were the result of the daily practice in the art of the kill. She was not into self-defence. To her, the only defence was the furious accelerated attack.

She is jolted out of her thoughts, by the sound of clapping and whooping, as the students rush down from the sides to swamp The Professor. The lecture has finished, and Tilda checks her watch, surprised that one and a half hours has passed so quickly.

She had vaguely paid attention to what he had been saying, but most of the time she had been watching his eyes and his movements, looking for angles of approach and trying to assess his balance. Clearly, he was impeded by the years of alcoholic abuse. He looked fat and out of shape, although she knew that he would retain a similar level of muscle memory to her.

Well, not like me, she thinks.

She's banking on the fact that he will be drunk by the time she approaches later tonight. Darkness shall be her ally and she will proceed cautiously. She has scoped out his place on *Google Earth*, so she understands the lie of the land. But she knows that nothing beats on-the-ground intel, especially of an assassins own backyard. She assumes he will have some kind of surveillance system guarding the dump he inhabits, and so she will need to understand and compromise it quickly.

So now she gets up, and makes her way out of the exit at the back of the auditorium to scout his land with her drones. She figures he will be buried in student questions for an hour at least, so she has some time to get ahead of him and complete her reconnaissance.

But the clock's ticking.

The Professor tries to get his students into an orderly queue as they bustle him into the corner, armed with their questions.

As he fights them off with answers, he catches a glimpse of a tall woman with dark hair disappear through the exit at the back of the auditorium. He pays no more than a passing glance at her, and goes back to fending off his student assault.

She goes back to the hotel, changes into her khaki pants and green sweatshirt, then collects her rental car that has been delivered.

She chose a small black Peugeot for its ability to blend into the traffic. Then she heads west out of Århus towards Hinge. She was not surprised that he had chosen to live so far away from his place of work, as remoteness was an asset for someone seeking to hide from the past.

She guessed the distance probably contributed to his tardiness. He probably fell out of bed most mornings, bypassing the shower, and hitting the road to get to his classes on time.

She had researched him carefully in the weeks before she drove up from Munich. According to multiple sources, his classes were some of the most inspirational in Denmark, and she had just witnessed the old aura he projected. She felt that he had become a man of extreme contradictions. His very public image was at odds with his extreme focus on privacy.

Like all the other remaining members of *The Unit*, he had continued to live under his own name. Well, it was a safe as any other. After all, they'd always adopted aliases when deployed on overseas on hits.

She pulls up at Hinge Kirke just after four p.m. and parks her car. She walks across to the beautiful church, struck by the memories of her homeland that flood back. She knows she doesn't have time for it, but the striking image of the white tower and red brick chapel draws her in.

She walks around it, assaulted by the sounds and smells of late summer, taking in the well tended hedges and flowers surrounding the burial plots, and she harks back to an age of *hygge* that she has lost forever.

Before I became a killer in a team full of killers.

That thought snaps her out of her nostalgia, and she strides back to the car and drives back to the road, turning left into Hinge village. She drives straight through, following the GPS toward his farm, a couple of kilometres to the west.

She has already chosen the spot to park her car, and survey his property, both from the land and sky. She pulls off the road onto a small track which she knows is a dead-end, and turns the car so it is facing toward the road. Then she reverses into a hidden space between some trees.

She gets out of the car and takes her backpack from the rear seat, then walks to the end of the track and looks out across a meadow. Next, she takes out the two drones, controller and a *HoloLens*, and begins to set them up. She has to set the coordinates for both drone missions. Each will swing round in a wide arc, take a high aerial run, then swoop down, and zigzag across the open land surrounding the farmhouse. The sophisticated sensor package should then pick up electronic signatures, beaming them back to her *HoloLens* as she tracks the drone's progress through video images.

The HUD will also allow her to scan the environment, and not have to look down at the controller, simultaneously allowing her to see beyond her own visual line of sight. It was a neat bit of tech that her team had picked up from a *startup* in Helsinki.

She puts the device on her head, standing in the shadows to reduce the glare from the sun, then fires up the drones.

The buzzing noise is not quiet enough for her, and she looks around, checking there are no passers by. Satisfied, she releases them, and watches as they shoot out of the small clump of trees that offer her protection from prying eyes.

She releases her hands from the controller, confident in the pre-programmed path they are flying, and begins to scan the two video images playing out in windows in front of her eyes.

Two minutes into the mission and she gets a red warning light from DRONE#1, which is scanning the rear of the farm. She interrupts its mission and takes manual control, allowing DRONE#2 to proceed on its own path.

She pulls down a menu and scans the sensor data. It has detected a light signature that is apparently criss-crossing the land at the back of the farmhouse. She pulls the drone back, and then flies it low across the wide open space from north to south.

Laser mesh, she thinks.

She locates the end points which are attached to small posts, where the laser field ends, and tags them to build up a *point cloud* of The Professor's defensive perimeter.

In the meantime, DRONE#2 has completed its sweep of the front, and has detected nothing except for a light sensor at the front of the driveway. She zooms in on the front of the farmhouse and can see a number of cameras and movement sensors arrayed at strategic viewing positions around the building.

She loads all of this data into her *point cloud*, then calls back the drones. Thirty seconds later they shoot back over to her position in the trees, lowering themselves to the ground in front of her feet. She packs them back into their small case and puts them into the back of the car.

Then she gets into the drivers seat and begins to review the digital map from her spies in the sky. She doesn't notice a third, smaller drone, hovering just above the long grass, about fifty metres from her car.

It takes him an hour to escape the clutches of his admiring students, but finally he's in his battered old BMW, heading west towards home.

He stops off at a store on the outskirts of Århus to pick up his supplies for the next few days. Ten frozen meals, some bread, milk, four bottles of moderately expensive red wine, and two bottles of whiskey.

He's back on the road in ten minutes and beginning to relax. He always gets a warm feeling when he heads home in the summer, across the green Jylland landscape.

He was born in Sjælland many years ago, but from an early age he harboured romantic dreams of a farm on the mainland. He could never quite put his finger on it, although it was probably something to do with growing up in such a crowded, bustling environment.

He liked his life in Copenhagen, but he yearned for a life on a farm. He always knew he would get into tech research and development. The telecoms and computing industry was exploding, and he had the ability to predict future trajectories. Not like these *Futurists* you see on the corporate circuit these days. No, he knew he had the ability to make it happen through his deep understanding of converging technologies. And more specifically, how they would open up realms of opportunity that hadn't even been dreamed of.

Then he got distracted.

He wanted to travel, but was not fortunate enough to be able to afford it. His parents had limited means of helping him, so he joined the army in the eighties. There, he discovered, not only the world, but the most cutting edge communications technologies used to monitor and secure it.

He immersed himself in the field, leveraging his rapidly accumulating skills to become the most celebrated technical operator that no one had ever heard off. Except those people across NATO who knew such things.

He pulled some juicy assignments across combined NATO engagements, and used his activities to build cutting edge relationships with the few key commercial organisations that had defence contracts.

But there was one other ability he had developed over his first five years in the forces, and it involved guns. He had become a master sniper.

It caused him and his management some challenges, as he was pulled in multiple career directions between competing branches of the military. Having aced several shooting competitions, word got out that he could take the wing off a bird at a thousand metres. But he could also break into any encrypted communications system the enemy could afford.

Eventually, the top brass figured why not use both skillsets? So he was bundled off to a Special Forces team where he spent a couple of years helping to remove bad guys from the planet.

During this time he caught the attention of a Dutch officer who was in the market for a new unit. The Professor got approached by The Dutchman one evening in a shitty bar in a hot country, where he was busy investing in a hangover.

He remembers that night with crystal clarity. The Dutchman was mesmerising. He had a way of making you feel like you were so special.

He asked The Professor what he would like to do after leaving the service. He responded that he wanted to buy a farm in Jylland.

"A beautiful part of the world," nodded the Dutchman. "I can help you realise that dream."

"How?" asked The Professor.

The Dutchman then proceeded to explain that he was building a unit of specialist operators who would take on jobs that were, as he put it, "not too official."

The Professor was no dummy, and he replied, "you mean spy shit?"

The Dutchman laughed and shook his head. He went on to explain that, "no, we will not be spying on people. We will be taking them off the map."

The Professor stared down at his whiskey and shook the ice, watching the brown elixir wash around the cheap glass.

Then he looked up and asked how this would help him buy his farm?

The Dutchman leaned back and rubbed the sweat off of his forehead. It was then that The Professor noticed the two small bumps on each side of his head.

Weird, thought The Professor. It makes him look like the Devil.

The Dutchman, sensing his recruit was getting distracted, put his arm around The Professor's broad shoulders and said, "you won't be paid by the military. In fact, you won't have to worry about money again. And you can help your parents pay off their debts on that bike shop in Nørrebro."

The Professor looked up and into the smiling eyes of the Dutchman. He was sold. He was in. All that was left was to meet the other members, of what the Dutchman called, *The Unit*.

He swerves and narrowly avoids killing a cyclist, and it gets him refocused. He grips the wheel with his left hand, and reaches down for the water bottle. He takes the lid off and splashes some water on his face, soaking his old jeans.

I need a drink, he thinks.

He calculates that he will be pulling into his yard in twenty minutes, and the thought soothes him.

He looks down at the bag of groceries on the seat next to him, and instinctively reaches down and touches the shimmering golden liquid, encased in the beautiful glass bottle.

Just then he gets a ping on his phone. It's from his surveillance system. He picks up the *Samsung* and opens it with his face.

Distracted, by the complex balancing act, he nearly rams into an oncoming truck and drops the phone between the seats.

He curses and then pulls over into the next bus stop, and spends five minutes trying to fish the phone out. Finally he manages to push it forward enough to grab it.

He pulls it out, and opens it up again. It's an *intruder warning* from his farm's surveillance system. He opens up the file and plays the video, getting a birds-eye view from his security drone as it rises up out of its charging station.

Something triggered it and now it's zoning in on the intruder. He can tell it's not an animal because of the speed and trajectory.

His drone flies fast and low over the field at the back of his farmhouse, and through the phone's small screen he can just make out two fast moving black dots ahead. Then they make a beeline for a clump of trees and come down to land. At the feet of a tall woman wearing a baseball cap.

His drone closes in slowly on the target, as it's been programmed to do. Then it stops and hovers, and he can see the woman picking up the drones and putting them into the back of a small black car. He thinks it's a Ford, or maybe something French.

He can see her get into the car and sit there, but from this range he cannot make out what she is doing. After fifteen minutes, she starts the car and pulls out of the trees and disappears down track. The drone, running low on battery, makes the decision to return to its charging station on the roof of the main building.

He rewinds the video and checks the timestamp on when she left. He kicks himself for not fixing up a live feed. This was forty-five minutes ago. He throws his phone onto the passenger seat, and pulls out in front of an approaching bus, flooring it to the sound of blaring horns.

She drives into Kjellerup and parks.

She's going to hit his farmhouse when it is dark, because, well it will be dark, and hopefully he will be half in the bag from his alcoholic meal. So she's got time to kill and hunger to sedate.

She decides on an Italian and wanders in, taking a table by the window. She takes her time with the order and starts with a glass of white wine. She knows she shouldn't, but fuck it, she needs it!

Tonight, she'll kill again. It has been a while. A long time to cool off and re-evaluate one's belief systems.

She knows she has changed, but not that much. She's still capable of taking a life again. Four of them for starters.

There were five, she reminds herself. But *he's* a ghost.

So number one of four gets the big send-off tonight. And that's why she needs the drink.

She's forcing herself not to think about the next one on the list. Partly, because *she* is the one Tilda is most concerned about, but mainly because she needs to be so fucking focused for what she's about to do tonight.

The waiter comes and she orders a starter, main course and desert, then she settles down for a couple of hours to plan, and practise speaking her mother tongue that she abandoned so many years ago.

She checks her watch. Sunset at twenty-one forty-five. She'll give it another thirty minutes after that, then she'll kill him.

The other cameras didn't pick her up, and the drone footage couldn't make out her features under the shadow of the tree.

He took a walk out to where she had parked but he didn't turn up anything.

Two drones. That requires skillsets to handle them both, he thinks.

He walks back toward the farmhouse to make his preparations in case she comes back later. But first he needs a drink.

2 - THE TRIPWIRE

Tilda doesn't park in the same lane behind the house on account of the noise, so she pulls off the side of the road five hundred metres before.

She's dressed in black and she knows she needs to get off the road as fast as possible. From her investigations into his security system she spotted a gap in his defences on the far corner of the farmhouse. It lies at the point where the laser mesh ends, and where there is a camera mounted on the wall covering the blind spot. Except the camera is clearly out of order, as it is hanging down as if it's been torn from its mounting.

That will be her approach.

She again enters the small lane and walks to the end where the field at the back of his farmhouse starts. She crawls between some bushes and then takes a wide arc around to the far end of the field. She takes her night vision goggles out of her backpack and puts them on, filling her field of view with the familiar green world.

Looking ahead, she can see the criss-crossing of the lasers as they fan out from the house. Satisfied that she's clear of them, she looks up at the broken camera on the corner of the building, and then stealthily moves toward it.

He's sitting at his old kitchen table, clutching a half-empty bottle of whiskey. He's got the TV on silent in the background, but he's not paying attention to it.

He's kept his lights low, allowing the flickering of the TV to be easily seen from the front of the house. *How many are coming, he wonders. If they're coming. Maybe she was a journalist or police? Don't be ridiculous.*

He takes another drink, knowing that it's reducing his capabilities further.

Fuck it, he thinks. *I'm better when I'm drunk*, he lies to himself.

He gets a ping on his phone and makes a grab for it, but it slips out of his hand and he drops it on the stone floor. He reaches down and picks it up, and sees another big crack across the screen.

"Fucking smartphones," he says, opening it up with his face. He clicks on the notification, and opens up his perimeter security system, selecting *live feed*.

He sees the dark figure approaching across the field of long grass at the back of the house. He can't make out any features, but the person is tall. He assumes it's the same woman who was scoping out the place earlier. He tracks her approach, then quickly flips to the front view to see if she brought company.

No signs.

He flips back to the rear camera.

She's smart. She must have figured out the laser mesh, and then spotted the broken camera, creating the only blindspot approach.

But that was a feint. He had installed another more powerful camera with night vision just above the broken one. It was hidden behind some guttering.

He knew it was effective because it had served him well a while back.

Three years ago, two drug addicts cut a swathe from Sjælland, through Fyn, and onto Jylland, robbing remote farmhouses to fuel their insatiable needs. Unfortunately for them, they selected his property.

He had sucked them in like a Venus flytrap, with the same broken camera. He didn't have the laser mesh back then. He added it a couple of weeks after he killed them.

He had followed their progress in the news, and he heard that they had hit two places in the region. Both places had been empty, with the owners away. So for a week he left all the lights off and operated as a functioning alcoholic in near darkness.

One night they triggered the rear camera sensor, and he was waiting. He had left the back door unlocked, and he heard their incompetent approach through his hallway, towards the kitchen.

He killed Crackhead#1 instantly with a high powered crossbow bolt that went through his head and pinned him to the wall.

Crackhead#2 was paralysed and stood there, with a small knife, limp in his hand, not knowing what to do.

Those last precious seconds of his life were his final contribution to humanity. All he saw was the shimmering light moving rapidly towards him from down the hallway. He reflected to himself, in is own drug-induced way, that it reminded him of one of those kaleidoscopes that he'd had as a child.

The big hunting knife embedded itself in his chest and lifted him off his feet with the force of the impact.

The Professor, half drunk, decided to bury them in pit at the back. It had taken him all night to dig because he was in poor condition. It was not helped by his continuous whiskey consumption, as he flung dirt out of the deepening hole. He was in a race with the sunrise, and he finished the job just before dawn.

He laid them in the pit, and then covered them with a lime blanket, replacing the dirt and then driving over them a few times with his tractor.

Over the next few weeks, the country noticed a significant drop-off in break-ins. No one ever figured out what happened to the *farmhouse bandits*.

He freezes the video feed on his smartphone, and he can see that she's halfway to the rear of the house.

Wait a minute.

He rewinds and watches her approach again, then pauses the feed again.

That walk!

The predatory stance when she stops. How she slowly moves her head side to side, taking everything in.

Jesus Christ!

It's her!

His heart begins to hammer through the alcoholic haze, and he rewinds the video five seconds, letting it play forward.

Yes, it's her, he confirms to himself, instantly realising he's wasted precious seconds.

He slides the video time bar forward to the live point, and watches as she disappears from the camera view, into the blind spot by the back door.

He forces himself to slow his breathing, and wipes the forty-percent proof sweat from his forehead. He closes down the security app and then sends off a message to four numbers that he'd hoped he would never have to use. Then he puts down his phone, picks up his loaded shotgun, and stands behind the table focusing on sounds.

So be it, he thinks.

She reaches the side door under the broken camera and carefully tests the handle. She's surprised that it is unlocked, given the security measures he has guarding the rest of the property.

The door lets off a small creak, then it settles into its hinges and opens the rest of the way silently.

She takes off the backpack and pulls out her GLOCK 26 Gen5, and takes her *iPhone* from her back pocket, laying the rest of her equipment on the floor. Then she slowly moves through the door.

The hallway is about twenty metres long, and she can see a soft light flickering from under the door at the far end.

TV.

She gingerly tests the floor boards in front of her for creaks, then opens up her phone and selects the *DJI* app, and slowly creeps forward.

He knows the rhythm of his house.

He's lived here alone for over two decades. He knows every sound and vibration. So he feels it as the intruder passes the great clock on the wall. And he knows what comes next.

The sound that has irritated him for so many years, and which he kept promising himself to fix.

Creak.

Two metres from the kitchen door. He raises the shotgun and aims it dead centre.

She bites her lip as she feels the wooden floorboard sink a centimetre under her left foot. It's followed by a light creaking sound.

Dammit!

She lifts her foot again and the creak responds. There is no sound coming from the kitchen. She's just under two metres from the door. She gently places her right foot in front, and tests the floor again.

No creak.

Then she moves forward the final two paces, with her back sliding against the wall. She can now see the old metal door handle, rusted from a lack of maintenance.

She stops, opens up her phone, and activates the flight path she had programmed in.

Ten seconds, she says to herself.

She grabs the broom handle leaning against the opposite wall, and reaches forward, pushing down the door handle with the tip.

The roar of the shotgun blast is deafening, and Tilda turns her head to avoid the splinters as they explode into the hallway.

That was only one barrel, she confirms to herself.

The kitchen door disappears into oblivion, and he's getting ready to fire the other barrel into the wall to the right.

Suddenly, something crashes into the kitchen window, and he whirls round, sending his remaining cartridge of buckshot towards the disturbance.

It obliterates the window, and the drone hovering behind it, and he stands there, alcohol-paralysed, trying to process what just happened.

Clarity resumes, as she bursts through the destroyed kitchen door, firing off rounds.

GLOCK, he thinks, even as three bullets hit him in the chest.

He doesn't feel the fourth blow through his right shoulder.

He's heard people tell stories of how you die in slow motion. He now knows that's not true.

The chest shots blow him back into the old iron stove, and he feels competition for pain as his spine slams into the immovable object. He tumbles over and lands on his back, staring up at the ceiling, vaguely aware of her approaching form.

She stands over him, looking down at his mortally wounded body. He thinks that she has nice black hair these days, even though her face is unrecognisable. But when she kneels down to get close to his face, he catches a glimpse of the past.

She brings her ear close to his mouth to try to hear what he is whispering. She turns to face him and nods, looking into his eyes with a cold stare.

He remembers a tune from an old movie called *American Beauty*. It was the most haunting, beautiful sound he had ever heard. He reaches down into the rapidly declining cognitive capabilities that is his mind, trying to bring that tune to the surface.

It is beyond reach.

Tilda looks down at The Professor as his eyes begin to flutter, as if he is searching for something.

She stands up, aims down, and puts two into his forehead. Then she drops her gun hand to her side and stands there, breathing in the night air which is blowing in through the shattered window.

After a minute, she recovers her posture, and goes to the kitchen table. She picks up his smartphone, but it's locked so she takes it back over to his body, and opens it with a scan of his bloody face.

The messaging app is still open, and she can see that he just fired off a text to four other numbers. It only contains two words.

Lærke's alive.

She sits down at the table and pours herself the remainder of his whiskey, and downs it in one.

Camilla's sitting on her terrace, sipping a cognac, staring out at the blinking lights on the *Storebælt* bridge, warning aircraft of the majestic structure connecting Sjælland with Fyn.

Ping.

She's about to pick up her phone, when Lucas wanders out onto the terrace in his shorts.

"You want some coffee?" he asks, wrapping his arms around her shoulders, and kissing the back of her neck.

She leans her head forward, inviting him to continue, and he obliges. She's still dressed in her business suit, having just got back from Odense after ten.

"Better not have any coffee, I'll never sleep."

Lucas leans into her ear and says, "who says you're allowed to sleep?"

She looks over her shoulder, and into his mischievous eyes, and kisses the tip of his disjointed nose.

"Good idea. Come and join me first out here for a while."

Lucas goes back in to get a jumper and Camilla reaches down to the side table, picking up her phone. Finally, those Americans have woken up, she thinks, opening up the message.

Lucas comes rushing through the terrace doors at the sound of the breaking glass.

"You OK, Milli?" he asks.

She's standing up now, with her back to him, facing south towards the great bridge.

The phone is dangling in her right hand.

"Milli, whats the matter?"

Camilla turns, and stares at Lucas, not saying anything. After an eternity, she walks toward him and rests her hand on his shoulders, then says "I...I need to go back to the office."

"Are you kidding me? At this time! It's nearly eleven."

"Yeah, somethings come up. I'll be back in a few hours," she says, planting a soft kiss on his forehead.

Before he can respond, she has walked past him, towards the front door, grabbing her keys and then goes out and gets in her car.

Lucas hears her burn rubber out of the driveway.

Camilla doesn't go to the office. She hangs a left onto the highway and aims her Mercedes towards Copenhagen.

Bekka and Simon are sitting in their living room. Bekka finally got the kids settled. As usual, she handled it because *His Majesty* was too busy playing with his stocks app.

They haven't said a word all day, except for common responses needed when the kids were around. Bekka looks over at him and thinks, *what the fuck happened to you?*

He senses her scowl and tries to hold her stare, but turns away, knowing he's in the shit, and that it's better just to ride out the storm.

Both their phones ping at the same time, breaking the tension in the air. Like addicts, they automatically reach for their sugar rush dispensers, opening up their messages.

They both look up.

"No, no, no...this is bullshit," says Simon, looking at his phone.

Bekka gets up and strides over to the other sofa. She looks over his shoulder, and then compares his message with hers.

"No number," she says.

"Who did this come from?"

"Only one person alive who would send a message like that," Bekka replies.

"But we haven't heard from him in going on twenty years," says Simon, rechecking his device. "Are you sure it wasn't Cami—"

"Don't mention that Funen bitch's name in this house where your kids are sleeping!" hisses Bekka. "Besides, she wouldn't tip us off. It's The Professor."

"Should we call him back?"

Bekka stands up again and walks to the living room window, peering through the curtains. She knows it's a totally irrational thing to do.

"No point. He's probably dead already," she says, not turning back to her husband.

"There is...*him*," Simon says, getting up and walking to the rear sliding doors, and looking out onto the garden as it disappears into the darkness.

Bekka shivers. She hadn't thought of The Dutchman in over two decades. Well, not quite true. She'd had a few nightmares, always the same. Always his face pressed in close against hers, breathing in his foul smell. She shivers again.

"We need to make some preparations, think this through. Things are different now. We can't just make a run for it, or go hunt her."

"Why not?" asks Simon, turning from the glass doors.

"Because of the kids, you wanker!" she yells, a little too loud. She catches herself, and then advances on him, causing him to back up.

"Of course I know that, but we can leave them with your mother or sister," he counters.

"And you don't think she would have considered that?" Simon looks into Bekka's eyes, almost pleading.

"But surely, she wouldn't go for the kids?" It was a half hopeful question.

"It's *Lærke*," says Bekka, answering his question, and causing the colour to drain from his face.

"No, we need to think this through. Unfortunately, we might need to call your old girlfriend," she says with disgust.

"She won't talk to me," says Simon, hoping that his wife will bail him out of the job.

"Fuck, no! You screwed her, you call her. Find out what she knows, and what her plan is."

Nikolaj's nurturing a potential hangover, thanks to the tumbler of whiskey that's running on autonomous mode.

He's spread out on his sofa, scrolling through his research on this Brit called Simon, and his boutique investment outfit. He'd made the decision to commit to the two-part project, and set the wheels in motion with the TV station. For the last twenty-four hours he'd had a couple of students from one of his classes go dig around on this guy.

And they went off the deep end. Turns out this guy's venture fund first saw the light of day around '07. It was gassed-up from an injection of Icelandic cash that came from London, freshly laundered, and hung out to dry in Copenhagen via some investments in obscure startups.

Obscure because they were basically vapourware running off the *fake-it-till-you-make-it* genes that had becoming de rigueur.

But somehow, this guy's early infusion of cash enabled the three companies to pump their valuations, creating exits to global corporates that really should have known better. With a hefty war chest of two hundred and fifty million dollars from those exits, Simon and his two cronies ploughed it all into a new fund, this time focused on financial services.

Disco.

He did it again.

Pawning off some dodgy new financial apps to international banks after another five years, only for them to be written off quietly by the bank's accountants a year after the acquisitions closed.

Another three hundred and twenty million, thank you very much. This time it's in Euros.

Then another new fund in the late twenty teens. This time healthtech's hot. So Simon's mob venture out of Denmark and go shopping in Finland and Sweden.

Two years later, same gig. Big Pharma are the ones this time on the end of the screwing.

Nikolaj's thinking, *this guy is really good. At fucking people over*. He fires up a couple of *YouTubes* of the Brit speaking at a few startup and venture funding conferences. Silky smooth, with charm dripping off the threads of his fifty thousand kroner suits.

He's in pretty good shape too, Nikolaj thinks. Simon's even got three years on Nikolaj, which pisses him off.

Nikolaj goes further back in time. Pre-'2000 and his *LinkedIn*'s a bit on the vague side. More like non-existent.

Seems he just appeared out of a bottle like a genie in the early two thousands. A few scattered references to a career as a British officer, but light on the details.

Nikolaj goes sniffing round his two partners, who are pretty vanilla. They went from being office clerks to financial *Senior Executive Vice Presidents* in the space of a year.

Around the time they hooked up with Simon.

Next he digs into his family. Married to a Dane with two kids. Been together a long time. She can look after herself. Runs a karate and yoga school. She's got steel in her eyes, he can see from the glamour pics. Seems they bought their way up in the world. Now they've got a Vedbæk address, and are regular hosts for the Copenhagen in-crowd. Seems they also share a few joint acquaintances.

Hmmm, maybe I can leverage my way in.

He reckons he'll try to score and intro with Simon before this Saturday's part one. If not, he'll chase down the wife, Rebekah. If he can't get anything out of them he'll run the positive angle on the amazing venture firm with unbelievable returns.

That'll be the set up, and it will flush out the whistleblowers. Then the following Saturday he'll go to town on the guy.

Or maybe not. Maybe he's clean, but Nikolaj's got a feeling about this guy.

And an itchy mouse finger.

The Devil is powering through the surf in his new *Scarab Jet 285 ID*.

The wraparound *Oakleys* are protecting his eyes from the warm wind as he makes a hole in it.

He spent the early afternoon snorkelling a couple of kilometres off shore, then he went back to the villa to freshen up for the evenings entertainment on St. Maarten.

He looks down as his phone begins to move on the dashboard from the vibration of an incoming message. He grabs for it, and raises the shades onto his forehead.

When he reads the message, he slams the throttle back, causing the boat to come to a rapid halt.

He sits there, reading the message again, as the powerful boat idles halfway between the two islands.

He gets out of his seat, and makes his way to the back of the boat, and stands there, gazing out at the horizon. He checks his watch, then goes onto the *KLM* site and looks up flights. The next flight out to Amsterdam is tomorrow, late afternoon, so he makes a reservation.

He looks out to sea again, rechecking his watch. He figures he has plenty of time to make some investigations and put some assets into play.

He has one *Unit*, working out of Goteborg, that's just rotated out of the field. They won't be happy, but they're the closest assets he has to Denmark.

He then reminds himself of his evening's entertainment that he'd ordered special delivery from Arkansas.

He rubs the bumps on his forehead. *Shame to let that little investment go to waste.*

So be it. He will continue on to St Maarten, satisfy his carnal urges, then return in the early hours to Anguilla. There, he'll make his preparations, then be back over at St. Maarten airport by early afternoon. He can catch-up on sleep in First Class. His plan is set, so he climbs back into the drivers seat and opens up the throttle.

Lærke. Well, well, well...

Tilda spends the next four hours cleaning up the mess. There's not much she can do about the window or the door, but she goes to work on the bloodstains after dragging The Professor's body out the back door on a sheet.

Next she starts going through his drawers. She finds his laptop but can't access it. She puts it in her backpack with his phone, confident that she can get into them later. She goes out to the front, and picks up the remains of her disintegrated drone. After that, she goes round the house to the back field and begins to dig.

She's in her car two hours later, heading towards Århus, when she hears The Professor's phone ringing in her backpack. She pulls over and takes the phone out. It's a blocked number.

She answers the call, and puts the phone to her ear. All she hears is the background sound of a car in motion. She sits there, listening and breathing for thirty seconds, then she closes the call.

So the game is on, she thinks, pulling out onto the quiet road and heading east.

She doesn't go back to her hotel. Instead, she goes to the Airbnb and parks her Peugeot rental in front of her Tesla. She enters the house, gets undressed, and runs a bath to wash the dirt and familiar old smell of death from her body.

At two-thirty am, a car's headlights flood the living room of Bekka and Simon's villa.

Bekka has been sitting at the kitchen table for the last two hours, interrogating her laptop. She's been growing more and more frustrated as all of her former passwords to secure systems have expired. Gradually, over the last ten years, they became more and more comfortable with their new life. They lapsed in their paranoid focus on precautionary measures, as their priorities got adjusted towards their children. And keeping up their increasingly lavish lifestyle.

Simon had gained a bit of a fold-over, and Bekka constantly nagged him about it. For her part, she took pride in her physical condition, and would sometimes smile to herself when she was giving her demanding yoga classes.

If any of these women knew what I was truly capable of... well...At fifty-six, Bekka was still a match for many combat veterans. Especially if knives were involved.

She looks up from the laptop as the full beam of the lights penetrates the front room.

"What the fuck?" She goes over to the locked drawer above the drinks cabinet, and takes out her pistol. Then she walks back through the living room and shakes Simon out of his sleep.

"Get up. We've got company," she whispers, walking over to the curtains, and peering through at the blinding light.

Simon gets up and rubs his face, walking up behind his wife.

"*Lærke*?" he says under his breath. She turns on him, and looks directly into his eyes.

"You really think she'd announce herself? No, when she comes, we won't see her. This is someone else. You go out there"

"Me?" Simon says in a squeaky voice. "Why me?"

"Because it's your fucking girlfriend," rasps Bekka.

Simon knows it's the smart thing to do. Bekka and Camilla always were a combustible cocktail and needed to be handled with care. He was handy with explosives, but he couldn't disarm those two if they got into it.

He goes to the front door, and turns to look at his wife.

"I got your back, babe," she says, suddenly concerned about his safety. He nods and opens the door, closing it quietly behind him.

The headlights shut down their full beam, leaving only the side lights on. He can see a black *Merc* wrapped in an *AMG* sports package, squatting low like a big cat, behind the gate. Behind the steering wheel he can make her out, staring directly at him, with her eyeballs on full beam.

His pulse begins to race, then he catches himself, reminding himself that his wife is standing behind the curtains with a gun. He opens the gate with his phone and Camilla cruises into the driveway. He closes the gates behind her, and a thought occurs to him that maybe they are now boxed in. She pulls up behind his 911, and gets out.

It seems to take an age for her to lift her long limbs out of the *Merc*, exacerbating his stress levels. Or, is it sexual desires.

Focus, you wanker, he demands of himself.

"It's been a while," she says in her deep, throaty voice, as she approaches him.

"Indeed, you should have dropped by before," replies Simon, trying to sound nonchalant, but not quite pulling it off.

"I'm sure your wife would have loved that," she says, nodding towards the house. "She got a gun on me now?"

"Naturally," says Simon.

"So it seems twenty-seven years ago we screwed up."

Simon doesn't respond. He just looks at the window and then says, "you better come in."

"Love to," says Camilla striding past him, catching off guard, and causing him to try to run after her before she gets to the door.

Bekka opens it, with the pistol dangling from her right hand.

"That a welcoming present for me?" asks Camilla, climbing the three steps to the door.

"It depends how this conversation goes," responds Bekka. "I'll hang-on to it, if you don't mind."

"It's your house, but no, you won't need it. But I do need a drink."

"Come in then. Cognac still your tipple?" asks Bekka.

"Yep, I'm predictable that way," says Camilla walking through into the hallway.

She glances around, then walks into the big living room. "Impressive place. You keeping up with *the Joneses*?" she adds, sarcastically.

Simon walks in behind and says, "can you two please speak english?"

"Sure babe," says Camilla, catching Bekka's look, and causing Simon to wince.

Jesus Christ, it's like a fucking Mexican standoff in the middle of Vedbæk, he thinks.

Camilla walks over to the drinks bar, and helps herself to a healthy dose of *Louis XIII*. Simon's about to tell her to go easy, but Bekka grabs his wrist, and gives him the look that says *now's not the time to start measuring your fucking cognacs, dear*.

Camilla turns, raises her glass, and says, "to old times," and takes a big swig.

"So she's back, then," states Bekka.

"She's back. And more to the point, she's already taken The Professor off the grid."

"How do you know?" asks Simon.

"Because I called him," responds Camilla, in a matter of fact way.

"You got his number? How? We couldn't see the number the message came from," says Bekka advancing toward her.

"Our old colleague was a silent partner in my business. He wasn't an active investor. He just lived off the passive income I generated for him. It allowed him to live out his fantasy in that shit hole on Jylland. So yes, I had his fucking number."

"So how do you know he's dead?" asks Simon again.

"Because our long, lost friend answered," says Camilla, finishing off the rest of the cognac. She goes back to the bottle and pours herself another triple measure, then turns and raises her glass at the two of them.

Bekka's waiting for her to go on, while Simon's staring at the rapidly disappearing golden liquid in the bottle, thinking, *that's a month's mortgage she's chugging*!

"She didn't say anything. But I heard her breathing." Camilla looks down at the ground, and mutters in Danish, "it's like she was breathing directly into my soul."

Simon looks at Bekka, waiting for the translation. Bekka pays him no attention, and waits for Camilla to regain her composure. She doesn't say anything. She just stands there, staring at the floor.

Bekka, growing impatient says, "OK, so what do we do now?"

Camilla looks at the wife of her ex-lover and says, "we take her out, and finish the job that we fucked-up on that Minorcan beach a quarter of a century ago."

"What about *him*?" asks Bekka.

"If he's still alive, then he has assets we could put in play."

Simon's face drains of all its blood, and Camilla looks directly into Bekka's eyes. "For sure he's still alive. And I'm sure he got the same message. The Professor could find anyone. I would bet my company that he's on his way over here now."

"Fuck!" says Simon.

"I need to get back. If she took out The Professor at his farm, then she could be planning to work her way across the country."

"And if she is?"

"Then I'll welcome her onto Fyn, and you two won't have to worry about anything. Well, except when *he* arrives. But he's your problem. I'll handle Lærke once and for all," says Camilla, finishing off her second triple and dropping the empty glass onto the cream sofa.

"I won't be in touch," she says as she strides between the two of them and out of the front door, leaving it open behind her.

Camilla doesn't return home. Instead she blows straight past Nyborg on the E20, and goes to her office in Odense. She arrives around four-thirty in the morning, and goes to the gym to take a shower. She sets it to piping hot, and stands under it for ten minutes, then she flips it to freezing cold and takes two minutes of pain.

As she begins to dry herself off, her mind begins to clear, thanks to the alcohol wearing off and the assault on her senses from the harsh shower. She knows she needs coffee, but she needs sleep more, so she goes up to her executive suite and lays down on the sofa.

She wakes up around seven forty-five when she's disturbed by the cleaner, who is surprised to see the CEO half hanging off the sofa. She snaps to attention, rubs her face, and fluffs up her hair. Then she goes to her private kitchen, and puts the coffee machine on.

She wanders back out to the car park and takes her spare suit from the back of the *Merc*. As she's walking back into the building, she gets a call from Lucas. She sends it to voicemail. She'll call him after she's had her first caffeine infusion.

Her mind is a bag of nettles. Everything's turned upside down since yesterday evening. The consequences of Lærke being alive, and out there, are too much for her to process. And being forced to bring those two idiots back into her life is almost as bad. She hated Lærke as much for that, as for disrupting her perfectly balanced existence.

There are many implications to consider. Camilla always liked to make lists, with business at the top, and personal stuff at the bottom. But Lucas had given her a whole new outlook on life, and she loved him dearly. She knew she could never tell him about Lærke, because then she would have to tell him everything. And that would open up the whole can of worms.

How do you explain to your sweet husband, who is twenty-one years younger than you, that you used to be an international assassin?

It's of course possible he might get past that, but his reaction would probably be male-orientated. He would want to protect her. And there was no protection from Lærke. She would not stop, and she would kill everything in her path to get to Camilla. After all, Camilla had *killed* her on a beach a generation ago.

That worked out well, she thinks.

Then there are the others. *Well, fuck them.*

But she could use them. They were, probably still are, useful assets. *Decoys? Possible.* Simon and Bekka have kids now, so they're even more motivated than her. With The Professor off the map, that leaves only *him*.

She shivers with the thought, and puts *him* to the back of her mind. *No, what I need to do is get Lærke out in the open. And away from Lucas.*

She sits back in her chair and sips her coffee, thinking through all the variables. Then she calls Lucas to apologise and promise him a week at their Tuscan villa in a couple of weeks.

Tilda slept until noon, then crawled out of bed to make some coffee. Now she looks in the bathroom mirror and thinks about *Lærke*. It's been over fifteen years since she raised herself above the level of Tilda's subconscious. She's worked hard to suppress the nightmares of the life she once led.

Well, they were not all nightmares, she thinks. *There was... Nikolaj.*

She looks down at the sink, splashes cold water on her face, then looks back up to the mirror, trying to banish his long buried image again.

She had tracked his movements for a while in the early 2000s. Over the last five years, his name kept popping up thanks to social media, and his increasingly successful public profile. She rationalised that *Tilda* didn't even know him. *Lærke* did. But she never won that argument with herself whenever he visited her half-dreamy state in the late hours.

She needs to get some air and food, so she decides to go the local store and get some groceries, and then come back and take a look into The Professor's devices. And then she needs to start re-planning. His message to the other members of *The Unit* will have them all running around trying to predict her next moves.

She came into Denmark with a detailed profile on their locations and regular movements, but for sure they would now adjust those. And probably call in extra security.

I can't think straight on an empty stomach. She goes to the bedroom and gets dressed, then exits the house from the rear, checking the road for anything suspicious.

He exits the villa on St. Maarten in the early hours, and he knows he is way behind schedule.

He runs down to the harbour and jumps in his Scarab. As he goes to release the mooring lines, he notices the blood on his hands. He puts them into the water and washes off the girl's existence. He realises he got careless because he was distracted by the clock. Still, he got his fix, and it put his vile urges on hold for a few days.

He considers the look in her eyes, when she realised who she had been sold to. Her fear fed his desires, and only served to bring out his most evil tendencies.

Well, he corrects himself, *I am evil. Whatever that means.*

He doesn't consider himself operating on the same plane of existence as other mortals. Unfortunately, he is also mortal, although he has also been working on solving that problem. He's sunk close to three hundred and fifty mil into life extension tech. Some of it has shown real promise, but nothing to set his life clock back the decades he needs. So he's been hedging his bets with *The Dark Lord*.

As a rational devil worshiper, he knows these sacrifices, and other activities, yield little return, except for temporarily satisfying his carnal needs. But on a deep, primal level, he senses something down there, in the darkest pit of his mind, that he can grasp the longevity he requires through the suffering of others.

The fresh breeze from the boat blasting through the surf reorientates his mind. He has business to take care of in Denmark, so now he's all about preparation. He'll connect to Amsterdam via Paris, then he figures he'll be in his rental, heading east from Amsterdam toward Denmark by the end of tomorrow.

He's decided not to tell the other members of *The Unit* of his imminent arrival. He wants them disorientated when he appears in their mist. They may wonder if he is coming.

Well, let them marinate in their own fear. He doesn't actually care about them. Only one thing concerns him. *Lærke.*

Simon's freaking out because he got word that someone's doing a hit job on him.

Not one of those assassination types. It seems his insatiable greed and desire to be seen in the right circles has ensured that he flew onto the radar of one of those TV exposé journalists.

And not just anyone. Simon's watched this guy Nikolaj go to work on his victims, carefully building them up, then dropping the hammer with a Saturday night special.

Simon got a tip off from one of his *Café Victor* crew who was trading business gossip with someone who was sleeping with someone they shouldn't have been, who'd overheard something at the *Palæ Bar*. So by the time Simon got the word, half of Copenhagen knows that he's getting shit-canned.

Then it's confirmed when his assistant tells him that he's had a request for a meeting from this fucker, Nikolaj.

Shit, he thinks as he drives through Klampenborg, oblivious to the sun, sea, or the *Swedish Unit* that were googling him just over the bridge to the east of his location.

He knows Bekka's going to freak. Especially if they've got anything on him and it plays out on the TV. From there it's a short hop onto social media, then he's viral.

Now, we are fucking viral, he can imagine Bekka screaming.

After that, it's a six month vacation down to their place in the south of France, and off every dinner party list for the next three years as they go through social rehab. If they make it, that is.

All members of *The Unit* had carefully crafted their legends. And thankfully, their antics pre-dated the age of social media. So not too many bread crumbs. But Simon knows that if this Nikolaj is as good as they say he is, then something could turn up. Then it goes from being a personal embarrassment, to possibly life threatening for himself, Bekka...and the kids.

Jesus!

He almost banks the car on the sidewalk, nearly taking out a rollerblader. He jerks the wheel to the left, skidding the car back onto the road, to the sound of horns.

He's sweating now. Trying to process all the possible scenarios and options.

What if I just took this guy out?

Well, he wouldn't actually do it himself. He hasn't got his feet wet in over fifteen years. But he knows a few guys who know some guys...

Forget it. This is Denmark! Those kinds of things don't go on here. But still... Keep it on the back burner, mate.

Maybe he should meet this guy. Invite him to a long lunch down at *Address*. Get him lubricated and see how it plays out. He calls his Assistant and tells him to put the word out to Nikolaj that he would welcome a discussion.

He sighs with relief, and focuses on the road as he slips through Skodsborg.

Now all I have to worry about is that fucking Dutchman and Camilla.

And Lærke...

3 - IT ALL GOES SOUTH IN MINORCA

They didn't all arrive together.

Bekka and Lærke brought the weapons and other technical equipment in by boat from Barcelona, then proceeded to the villa to start making preparations.

The Professor, Camilla and Simon all flew in a day later. No one knew when The Dutchman would show up. Apparently, he was already on the island, staying with some acquaintances. The team were happy if he could delay his arrival as long as possible. Even though they were hardened killers, he repulsed them. His handsome features at odds with the vile smell he excreted.

They had chosen the villa on the south coast because it was five hundred metres away from where the American family would be staying. It was one of the largest on the island. It needed to be in order to accommodate the heavy security detail that protected them at all times.

The Unit's latest INTEL from stateside suggested that the American guests were staying for at least another two weeks. That gave them plenty of time to plan the operation.

The trickiest part was to separate the kids from the adults and take care of their security. They were after three couples who had been sanctioned by CORP-ROGUE. They didn't know precisely who, or why, these individuals were to be terminated. Only The Dutchman knew. They didn't actually care. They just wanted to get the job done as fast as possible and get off the island.

They were an odd crew.

This was their sixth operation together, and they were considered to be the most efficient assassination squad in the west.

Not that anyone kept lists.

Yet, despite their extreme effectiveness, they were highly dysfunctional. It was partly due to the fear that The Dutchman engendered upon them, but mainly it was due to sexual tension.

But their competencies over-compensated for their indiscretions, and they respected each other's capabilities.

Nineteen ninety-five had been a bumper year for them, especially on the corporate side. The business world was flush with cash, and communications and the early internet were beginning to rock and roll. Depending on the layer they were working for within the CORP-ROGUE hierarchy, defined the type of target. Corporate or financial hits always came from layer three. Military from layer two, and political from one.

It was like an MBA's wet dream for subversives. The Dutchman handled sales and purchase orders, which left all of them with the uncomfortable feeling of being puppets on his strings. They had whispered during the drunken winding down sessions after missions, that they should break free of him.

Those ideas were quickly dismissed out of fear of his reach. And there was a darkness about him, that spooked even these most ruthless of killers. They considered themselves slightly moral, in that they did not take out children, although there had been one *accidental* death where a small boy was collateral damage.

Well, he wasn't collateral. The Dutchman had pulled the trigger, knowing full well the spread of bullets from the automatic weapon would annihilate everything in the vicinity.

The Professor had been particularly distressed, and it was Bekka who had prevented him from committing suicide by leaving *The Unit*.

If the Professor was the conscience, then Camilla was the polar opposite. She would not hesitate to terminate on command, then kick-back and party hard. Cognac and dancing was her way of working off the tension.

Simon was a pretty decent allrounder with guns, explosives and hand-to-hand, but the considered opinion of the rest of *The Unit* was that he was a bit of a wanker.

He was also responsible for the tension between Camilla and Bekka.

Bekka was the one that held everything together. She was short, rugged, extremely proficient, and the problem solver. Harmony was her middle name, and while they left murder and mayhem in their wake, Bekka always tried to get everyone to patch things up for the benefit of the team.

Lærke was the youngest by a couple of years. She was the only one who came close to Camilla's level of ruthlessness.

She kept her own counsel, although Bekka had got her to open up a few times after intense actions. Lærke had a preference for hand-to-hand and the long rifle. She executed every task with precision, which annoyed Camilla, because she always wanted things done fast.

That left The Dutchman. And the consensus was that he was pure evil.

Their cover was as a European corporate management team on an extended jolly. That way they could be discrete while being indiscrete. They turned up at the same restaurants as the American party on a couple of evenings, though they didn't push their luck. It was a useful observational tactic, as they quickly learned the characteristics and synchronisation patterns of the four armed guards.

The biggest problem was the alcohol. To blend into the noisy restaurant scene, they had to drink. And Camilla and Simon took that seriously, which made their post-dinner analysis all the more complex.

A couple of times when they got back to the villa to review their findings, Camilla and Lærke would get into it. Bekka always had to calm things down by getting between them.

By the fourth evening together, they had the genesis of a plan. They would take out the targets at the villa when, hopefully, the kids would be asleep in the wing across from the adults. They had actually discovered that there were six guards, and they operated on a rotational basis, ensuring twenty-four hour coverage, with rest built into to their daily regimens.

Two of the guards were Brits, one Spaniard and three Americans, and they comprised of four men and two women. As a professional courtesy, *The Unit* studied them closely, and could discern that they were competent and efficient, but they had a preference for outward aggression and machismo. This, *The Unit* decided, was their weak spot.

The time was set for two-thirty in the morning of the sixth day. *The Unit* would split into three teams. The Professor and The Dutchman would coordinate from the north side of the compound, which had the advantage of a grove of orange trees and high ground. The Professor would neutralise the two guards on the early shift with his silenced long rifle, when they were walking in opposite directions.

Camilla and Simon would approach from the east, and situate themselves behind a low, white-washed wall between the adult's and children's wing. The logic being that any surviving adults from Bekka and Lærke's assault from the west side wing, would be flushed out into a hail of gunfire.

It all centred on first neutralising the on-duty guards, followed by their resting comrades, then the real targets.

It seemed like the most optimal plan.

Then it all went to shit.

Specifically, they hadn't counted on the fact that one of the children would be sleeping in the parent's bed.

So when Camilla and Simon assaulted the adults wing, the child woke up and ran out towards the swimming pool, followed by his mother. One guard who hadn't been taken out, came sprinting out of the complex. He was obliterated by The Dutchman from the elevated position. He also killed the mother and child, in an extended burst of fire.

Lærke leapt over the low wall and began screaming at The Dutchman to cease firing. But he kept blasting rounds into the mother, even as she tumbled into the pool after her dead son.

Finally, the shooting stopped, and Lærke stood there with her submachine gun dangling from her shoulder. She looked into the red pool, and vomited on the tiles.

Bekka came up behind her and looked into the water. Then she looked up into Lærke's eyes. But Lærke wasn't looking at her. She was staring up into the darkness, at the clump of trees where The Dutchman was firing from.

Bekka grabbed her forearm and said, "let it go. We need to move. Now!"

But Lærke was rooted to the ground, continuing to stare at the orange grove.

She saw The Professor emerge, followed by The Dutchman. Who was grinning. At the same time, Camilla and Simon emerged from the adults wing, still aiming their weapons, but lowering them when they saw that the action was over.

Camilla strode over to Bekka and Lærke and said, "what the fuck is up with her?"

Lærke's left fist connected with Camilla's temple, and sent her down on her knees. Then Lærke was on her in an instant, reigning punches and knees to Camilla's body.

Bekka grabbed Lærke from behind in a bear hug, and Simon ran over and braced Camilla.

"Fucking let me go, you wanker. I will finish her now," Camilla screamed.

But Simon held her firm. Lærke's eyes were bulging out of her sockets, but she turned her stare from Camilla and aimed it at The Professor, who was jogging over.

"Where is he?" asked Lærke, looking round for The Dutchman.

"He bugged out," The Professor replied.

"Where?"

"He's on his way to the place he was staying at to get his gear. He said he would meet us at the boat."

Lærke stood there staring into the darkness beyond the shimmering pool. Then she took her pistol from her holster and checked the magazine and spares in her belt. She walked across the terrace to one of the slain guards, kneeled down, and opened up his blood-soaked shirt.

She took out two more magazines and checked them, stuffing them into the long pockets of her khaki pants. The others stood there watching her, as she strode past them toward the front of the villa.

"Don't do it," said Bekka, making a grab for Lærke's arm.

"Fuck her, let her go," said Camilla, rubbing the side of her head.

As Lærke disappeared down the steps, Simon said, "we need to move now. The boat won't hang around for long."

"And it looks like we woke up the neighbourhood. Lights just came on in the villa down the road," added The Professor.

That focused them, and they gathered up their equipment and made a hasty exit out the rear of the villa, circling wide, back to their vehicles.

Then they heard the screeching of wheels as Lærke peeled out of the driveway.

Lærke being Lærke didn't over-engineer the assault on The Dutchman's villa.

She put one in the head of the female guard who was pacing the perimeter, with her silenced pistol. The guard fell sideways into a small bush, creating a disturbance, causing the second guard to peer around the corner, directly into Lærke's gun barrel.

She blew out the back of his head, catching some of the spray on her face. She wiped it off on her dark shirt, then looked round the corner.

Two down, how many to go? She paused, slowing her breathing, listening. She could hear the sound of men talking and laughing from within the villa.

She back-tracked past the other dead guard and snuck round the whole perimeter. Satisfied there was no more security outside, she climbed up onto a low wall, then pulled herself onto the first floor balcony. She looked through the terrace doors and could see the room was empty, so she opened them and slipped into the bedroom. She padded across the floor with her gun raised in front of her, tracking her vision. She reached the bedroom door and could now make out the conversation from the open living room below.

She slowly opened the bedroom door, but only enough for her to squeeze her body through. She put the gun in the back of her trousers and crawled through the opening on her knees.

She reached the wall overlooking the living area and could see the shadows from the big open fire dancing on the ceiling. The Dutchman was speaking english slowly, in his precise, clipped accent. Lærke knew that she should wait and listen to what was being said. But her mind was being assaulted by the images of the bullet-riddled body of the child as he fell into the pool, followed by his mother.

Lærke went into a dreamlike state. It was if she was an observer, unable to influence the actions she was about to execute. The bald, fat man took two in the upper chest before anyone could react. As she pulled her aim round to the elder white-haired man, she sensed movement on the opposite sofa, followed by a hail of bullets that rained down on her position.

She continued firing, blindly, even as she ducked back behind the wall. The smell of gunpowder was all around, as well as a deafening silence as the gunfire abated. Then she heard the moans of a man, clearly in agony.

She raised her gun over the top of the balcony wall and fired off another three rounds in the approximate direction of where the shots came from.

No response, except for the man's moaning. She released her magazine and put a fresh one in, then slowly raised her head and peered over the wall down into the living area.

The fat guy was sprawled over a sofa, still clinging onto his last whiskey. On the opposite sofa was the white-haired man who was curled up in a ball. He had taken one in the upper part of his leg.

There was a third man and he was crawling behind the sofa, making a line for the rear door. None of them were The Dutchman.

Lærke raised herself to a crouch, then quickly moved to the staircase, sweeping the living area with her gun as she came down the stairs silently. The sound of the crackling from the fireplace filled the room, interspersed with the moaning of the white-haired man.

She got to the bottom of the staircase and walked up behind the crawling man. He sensed the shadow as it extended over his prone body. He half turned to look up, and saw the figure of a tall woman standing over him. The light from the fire hitting her back sent a chill through his body, causing him to piss his pants, and resume his hurried crawl toward safety.

Lærke put one in the back of his leg to slow him down, then, when he rolled over in agony, she sent two more, first class delivery into his forehead. That just left the white-haired guy on the sofa.

And The Dutchman.

One bastard at a time.

She swept the room again, as she walked past the raging fire towards the figure rolling around on the sofa.

"Who are you?" Lærke asked, kneeling down and prodding the man's wound with the silencer on the end of her pistol.

"Do you realise who we are?" responded the old man, half pleading with her.

"Last chance," she said, parking a round in his right ankle.

The man let out a howl as tears streamed down his face. He started to howl again, then choked on his rising vomit, muffling his scream.

"Where's The Dutchman?" Lærke demanded, bringing her face in close on his.

"He...he's...I don't know. He–"

Lærke stood up, realising it was useless, and fired a burst into the side of his head. Then she looked around the devastating scene. Three bodies, a lot of blood and flames dancing around the white walls and high ceiling. It was a charnel house.

She knew she should get out fast. The Dutchman was in the wind. *Would he go to the rendezvous on the beach*? She doubted it. But she wanted to know what the connection was between him and these other three men.

She searched around the rooms downstairs and found nothing. Then she went back up the stairs and started going through the other bedrooms. She came to the fourth wooden door at the far end of the hall, and tested the handle. It was locked.

She took aim and blew out the lock, then kicked in the door. The smell almost floored her, and she recoiled, retching up nothing but a dry cough. She recovered her composure, then walked into the room.

Lærke dropped the pistol to the floor, as she brought her hand to her mouth. The tears came next as she tried to process the scene of utter destruction that had been wrought upon the young bodies. She began to waver, and had to steady herself on the wall, then she lowered herself into a squat, and started to cry.

She set the fires in the rooms on the first floor, then made her way downstairs, setting the drapes and other furnishings alight. Then she exited out of the back of the villa, and ran down onto the road where she had left the car.

As she climbed in, she looked over her shoulder as the flames began to fan out of the building, consuming those tragic souls on the upper floor, who had the misfortune to have been sold to The Devil.

The four of them had gathered on the beach behind some rocks, just up from some locals who were working on their boats which had been dragged onto the beach.

The Unit had decided against boarding their boat in the local harbour because of the danger of being observed by the port authorities. They had changed into tourist gear, and stashed their weapons and comms gear in some long bags.

Tension was rising, for a number of reasons. Firstly, their ride had not yet arrived, and he was already twenty minutes late. Secondly, Lærke had not shown up since she bailed out on them at the villa. And thirdly, neither had The Dutchman.

For the last forty minutes they kept hearing sirens from emergency services, then they saw a big column of smoke rising behind a hill a few kilometres off. The Professor noted that it was in the rough direction of the villa that The Dutchman was staying.

Bekka saw the motor launch first. "There it is," she said pointing, as the motor boat made its way through the early morning surf.

They all looked round and started gathering up their gear, just as a car screeched to a halt in the car park above the beach. They looked up and could see Lærke climb out of the drivers seat, grab her backpack, and run down the steps to the beach.

She had not changed, and they could make out the dark stains on her shirt and khakis.

"What did you do?" yelled Camilla, turning on her.

Lærke brushed past her and went up to The Professor, poked him in the chest, and said, "did you know about their fucking cult up there?"

The Professor shook his head and said, "I have no idea what you are talking about?"

"I'm talking about human sacrifices!" They all looked around at each other, silently.

"*What did you do?*" asked Camilla again, in a whispered voice.

Lærke looked directly at her and said, "I sent them off to meet their Lord."

Bekka walked forward and asked, "and The Dutchman?"

"I missed him."

"Christ! That means he's going to come after us with everything he has!" screamed Simon.

"No, you prick. He will come for me. He only saw me."

"Well, you are with us, genius," sneered Camilla, "that means you dropped this on us too!"

Lærke, looking at Bekka said, "listen, all I want is a ride out of here. Then you won't see me again."

"You're not getting on that boat," Camilla said, getting in Lærke's face.

Simon said, "she's right, Lærke, you're gonna have to find your own way off the island."

"Screw you all, I coming," she said, bending over to pick up her backpack.

As Lærke stood up, there was a small popping sound and she stumbled backward, clutching her stomach.

"Jesus! What the fuck did you do!" screamed Bekka.

"We have to move now," said The Professor, nodding toward the boat bobbing up and down in the waves.

"She's not dead!" said Bekka, kneeling down over Lærke.

"Finish her off," said Simon, looking over at Camilla.

"No problem. Out of the way, Bekka," Camilla said as she stood over Lærke, aiming her gun at her head. Then she froze, and put her gun behind her back, as a group of locals rounded the rock and stopped in front of them.

"Our friend is sick," said Simon in pigeon english, that none of them seemed to understand.

Camilla put her hand on his shoulder, whispering, "let's get out of here." She picked up her bag and started jogging to the surf.

By now, the group of locals had been joined by others, and they were edging towards them to see what was wrong with the woman on the ground.

The Professor looked at Bekka, who was distraught, and said, "we are leaving, now!"

He took off after Camilla and Simon, quickly followed by Bekka. They waded out into the waist-high surf, and one-by-one climbed into the motor launch. When the last one was in, the pilot opened up the throttle, and it roared off out to sea.

The locals crowded round the woman who was curled up in a ball on the beach. They could see the dark brown stain that was expanding in the sand around her belly.

Just then, there was some shoving, and a middle-aged woman in working clothes and an old cloth cap fought her way through the crowd.

Her name was Isabella, and she gave life to *Tilda*.

A kilometre out to sea they killed the boatman and dumped him over the side. Then they sent the guns and comms equipment down after him. They made their way back to shore after a while, but Lærke's body had disappeared.

After searching the island for news, they were ordered to get out of there, and made their way back to the boat. Simon steered them three kilometres to the south-west, where they met up with the cabin cruiser that would carry them to Barcelona. They sat in silence for the entirety of the trip.

Then, when the port came into sight, The Professor said, "you know, he's going to come for us anyway." It was a statement.

No one responded, so he continued, "Unless he can't."

Bekka looked up, "explain?"

"I have access to all his networks, agreements, coded messages. It's leverage."

"What are you suggesting?" asked Camilla, already knowing the answer.

"Simple," The Professor said, "a mutual destruction pact. We each hold a copy of all his files. If any one of us has an unfortunate accident, then they create a mechanism for releasing the information."

"That could blow back on us. After all, we've been doing a lot of his cleaning," said Simon.

"True, enough, however, there's also a lot of useful contacts that we can profit from. And The Dutchman has considerable leverage over some very influential people," added The Professor.

"I like it," said Bekka.

"Agreed," nodded Camilla, "it's making the best of a bad situation."

"And...Lærke?" asked Simon.

"She's dead," said Camilla, firmly.

"How can we be sure?" replied Bekka.

"You want to go back again? Half the fishing community on the island saw us. And did you not see her guts hanging out? She's gone."

"And what about what she said she found at The Dutchman's villa?" Bekka asked.

No one responded.

"One things for sure, we need a new line of work. We need to exit from The Dutchman's activities," says Simon.

"Well, I'm out. You can all do what you want," said Camilla, adding, "it's been fun, but I'm done with all of you, and I have my own plans."

"Good riddance," muttered Bekka under her breath, but loud enough for Camilla to shoot her a look.

The boat cruised slowly into the harbour and pulled up at a wharf. The two-man crew tied it off and *The Unit* jumped ashore. As the others headed off to the taxi rank, Bekka stood and gazed south-east across the Balearic Sea, towards the island of Minorca. She had an uneasy feeling.

4 - ISABELLA & TILDA

Isabella was a force of nature.

A headstrong woman with considerable influence, both on and off the fishing boat. In her fifty-five years she had never left her island home, except for that one trip to Barcelona with her mother, so many decades ago.

For close to forty years, she had lived a schedule that would have broken most people. She had grown up working the fishing fleet, first helping her uncle, and later crewing for bigger vessels. She was a keen learner which complimented her work ethics, and her value soon increased, thanks to her abilities with numbers and schedules.

She lived sparingly and saved as much as possible, eventually investing in her own fishing vessel. She was a hard taskmaster, but a fair captain, and she attracted a crew who became her extended family. They were a tight outfit, and more than a match for predators seeking to illegally profit from other people's hard graft. Knife skills were a core competence on this boat, and it was said that Isabella's crew could gut a gang as fast as they could gut a net-full of fish.

As the profits rolled in, she expanded into the fish market business, vertically integrating her operations, capturing all the value, and compensating her workforce well, ensuring their loyalty.

As the market activities took up more of her time, she spent less and less on the fishing side of the business. She made sure she still went out at least once a week, not just to monitor the operation, but because the wind and the waves filled her senses with a feeling that she missed.

On this morning, she had been helping out with cleaning the underside of one of her boats on the beach. The crew had started early, and now they needed their breakfast and infusion of strong coffee.

As Isabella followed them back towards the town, she noticed that they had assembled in a group by some rocks. As she fought her way through her men, she found some tourists who were standing in a circle around one of their group who was lying on the sand. She was spewing blood from her stomach, and appeared to be lifeless.

Isabella did not speak english, so she could not understand the conversation they were having. After a heated exchange between two of them, one woman broke off and ran with her bag towards a boat that was bobbing in the surf just off the beach.

Isabella strained her eyes to make out the owner of the boat, but she did not recognise him, nor did the boat look familiar.

I wonder where that came from, she thought. Then, the other three tourists picked up their bags and ran after the woman to the boat.

Isabella and the crew turned back to the lifeless woman on the sand. She kneeled down and brushed her blonde hair away from her face. She looked German, or from one of the Scandinavian countries. She had seen many similar looking tourists over the years, and they were frequent customers at her fish shop, which now had a small café on the side.

She reached for the tourist's neck and checked her pulse. *Nothing*. Then...*wait! A faint beat.*

Isabella looked up and yelled, "she's alive! Go phone for an ambulance now! And call the Doctor. He will probably get here faster. Go!"

She rolled the woman over onto her back and pulled up her dark shirt. There was a collective groan from the men leaning over Isabella. The tourist had what seemed like a small wound, but it was producing an enormous amount of blood. Isabella took off her old shirt, and pressed it gently over the wound in an attempt to plug it.

It took another one and a half hours for the ambulance to arrive. By that time, the Doctor had been on the scene and managed to apply a temporary bandage around the woman's waist. It was already soaked through.

They transported the woman to the hospital, accompanied by Isabella, and sedated her for the operation. Isabella had sat outside the operating theatre for hours, dozing on and off.

Eventually, the surgeon had come out and said she should leave, and that it was highly unlikely that the tourist would survive through the night. Isabella nodded, then stood up, stretching her aching body, and walked out to find a taxi to take her back to her apartment above the fish shop.

She returned the next day, late in the afternoon, after shutting down the café. The woman had now been moved to an open ward, and was still heavily sedated. She found the shift Doctor at the Nurses station and enquired after the woman.

The Doctor said that it was likely she would be sedated for another few days. The bullet had done significant internal damage on its journey through her belly, before exiting out of her lower back. The Doctor asked Isabella if she knew anything about the woman. Isabella said she did not. The Doctor said that the police had turned up because of the nature of the victim's wound, and the fact that the victim had no ID or credit cards. From descriptions given by witnesses at the beach, they had come to the conclusion that the woman was German, but they were unable to verify this.

A search at the scene of the crime had failed to find the bullet, probably because the sand where she lay had been heavily disturbed. The Doctor told Isabella he did not think the police would investigate further, because of their limited resources. Isabella told the Doctor that she would return in a few days to see how the woman was doing.

A week later, as Isabella was just getting up from the bedside chair following her daily vigil, she almost jumped out of her skin as the woman suddenly grabbed her wrist.

Isabella spun round and looked down at the woman who was staring directly into her eyes. Isabella made a move to get the attention of a nurse, but the woman's iron grip on her hand would not release her.

Isabella leaned over and asked how she was feeling and what her name was, but the woman was unable to answer, either because she could not speak the language, or could not speak.

Probably both, thought Isabella.

After a few minutes, the woman's grip opened and Isabella rushed out to the Nurses station. She explained what had happened to the Doctor, and he said that it was a positive sign, but he was not surprised she had slipped back into unconsciousness.

Over the next three weeks, the woman's progress greatly improved, and she was able to sit up slightly in the bed. Whenever Isabella would visit her late in the afternoons, she would break out of her fixed stare at the ceiling into a broad smile at the approach of the Minorcan. She would hold Isabella's hand as she listened to her stories of the day, even though she understood nothing.

One day, in the fourth week, Isabella entered the room as the Doctor and Nurse were helping the woman to stand for the first time. Isabella could see the pain on the woman's face as she sat on the side of the bed, and then placed her feet on the floor. As she tried to raise herself, she needed the stability of the Doctor and Nurse in order to stand up and remain there.

She towered over the Minorcans, and she was heavy for them to support, even though she had lost considerable muscle mass since she was admitted to their care. They helped her walk to the bathroom and it took a long time, consisting of small, slow steps. At one point, the Nurse had pointed to a wheel chair, but the woman shook her head violently.

Over the next two weeks, the woman made good progress and was able to pad about on her own. One day, Isabella came in and the Doctor pulled her aside. He told her that the woman would have to leave in three days because they could no longer afford the space. He told Isabella that they were going to call the German Consulate in Minorca, and ask if they would help with her transportation back to Germany.

Apparently, the woman understood the gist of the discussion, because she threw a Spanish phrasebook at them to catch their attention. They looked round and she was shaking her head.

The Doctor asked Isabella what to do. Isabella looked out of the window for a moment, then said firmly, that she would take her. She explained that she had a spare room above the fish shop and café, and she could rest there for a while.

The Doctor thanked Isabella, smiling at her. He had seen the dedication she had shown towards this poor stranger, and he had also heard of Isabella. She was known to be a formidable woman who did not suffer fools lightly.

It was also said that she was much loved by her crews, and that her influence in the local town's affairs were considerable.

Three days later, Isabella returned with two of her crew, and they helped the German woman into a wheel chair and proceeded to the entrance of the hospital. Isabella had managed to find some second hand clothes that almost fit the tall woman, which had not been easy.

The Doctor walked with them to the entrance and he shook the German's hand as he looked up into her blue eyes. She gave him a warm smile, and, with great effort, she leaned over and kissed him on the cheek.

The ride back into town in the van was one of the most painful experiences that Isabella had seen anyone endure. She could see the agony the woman was in every time the van bounced over a stone or hole in the road. Isabella yelled at the driver to be more careful, and there was much waving of hands and apologetic gestures as he tried to make the trip more comfortable.

Finally, they pulled up in front of the shop, and the crew helped the woman climb the steps at the side to the apartment above. After they had gone, and Isabella had made the woman comfortable in a stuffed chair by the window, she brought her some tea and sat down opposite her.

Isabella handed the woman a piece of paper with the word *name?* scrawled on it. The woman looked at it, then out the window. Then she took the pencil from Isabella and wrote some lines in english.

My name is Mathilda. Call me Tilda. Thank you.

Isabella looked at the writing and then she picked up a Spanish/English dictionary and constructed another sentence.

Can you speak?

Tilda shook her head and pointed to her mouth and then stomach, indicating that it hurt when she tried to speak. Isabella nodded, then consulted her dictionary, before writing again.

Who do I call?

Tilda shook her head and waved her hands.

So that's definitely a no, thought Isabella. *She's afraid.*

And so it went for a few weeks. Isabella would disappear in the early hours, and return after the café had closed. Tilda became stronger and more mobile, thanks to the hearty food, good rest, and most importantly, Isabella pushing her each day.

During her long hours alone, Tilda would study the Spanish phrase book and dictionary, and consume the television shows. As the pain reduced in her belly, she began to mutter words in English and Spanish, and the two women began to semi-communicate as they prepared their evening meals.

The day came when Isabella wanted Tilda to walk down the back stairs and out onto the street. Tilda asked if Isabella had a hat that she could wear. Isabella could see that Tilda was nervous of being seen. She helped her slowly down the steps, and then walk around to the front of the café. Then they returned and carefully climbed the steps back to the apartment.

When Tilda got back up there she was exhausted and in considerable pain. The next day Isabella returned in the late afternoon with some black hair dye. She then went to work, cutting Tilda's hair into a scruffy short look, then dyed it jet black.

It was a shocking sight for Tilda when she looked in the mirror, but at the same time offered her some relief. That night, as they ate their evening meal on the small balcony over the busy street, Tilda took her first sip of wine, and they both smiled and clinked glasses. Tilda told Isabella that she wanted to work, and Isabella, laughing, said slowly, "it was about time!"

Once Tilda got it, they both erupted in laughter, but it was cut short by Tilda grabbing her belly.

"No more jokes," said Tilda.

"I wasn't joking," replied Isabella, laughing.

Tilda started helping Isabella's assistant in the back of the café the next morning, washing cups and dishes, but staying out of sight. She was not well enough to serve, and it suited her that she could rest herself against the sink.

She had visited the hospital for a number of check-ups, and the Doctor, after examining her, had explained that he was pleased with her progress.

Isabella accompanied her on every occasion. One time, Isabella and the Doctor engaged in a long discussion, and she came back to Tilda with tears in her eyes. Tilda asked what the Doctor had said, and Isabella, after wiping her eyes, and pointed to her belly and said she would not be able to have children.

Tilda did not react because she already knew. She asked Isabella why she was so upset, and she responded that she had never being able to have children herself, and she never wished it on another woman. Tilda put her arm around the Minorcan's shoulders and kissed her on the top of the head, hiding her own tears.

As the months rolled by, Tilda became stronger, and more confident in her rudimentary language skills. She ventured out of the back room and into serving and helping with the customers. Many tourists came and she was able to help the café revenues improve with her English and German skills.

Whenever Scandinavians came in she would speak English, although she would listen in to every word that the Danes, Swedes and Norwegians would say.

She began to take long walks, and started performing elaborate stretching exercises before and after. Isabella noticed the return of Tilda's muscle tone, and so did many of the local men. But it was known that the German was living with Isabella and that she was a very private person. The locals knew well enough to avoid incurring the wrath of Isabella.

Or Isabella's fishing vessel crews. For it was said that they could gut a person like a fish and not blink.

As Tilda evolved, Lærke kept her demons at bay. The night and the early mornings were the times when The Dutchman would appear.

A fractional moment, often at the false dawn, where her consciousness would balance on a precipice between light and dark, was when she was at her most vulnerable. Her nightmares were not always the same, for they varied in degrees of intensity. It was not that she feared The Dutchman physically. But she feared reliving the sheer terror he had visited on those poor souls who happened to have been procured for his satanic pleasures.

Lærke always woke up before Tilda. During that first year of recovery, her first sensation on waking, would be the wet sheets that she lay on. It was the reminder to her that he had, indeed, visited her during the dark hours, and drenched her in his evil doings.

Lærke would spend the first thirty seconds of consciousness fighting off the packs of black dogs by replacing her fear with anger, and supporting that anger with schemes of vengeance that she would visit on him and his evil cabal.

Then the mists of anger and retribution would fade away, giving space for Tilda to find new purpose. As Lærke receded into the night, Tilda would focus on the tasks of the day, such as helping Isabella to make preparations for the return of the catch, and then setting up the café in time for the early tourist trade.

First, she would hang-up her damp sheets in the window to dry them out, then she would go into the kitchen and take a coffee from the pot that Isabella had prepared before her departure. Tilda could never figure out how Isabella always got such a head start on her. But it always made her smile. This woman had first saved her life, and then given her a new one.

By the eighth month, Tilda could jog slowly, albeit painfully, but she persevered and by month eleven she was running smoothly. Her wound was tender, but gradually she built up protective muscle around it.

Isabella noticed the changes in Tilda as she began to acquire her fitness and levels of confidence. She was still cautious in public and always wore a hat that covered her scruffy black hair. She kept her eyebrows dyed black, and her suntan gave her a Mediterranean look. But her height and muscle tone commanded attention, and she sought to minimise it by wearing baggy long sleeved vests and stooping her shoulders.

Communication became easier, both with Isabella and her crews. Tilda started to venture out onto the early morning sea with the fishermen, learning the ropes and bringing food to the island. She became tight with the crew, and they formed a protective bond around the mysterious German woman who had steel in her eyes and iron in her arms.

The first time she dreamt of Nikolaj was early into her second year.

That particular pre-dawn awakening was characterised by the lack of sweat on her sheets. Tilda sat up, confused that Lærke was nowhere to be found.

She stood up and performed her stretching routine, then grabbed her breakfast and coffee, and made her way down to the harbour. As she walked toward the boat, she kept trying to grab hold of the thin strand of the dream, as if it was a blind that she could pull down. All she had was a vague half-memory of sitting on the side of a low wall in Nyhavn in the summer sun, and feeling the cold ice cream that the little boy spilled it onto her leg.

That was the first time she met Nikolaj. It was the first, and only time she fell in love. She wondered where he was now. They had been inseparable.

Well, apart from her *Unit* rotations abroad with UN Peacekeeping missions which she had lied to him about.

But whenever she returned to Copenhagen, they would live out of each other's pockets. And she learned to love Lucas, Nikolaj's son.

As she approached the boat in the darkness, the crew waved to her, and she hoped that she would dream the same dream tonight.

Years passed, and seasons cycled through the Mediterranean waters. Tilda became a part of Isabella's family, and an integral member of her fishing and tourism operation.

One evening, Tilda and Isabella were walking back to their apartment, when they ran afoul of a group of English hooligans who were rampaging through the beautiful old town. They were part of the unfortunate trend that had infected their beautiful island paradise in recent years, disrupting the tourism industry and putting fear into the local business owners.

That night, as Isabella and Tilda rounded a corner, their access to the stairs was blocked by the tattooed gang of vandals, who were hurling abuse and vomiting in the street.

Tilda tried to shepherd the smaller Isabella around two of the gang, but one grabbed hold of her arm, trying to stop her progress. Tilda put her body between the hooligan and Isabella, then, taking a step back, snapped her leg out, driving it up into the thug's balls.

He collapsed on the floor in agony, giving his nearest accomplice a cause for concern. He froze as his mate rolled around the cobbled street in a ball. Then two others ventured over and emboldened him, giving that artificial courage that strength in alcoholic numbers often provides.

They closed in on the two women, throwing half-drunk cans of beer, as Tilda spread her arms out to shield Isabella. One full can hit Tilda in the side of the face, causing her to protect her head as blood started to seep from a small wound.

Just as the gang started to move in, Isabella swept in front of Tilda, brandishing a small knife. It had the effect of pushing the semi-circle back a pace. As Isabella swept her knife in a wide arc, several knives appeared in the gang's hands, and they began to close in.

Just then, a group of Isabella's fishing crew rounded the corner. They ran yelling towards the two surrounded ladies, causing the hooligans to break off. As they dispersed, one of the leaders hurled a chair, that was stacked up outside the café, through the large window, shattering it.

Then he screamed that they knew where the women lived, as they ran with their tails between their legs, followed by Isabella's furious cavalry.

Tilda and Isabella spent the next couple of hours cleaning up the glass, then helping to board up the window. Exhausted, Isabella then went to bed, leaving just Tilda and Gabriel to finish off.

Gabriel was in his late thirties, and he had been with Isabella since she found him as a ten year old stray. He was silent, all wiry muscle, and deadly serious. He had a fearsome reputation, both within the fishing community and across the island.

No one had ever seen him commit any acts of violence, but stories were whispered and passed around. It was said that he would kill to protect Isabella, and indeed, had done so on a number of occasions.

Another story goes that two of the visiting English tourists were reported missing by their mates sometime in the afternoon of the next day. The police were not that inclined to react, but the poor hotel owner had reported that blood was found on the sheets in their rooms, but they were nowhere to be found. Their luggage and belongings were all gone, including travel documents, cash and all other signs of their existence.

Their associates contacted the British Consul, who contacted the local police who responded that it looked like the men had returned to England. When the Consul proceeded to push the matter, he was told that no one gave a shit and the island was a better place for their disappearance.

Nothing more was heard about them, and investigations fizzled out. But rumours spread of the watery grave that had welcomed two barbarians from the north. It was said that they had been slain in their beds and wrapped in nets before being fed to the creatures that roamed the deepest parts of the Balearic Sea.

There was a notable drop-off in such groups visiting the town, as word had spread back to the cold island in the far north of the warm welcome for anyone venturing into the region with ill intent.

Isabella never asked Tilda about what happened that night. She didn't have to. She could read the eye contact between Tilda and Gabriel. It warmed her heart.

Isabella invented a birthday for Tilda.

On her fourth birthday, Isabella gave her a ferry ticket to Barcelona, and an envelope. Inside the envelope was an introduction to someone she knew, who knew someone else. That someone else also happened to be able to obtain passports and assorted documents to those in need.

Tilda's birthday present was a German passport. It was the first time that Isabella had seen Tilda cry. Then she burst into a big smile. For Isabella knew that Tilda would not stay forever on this Mediterranean paradise. She knew that there was a fury that drove her, something that needed to be purged from her system. And the answer to that was somewhere on the vast mainland of Europe.

Isabella had grown to love Tilda like the daughter she was unable to have. But it was more than that. There was a sisterly bond that existed, which allowed them to exist on a different plane to most people. They had both developed an almost psychic ability to know what the other needed, without having to ask.

When Tilda returned from Barcelona with her new freedom document, Isabella knew that she would not stay for long. Tilda, for her part, was determined to help Isabella see out the season, even though this gift had given her the ability to finally begin to put her plans into action. Eventually, the day they both dreaded approached.

They did not say anything to each other as they went through their morning routine. Then Isabella drove Tilda to the ferry in the van, together with Gabriel and two other crew-mates.

Tilda hugged each of them, and there were tears in all their eyes. At last she came to Isabella, and she took her head in her hands and looked deep into her eyes. They did not need to say anything, for their love was communicated through their water-filled eyes.

As the ferry's horn sounded, Isabella hustled Tilda to the passenger gangway. Tilda entered the boat, and made it to the upper deck, and looked down at her friends. They all waved and waited there until, the ship was exiting the harbour.

Tilda watched as they turned their backs and made their way back to the van. A wind chill ran through her body. But at the same time, the recognition that she had a purpose that needed to be fulfilled.

She walked to the stern of the ship, and watched as her Minorcan home disappeared into the horizon. She had a plan. She would make her way north into France, then cut across the coast to Italy. Then she would venture up to Austria, and on into Germany. When she reached Munich she would consider her next steps.

She had enough cash to live for a year. Isabella had seen to that.

5 - THE DEVIL IN THE SKY

He's sitting in his first class throne, up at about ten thousand metres, sipping a scotch and trying to corral all the vipers crawling about in his head.

The Dutchman's brain is usually a calm sea filled with the purest evil, but Lærke's return has raised a spectre that even he has problems dealing with.

Then there was last night. He rushed his desert, and it put him in the foulest of moods. Which meant he took it out on the poor creature who had the misfortune to cross into his world. And he got careless and messy.

The house had been used before for his purposes, and the owners were an offshore entity with multiple layers of deniability. The cleaning crew were amongst his most trusted disciples, and service was always guaranteed, because he had their families under constant threat of annihilation. And he paid them handsomely.

He will check in on them when he lands in Amsterdam. He doesn't trust airline WiFi. Or more specifically, who could be sitting in the cabin.

As well as last night, all his schedules have gone down the toilet. He had some visiting dignitaries who were flying in for some CORP-ROGUE discussions, and the apres that he had ordered from the north.

The Dutchman didn't like change. He liked precision. He didn't even know why they called him *The Dutchman*. He wasn't even Dutch, and it's not like he had a fucking business card with *The Dutchman* in *luminari* font with his mobile phone number!

It had caught on way back, in the ass-end of the seventies when he was doing things he shouldn't have been doing, in a place he shouldn't have been. A Brit mercenary squad he was hanging out with, thought he sounded Dutch so he adopted it, affecting the accent. He felt it gave him a certain *je ne sais quoi*.

He raises his glass and catches the attention of the stewardess. He can see her nervous look. The first time she served him, just before takeoff, she was all smiles. He seemed like a charming, handsome, older man with bright eyes and a nice smile. But when she leaned over to place the drink on his table, she was met with the most vile smell imaginable.

The Dutchman liked that. He lived for the revulsion and fear that he could drive into people.

The stewardess approaches quickly with his scotch, and she extends her arm as far as possible to place it on his tray. She's just pulling her arm back, when he grabs it, and gives it a tight grip. She looks down at him, helpless, feeling the pain from his clammy hand.

"Haven't you forgotten something, my dear?" he enquires, looking into her nervous face. The tip of his tongue just poking through his wet lips.

The stewardess freezes, paralysed by an unexplained fear that's flooding her body. She can feel the cold sweat beginning to run down from her neck and imprint on her shirt. The Dutchman also notices it, and he lowers his gaze, taking in her figure as if he was studying an ornament. He pulls her closer and exhales right into her face, watching as she fights to keep from retching.

"The empty glass, my dear. Here you go," he says, releasing her wrist, and taking her hand and unfolding her fingers. He then places the empty scotch glass in her hand, then goes back to his iPad.

The stewardess rushes back to the kitchen, drops the glass, and makes it to the toilet, just in time to vomit. The Dutchman looks up at the sound, and smiles to himself.

Sweet thing. Shame I'm in a hurry. Which reminds him. *Lærke. How the hell had she managed to stay off his radar for twenty-seven years? Where had she been?* He was more fascinated than angry. The explosion of social media and surveillance made it almost impossible to hide. He figured she had either been on the moon, or transformed her looks.

But she was a striking woman, as well as being a *striking* woman. If she had changed her looks it would have been a long and arduous process. And expensive. He was even more intrigued, and he felt himself getting hard.

He saw the stewardess emerge from the toilet, and he stood up, making sure that she saw the bulge in his pants. He smiled as she recoiled and disappeared into the service area.

I wasn't thinking about you, sweet thing, he thinks. *But maybe we'll meet again on the return.*

He sits back and brings Lærke back into focus. He had seen her first in '92. She was operating out of the Balkans. He had been tipped off about a serious potential asset, by a Colonel on his payroll, and he made plans to be in the same location when she came back off a mission.

He introduced himself to her in the officers mess, and she blew him off by telling him to go fuck himself. He liked that. So he fucked-off, then had her dragged into her Commandant's office the next morning. After dismissing the officer, The Dutchman proceeded to ask Lærke what she wanted out of life.

She told him to go fuck himself.

Then he started to tell her all about herself. About her considerable assets in the field, her misdemeanours, her family problems back home in Denmark, her needs.

"What do you know about my needs, you pervert?" she asked, getting in his face.

"I would like to offer you an opportunity to join a new military unit we are forming."

"You're not military," she stated.

"Not anymore, but I help facilitate operations that are outside the normal channels."

"In other words, Black Ops. No thanks, not interested."

It took him seven months. But he got her interested. And he fashioned *The Unit* around her.

She was the fulcrum, although she didn't realise it.

The Dutchman did wonder if he had been obsessed by Lærke. He knew he didn't love her, or even lust after her, like he did for Camilla. No, Lærke reminded him of, well, himself.

Minus the human sacrifices and other peccadilloes.

She reminded him of himself because she was like a cruise missile that, when locked on, would not deviate from its target, regardless of the obstacles in her path.

The others knew this too, which is what drove their respect and fear. He had not been certain that *The Unit* could work with Lærke and Camilla in the same team, and for a while it was touch and go. But out in the field they put their hatreds and jealousies aside to fuse the most efficient killing force he had ever run.

And now she's back, and she's already taken The Professor off the grid.

Tic-tac-toe, she's got his digital files. The question is... who's next? He would bet on Simon and Bekka. Even if there were two of them, they'd be an easier hit than Camilla.

It could go either way between them. He would not like to bet on the winner.

He'd made his decision to drive from Amsterdam to Copenhagen. It would take a lot more time, but he wanted to drop by The Professor's farm on Jylland and see what he could dig up.

Then he would hop over to Fyn and get Camilla into the game. Although she probably was already.

Lærke will go to Sjælland and take out Bekka and Simon. Or at least try. But she would find a welcoming committee, he thinks.

Because The Dutchman had already tasked *The Swedish Unit*. And they were spinning up now, even as he raised his glass to the stewardess for his next scotch.

The Swedish Unit were not Swedish.

Well, one of them was, but they got their catchy designation because they operated out of Skåne. Apart from the Swede, there was a Finn, Norwegian and a Brit.

They didn't like each other, and that's just the way they liked it. They were an efficient outfit, having rotated around the globe on mainly jungle or forest-type missions. In fact, they didn't like urban jobs on account of one of them being a bit anthropophobic. Which was not necessarily a problem for a sniper.

They found that Skåne was a good staging point for them because it was close to Copenhagen, which they used as a hub to pretty much get them anywhere in the world in twenty-four hours. As rural dwellers, Skåne had the side benefit of plenty of space, thus ample warning and security, in the event that the hunters became the hunted. Which was not an uncommon feature in this line of work. Still, they'd been at it for four years as a *Unit*, and they'd only fucked up one mission, which had been double-booked.

What was supposed to be a simple long distance hit-job, turned into a firefight with a competing *Unit* being run out of South Korea. What a shitstorm that turned out to be. They missed the mark, and one of them came out minus some fingers.

Which limited his sniping activities to the *Playstation 5*. Still, he had other skills, and one of them was being the self-proclaimed leader.

He's the Swede. So now Sven, let's call him that, is on a secure line with The Dutchman who's at cruising altitude calling the shots.

Mission profile is crystal. Three, possibly four targets, at these last known locations. Exercise extreme caution, because they were *The Unit*.

Which didn't impress the Swede. He'd heard all the war stories about the original team. It was all fucking nostalgia as far as he was concerned. They were well past their sell-by date, and his *Unit* would happily take the commission.

If the price was doubled. The Dutchman tripled it for insurance purposes.

Their conversation over, the Swede calls the Finn, then the Norwegian, and finally the Brit. He's the last one Sven always calls on account of him being a pain in the ass. He's also the not-people person, so he handles the really long shots. He's also not too happy when she finds out the job is across the Øresund bridge. In civilisation.

"I don't do jobs in civilisation," he yells in his south London twang.

"For triple the standard fee you will," replies the Swede, hoping he refuses.

"OK, for that I will. But I'm not going into a fucking city."
Shit.

He arranges for them to drive over to his farm which is close to Lund. There, they will plan the mission, and synch-in with The Dutchman when he lands in Amsterdam. The Swede's thinking about The Dutchman a lot. He ponders over the devil-worshiping rumours.

Well, each to his or her own, he thinks. We're no fucking angels.

With the *Unit* spun-up, he goes out to his storage hut to begin checking his gear. If the original *Unit* is as good as they're hyped up to be, then three-finger Sven's going over the bridge tooled up for a war.

6 - AMBUSH

Simon gets there first.

He pulls up next to a row of Teslas, Bentleys, Porsches and the odd Ferrari. The outside terrace is packed and he curses himself for selecting *Address*, especially after twelve-thirty. Although it's his favourite watering hole when entertaining clients, he's well known. But not as well known as Nikolaj. And so when Nikolaj cruises in, heads turn. Simon spins away from admiring the big bike parked next to the bar, and immediately sizes his guest up.

Similar age, looks confident, cheeks a bit too red, probably from too much booze. Looks like he may have been fit, once upon a time. Got a comfort tyre going round his waste now.

But his eyes. Now they're sharp.

Simon can see Nikolaj running the same inventory check on him, and simultaneously scanning the big dinning room for anyone he knows.

You are a stupid wanker, Simon thinks to himself. *Should have gone to the Marriott or Radisson Blu. Well, it's too late. Time to find out what this fucker is up to.*

"Good to meet you!" says Simon, offering his hand to Nikolaj, who grabs it in a vice-like grip and gives it a pump. Simon reacts a little too late and looses out on that battle. He curses himself as Nikolaj smiles at him.

"Yes indeed. My first lunch with a Venture Capitalist in many years," he says.

Was that a smirk, Simon's thinking. "We're not that fearsome, unless you're pitching a startup!"

"Yes, it appears you have quite a reputation in the startup world."

Simon gestures to the back of the restaurant. "Shall we? I reserved a table by the window. I hope that's OK with you?"

"For sure, I love the area by the piano. It's one of my regular spots."

Nikolaj gets the jump on Simon and leads him over to his own table that he booked. *Bastard*, thinks Simon, as Nikolaj shakes hands with a couple of guests at another table. Simon's now working on a sweat, and it's starting to fan out from his armpits and across his chest. He's desperate to take off his jacket, but he made another big mistake by wearing a blue shirt. So he's just gonna have to swim through this, and drink as much water as possible.

"You look like you're hot," smiles Nikolaj, as he takes his seat and removes his jacket.

"Just got out the gym," bullshits Simon.

"Better lose the jacket then, mate. You mind if I call you that? I love your colourful language."

"Of course not. I've seen you on a few shows. Always enjoy how you flip to English in the middle of an argument!"

"Your language is rich, and has so many different words and expressions for describing the same thing. For example, fake-it-till-you-make-it. Now, I love that one!"

"Well that's more of an Americanism that seems to have travelled over the pond."

"Ahah! The pond! Of course, you mean the Atlantic. The pond is so, how do you say, understated. Most charming. I do like to engage in rich conversations with the British. You are British? Or do you consider yourself English?"

"Well, I'm both, actually. We tend to slip between them depending on who we are talking to."

"I see, but you're not Scottish?"

"Most definitely not, although some of my best friends are from Scotland."

Nikolaj says, "so I guess you'll soon need a passport to go visit them!"

"Well, not for a few years," says Simon, taking a big gulp of water, and managing to spill some down the front of his shirt.

"Once *The Hair* and his enablers get blown out of town, and the next generation of younger voters comes in, then it's back off to the EU for the *Jocks*. I do like that name. It has such a ring!"

"Perhaps. To be honest, I don't pay too much attention. I'm more focused on the Nordic market."

"Indeed, and you have, how should I say, cleaned up. I have a question for you. May I jump straight to it?" asks Nikolaj, waving to the waitress.

"Be my guest," says Simon. He goes to speak to the waitress, but Nikolaj beats him to it.

"Hi, great to see you again. I'll have my usual, and my guest will have," he gestures to Simon who's flustering with the menu.

He goes for nonchalant, and says, "why don't I take same as you," throwing an over-cooked smile across to Nikolaj.

"Splendid! Two bloody rare steaks, please," he says looking up at the waitress. "And a bottle of your finest Rioja."

Nikolaj gets distracted by another acquaintance, and he gets up to shake a woman's hand. Then he sits back down and apologises to Simon, who's actually beginning to calm down. He knows it's a Danish game that often gets played out in many of the meetings he attends. They try to get you off your guard, and see how you fluster. But they do it with a big smile. It had taken him a few years to figure it out, but after a while he began to enjoy the charade. It was quite refreshing to have the metaphorical grenades hurled at you when you were on stage, and batting them away with your own opinions. So much more engaging than the sterile discussions that permeated his duplicitous, London-based meets.

Simon realises that it's not this guy that's got him on edge. It's the timing. Specifically, The Professor's demise, The Dutchman's imminent arrival, and his ex, Camilla, showing up in the middle of the fucking night. Oh, and Lærke at the centre of it all. Without all that shit going on, Simon knows he could handle this clown. So he resolves to try to focus on the next hour, and enjoy this engagement. He reckons if he can loosen up a bit then he won't give this guy any fresh angles. And maybe discover a few of Nikolaj's hidden ones.

"Anyway, back to the question I was going to ask you. How is it that you British pulled off this Brexit trick?" asks Nikolaj, as he takes a sip of the Spanish red, nodding approvingly at the waitress. "Cheers, by the way!"

They clink and each take a sip, then Simon puts down the glass and says, "well, if you wanted to go about it, of course this is hypothetical, then actually it would be a remarkably simple plan, if it was executed flawlessly. Great choice by the way," he smiles approvingly at his guest. "Flawlessly, how so?"

"Well, basically you would need a small cabal of interested parties, wealthy and clubbed-up of course–"

"–clubbed-up?" interrupts Nikolaj.

"Yes, a tight network of industrial, political and other influential people. People who have an agenda and an interest, in this case, getting out of Europe. Although most of them would probably still maintain or borrow their handsome villas in the south of France and Greece!"

"Yes, we have such networks here. In fact a lot of them are scattered around this dining room," Nikolaj smiles, and Simon winks back at him.

"Of course this is pure speculation, but then you would probably need a sprinkling of radicals who are prepared to do the shitty work for you in public. Then you would want someone to front it. It has to be someone that will bend to your will. Basically, a guy who will say anything to get what he wants—"

"—such as to be the Prime Minister?"

"Precisely. Even better if you have someone who has a history of making ridiculous statements about—"

"—bananas and condoms—"

"—amongst others. So you find some clown, who will say or do anything, then behind him you have a very skilled set of operators who carefully craft the messages and narrative. These people are so slick that whenever they get called out for spreading false information, they would simply pivot to the next big issue."

"*Pivot*?"

"Jump, or move. So the opposing forces don't have time to formulate a response, or get that across to the general public. And the public, or more specifically, the channels with which you communicate to the public, such as social media and a few key outlets, become crucial. Eventually, you could build up this unstoppable wave that sweeps you over the finishing line first. Then, if you could pull it off, you might be able to leverage that to gain the top job. Once in power, you can perform the same tricks. You just jump from issue to issue, exploiting the next big thing that comes up to distract the public and the opposition from the last self-inflicted disaster." Simon takes another sip, beginning to cool down, and looks across to Nikolaj.

"But how do you pull those same tricks once you are in power? Surely, you are accountable, no?"

Simon smiles and says, "well firstly you insulate yourself by surrounding yourself with your enablers who protect you. And you refuse to fire any of them when they screw up. Unless it's a last resort to save your own skin. And of course you could reward them with knighthoods and lucrative contracts. Then you would gradually begin to erode the norms and rules that previous generations of politicians and governments adhered to."

Nikolaj leans forward. "You mean you cheat?"

"It's not cheating if you change the rules. It's more like... magic! Then you just repeat the same strategy. Any time you get yourself into trouble, you go adjacent and create a distraction."

"But how did this, how do you say, cabal, ever get the thing moving in the first place? The British seemed to be OK with life as Europeans."

"That would be the easiest part, especially if the previous guy made a bet on behalf of the British public. His arrogance opens the door, and then it could be rapidly exploited. When he looses that bet, then he could fade away, without having to face any of the responsibilities for what he wrought. Can you imaging placing a bet on the future of your country, and those millions of lives. *Millions*! He was worse than the ones who exploited it after."

"Wow, that's quite a story."

"Yeah, it's just a story. It could never happen in real life, right?" Simon laughs, clinking glasses again with Nikolaj.

Nikolaj leans forward, grinning. "And are you part of this cabal?"

"Hell no! I'm European. I've been here in Denmark so long. My wife and kids are Danish. I love the how the Danes trade. I actually see that I have a responsibility to help maintain the strength of trading ties with the UK. We're not all wankers, you know!"

"One of my favourite words! May I quote you?"

"Be my guest," says Simon, warming to his new friend.

"And how do you help to preserve trade?"

"Through capital allocation. My fund, and the UK-based funds that I can tap into, can help grease the rails for new ideas and innovations. Usually ones that struggle to get the attention they deserve from the corporates or universities which they spring out from."

"And these ideas and innovations. Are they all real? We are back to this term *fake-it-till-you-make-it*."

Simon leans back. "Well that was a phenomenon for a while. But I would not paint whole startup ecosystems like that. Sometimes it worked out. But in some instances, that approach can be very risky. You're talking about playing with people's lives. Especially if you're building something in the healthcare space."

"Or financial and education?" asks Nikolaj.

"Indeed, in both of those sectors, you can end up ruining lives, savings and reputations. We are extremely diligent about how we invest other people, and our own money. Some may say we are too cautious."

"And yet you have, as they say, stellar results from your last few funds. And you have, to use your political metaphor, pivoted between technology, financial services and health-tech. Each time you have exited at the right moment, and moved to the next opportunity."

"Yes, we've been fortunate to be able to spot the next wave, then surf it."

Nikolaj laughs, and claps his hands. A little too loudly, attracting the attention of a few tables. "Surfing! I love that. So where did the money come from in the first place?"

Sidewinder.

Simon feels his face redden, and forces himself to slow his pulse. He takes a sip of water, then replies, "from my London network."

"Via a volcanic island in the middle of the North Atlantic, I have heard?" says Nikolaj, leaning in, with the biggest false smile Simon had ever seen.

"No, that was misinformation. All our initial funds came from British-based private investors," he says, leaning back, realising his sweat glands have reawakened.

"British-based. So not British?"

"Yes. I mean...yes they were British."

"Of course. And may I now...pivot to another interesting question?"

He doesn't wait for Simon to respond. "Since you exited the startups that were sold to the corporates, how have they faired?"

"Faired?" asks Simon, knowing full well where this is going.

"Precisely. What happened to the companies when you sold them?"

"Well they were integrated into the corporation's operations that bought them."

"Indeed. *Integrated*, is an interesting word. Isn't it more true to say that most of the value of all of the companies you sold, were in fact written off by the corporations who acquired them?"

Simon pauses, looks around, then fiddles with his meal that has since gone cold. He hadn't noticed that Nikolaj had been consuming his food in between his barrage of questions.

"Well, a few of them may have been. But that was more a case of the corporation not integrating the team and product into their operations, and–"

"–in fact eighteen out of the twenty-two companies you exited from were actually written down. Yet your firm profited with over four hundred and seventy million Euros! Simon, may I ask you, did you in fact fake-it-till-you-made-it?"

Now the smile is gone. Now it's the cold viking stare, and Simon's brain's going haywire, bouncing between *shit he trapped me, to should I consider killing this guy*?

Nikolaj goes in for his own kill. "Your own background before your financial adventures makes for fascinating research!"

Blanche.

"I understand that you left the Forces under a bit of a rain cloud."

"No I took an early retirement to move into business."

"Indeed, but that business was not financial, was it? I understand that you continued to engage in freelance military activities. Don't they call those people *mercenaries*?"

"That's outrageous! I don't have to stand for this," Simon says, getting to his feet and throwing his napkin on the table.

Nikolaj is looking up at his host, projecting calm. "Now come now, there's no need for such an overreaction. Sit down and enjoy the rest of the meal."

"Thanks, but I'll pass. You should know, that I'm tooled-up with some of the best lawyers in the country," he says.

"Indeed. Most of them are in this room," says Nikolaj, spreading his arms wide.

Simon's had enough. He slides his chair back under the table, and says, "we're done". Then he walks to the bar and pays the bill.

Nikolaj watches him leave, then looks around and nods at a couple of guests on another table. Then he settles back to enjoy the rest of the Rioja. Gotcha.

Simon knows he's fucked. The guy was as sharp as a knife and well prepared. At least now he knows what he's dealing with. The only thing he's nervous about is the bollocking he'll get off Bekka when he tells her how lunch went.

He heads back to his office downtown to catchup on the latest deals his junior partners are proposing. He parks his Porsche, then walks the rest of the way towards the office just off *Bredgade*. He feels a drop of rain fall on his head, and he looks up to see a thunder storm gathering above him.

7 - ENTER QUANTUM BARB

Tilda just made a big mistake and now she's cursing herself.

After filling up on food, she sat at the table in the Airbnb, and fired up her business iPhone. Big fucking mistake. She wasn't even thinking. The second it booted, she gets swamped by a torrent of texts, *WhatsApps* and other notifications. She knows she shouldn't dive into them because it will distract her from her mission. On the other hand, she's running a fifteen billion Euro business that doesn't sleep just because she's out on a murderous revenge mission.

She thought that she had left everything in an orderly state, leaving full control to Joss and his team. But now there's at least nineteen messages from Joss all asking her to immediately call him. Then a bunch from her Executive Assistant, plus a ton from customers and investors.

She leans back. *Scheisse.*

She decides to stick to her plan. It requires a lot of mental fortitude. She's got a bit of a reputation as being too hands-on. She tells herself she's not overbearing, but certain media journalists over the years decided to paint her as hard on her staff, driving them to burnouts. She'd commissioned external consultants to look into ethics and employee satisfaction, and they all indicated that her company was about average. But because of a couple of bloggers, the mantra stuck.

You still haven't got over it, she tells herself. *Put it in the trash. Besides, you have something else to do this week. Like, kill another three people. Or maybe four if I get lucky.* She fires off a couple of messages to Joss and her EA, repeating the story about a family tragedy, and that she's in Spain, *blablabla*. Then she turns the phone off and buries it at the bottom of her backpack, pretending that it's impossible to get at.

She looks at The Professor's laptop and phone in front of her. She'd got into the phone back at the farm by scanning his face. But it had shut down, and she'd buried his face in a field. She opens the laptop and stares at the password prompt. *How to crack this one?* She has assets in Germany that could get into anything, but that's out of the question.

Denmark. Hmmm. There's only one person in Denmark that she knows has the capability to do this discretely, and she's not even sure if that person is still around.

Quantum Barb.

Tilda knew that her *Unit* and others had used Barb to filter intel, and sort out the trees from the forest on many occasions. Barb had a diverse clientele, but she was known to be a bit choosey. She only had two criteria for accepting jobs.

Firstly, was it for a good cause? As *The Unit* was in the assassination business, that was always tricky. To get Barb onside, you had to convince her that the target deserved to go. Secondly, how much?

Barb was an entrepreneur above all else. That's how she ran the hottest café in Nyhavn, at the same time as hacking the world's most secure systems. Tilda once asked how Barb got away with it. The answer that came back was simple.

Leverage.

Barb had everything on everyone. And she didn't carry all the dirty secrets around in her handbag. Nope, it was all distributed globally, constantly on the move and booby trapped. That meant that if any of Barb's clients, be they governments, corporates or nefarious individuals such as The Dutchman, tried to fuck with her, then Quantum Barb would burn the whole house down.

So they left her alone. To run her little café by the canal.

It was an interesting joint, with a bizarre mix of clientele, ranging from students to startups to tourists to spies. As well as serving up the best half-kaf-double-dekafs in Copenhagen, Barb would personally serve up the richest smørrebrød of information that money could buy. And she had access to the systems that could do it. Hence the *Quantum* part of Quantum Barb.

The question for Tilda is, how to make the approach? Barb's no dummy. Once she opens The Professor's laptop, then she'll figure out who it belonged to, and what's on it. And that could compromise a lot of Barb's existing clientele.

But Tilda's already figured out how to incentivise Barb. If...no, when she kills The Dutchman, then he will not be a threat to Barb. It's a big assumption. Tilda doesn't know how tight Barb has been with The Dutchman's operations over the last two decades. But what she does know, is that Barb has moral principles. Well, kind of. And Tilda intends to take advantage of those to get Barb onside.

Next question is timing. Barb's in Copenhagen, but Camilla's in Odense or somewhere else on Fyn, and Tilda's gonna kill her before she works her way over to taking out Bekka and Simon. So to access The Professor's laptop, she's got to get across Fyn and over to Nyhavn, convince Barb, then hop back over the Storebælt, track down Camilla and then, assuming she lives, get back to Copenhagen to finish off those last two bastards. And all of this assumes that The Dutchman and his assets don't intercept her.

This plan is beginning to sound like a dog's dinner, she thinks. But Tilda's locked in. Like *that* cruise missile.

She gets up and grabs her backpack, then goes out the door and climbs into the rental.

Roadtrip.

Barb's hustling tables outside her café.

It's one of those warm September Copenhagen days that she lives for. The vacation season's dropped off, and a new type of clientele has flooded in. The type that spend serious money. And not just on the lattes.

It's not unusual to see Barb working the tables, indeed, for most customers she appears to be nothing more than the café manager. Little do they know that she's got another menu that ninety-nine point nine percent of her customers don't get to order from. That's just for her clients. See, Barb differentiates between customers and clients. The customers get the coffee and flødebolle, while the clients get the subversion and spy shit.

Those who are in the know, know how to do business with Barb. Those that aren't, are blissfully unawares that the person they maybe sitting next to, in this serene Nyhavn café, maybe trading in some really scary stuff.

And this diversity of business is how Barb likes it. It brings a little more spice to the job of running a café in this most cosmopolitan of cities.

Barb runs her side gig out of the top two floors of the bright yellow building, which is jammed between other brightly coloured buildings. She splashed out on it a few decades ago, and she's seen many changes during that period. Especially tech ones that helped her spin-up more business. The internet, smartphones, space-tech, and now everyone's banging on about *quantum*. Especially those people who know nothing about quantum computing. It's become the new buzzword bingo lingua franca. A bit like *cloud* was.

She's been into the *big Q* for a long time. Hence the nickname that few people actually know about. To most, she's just known as Barb. But to her clients, and suppliers she goes by *Quantum* Barb. She doesn't exactly know how it came about. She reckons it was some AI students who she'd helped source some serious digital juice to hack into a rogue bank many years ago. Those guys are still on her payroll. Not that she keeps an official one.

Most of her trade upstairs is done with digital currencies, which are just floating about in the air. Downstairs, you needed real kroner to get your *flødebolle* fix.

She's just walking back into the café, expertly balancing a tray of empty cups and plates when she gets a tap on her ass. She reaches into her back pocket and pulls out her Samsung and opens up the message from an unknown sender. Nothing unusual in that, she thinks. It just means they don't want the chocolate balls.

The message reads:

Enroute St.M. Need a coffee. Two days. Be available.

Shit. The Dutchman.

She hasn't had the displeasure of his custom for at least ten years. She'd hoped it would stay that way. She knew he was running his *Units* out of Anguilla. She also knew that he wasn't even Dutch. She knew exactly what his real nationality was. And his name. And he knew that she knew. That's how she'd remained alive for so long.

But what the fuck did he want? She remembers all those years ago when he would fly in. She'd always arrange for an isolated table for him outside, as close to the canal as possible, where his hideous odour had a chance to evaporate. She got a lot of complaints from the punters last time about the sewage system in the café.

Damm, what the fuck does he want?

Lillebælt.

Tilda's riding the E20 east, and she just drove over the bridge onto Fyn.

Camilla country, she thinks.

She focuses on relaxing her grip. She doesn't know why she's so tense. She's been in tougher situations than just hopping Danish islands. She knows it's not the geography. Well, partly it is. Every landmark and Danish sign bombards her with reminders of her formative years in her home country. But the tension, she rationalises, is all down to her proximity to Camilla.

What is it between her and Camilla, she ponders, looking into the rear-view mirror for the umpteenth time.

Maybe it's a Jyllander/Funen thing. No, it's more like a psychopath thing, she concludes. Then the debate in her head starts. *Hmm, one assassin calling another assassin a psychopath. That's probably a first*. But she rationalises to herself that there is a clear difference between her and Camilla.

For starters, Camilla tried to kill me, and left me for dead. But so did all of them. Yeah, but Camilla's different. She's special. Tilda wonders to herself if she hates Camilla so much, because she actually likes her? That's too deep. She opens the window and lets the wind blast in, and reorientates her mind around the job for the day. Tracking down Quantum Barb. Well, tracking her down won't be a problem. It's Saturday and she's probably outside serving cappuccinos. But getting her help is a whole other challenge. Barb is the smartest person Tilda ever knew. She knows Barb treads a fine line on all her transactions. She is the world's master at leverage. Any request she gets, and accepts, adds to her considerable mountain of power.

Tilda's amazed at how she has managed to survive for so many decades, working out of that café. But even the most hardened assassins won't touch her. It's partially because of her legend, but more likely because Barb has the informational and financial capabilities to go after anyone's loved ones. No matter who you are, there's always someone that you care about. Not that she's ever done that. But the implicit threat is there. She's like a human no woman's land where certain protocols are observed, no matter how vicious the clientele.

Which is why Tilda knows that The Dutchman will have reached out to Barb for help after that message was sent out by The Professor. The question is, where does Barb stand? Will she help Tilda or the Dutchman? Or both? Tilda won't know till she meets Barb face-to-face.

She reckons she'll be in Copenhagen late afternoon. She'll dump the car on the outskirts, and then ride the metro to Kongens Nytorv. That will give her the opportunity to scope out Nyhavn from both sides, taking her time, looking for people who are looking for her.

Well, that won't be easy, she knows. It's going to be packed at that time, especially with this weather. Still, she's not going to march straight into the *Quantum Central* and place an order for a laptop hack.

She needs to dial down her mental machinations. She punches the radio and scans through till she gets a hit on something to numb her brain.

Feel it still, floods the car, fighting with the noise of the wind, as she charges across Fyn towards the Storebælt. And Sjælland.

Amsterdammed.

The Devil gets out of his seat and stretches his long limbs. He checks his watch. Too long. The Paris stop was a pain in his ass. He regrets not tasking a private jet. *Get over it*, he thinks.

He walks toward the plane exit, and makes a point of moving in close on the stewardess, who is standing at the door saying her goodbyes. He sees her catch his approach out of the corner of her eye. He smiles to himself as he sees the colour drain from her face.

He leans into her as she tries to maintain the plastic smile, and breathes onto her face, saying, "I hope to catch you on my return flight." He sees her visibly retch, and he gives her arm a painful squeeze. Then he's gone. Disappeared up the gangway, leaving another unfortunate soul in his wake.

As he enters into the terminal, he thinks she was a sweet thing. She'll probably resign the minute she gets off the plane.

Such a shame. Still, perhaps he'll track her down one day. It wouldn't be difficult.

He zones out of his primeval needs, and focuses on business. He walks through the controls, and then goes to pick up his rental. Twenty minutes later he's in his black seven-series Beamer, heading east toward Hamburg.

He's got a couple of stops to make enroute to The Professor's farm, just west of Århus. He already tasked an asset to take a look around. The response came back that the Police had still not been there. All the asset found was a blown out kitchen window, and damage to the walls and door. He reckons he'll be there in six hours, if his two meetings along the way go according to plan. One is business. The other is to satisfy the carnal lusts that overcame him during the flight.

Somewhere in northern Germany, some poor soul is enjoying her last day on earth.

Camilla's working in the back garden, tidying up some plants.

She loves it out here. She's so happy they bought the new place. Just opening those terrace doors on weekend days, and feeling the sea air gust in from the *Great Belt*, then stepping out and looking beyond the garden to the sea.

Camilla used to work weekends like a robot, but since she met Lucas she made the firm decision to commit to not working Saturday and Sundays. Most of the time it works out. She lives for Lucas now, and the new sense of balance he has brought to her life.

She glances down the garden, and can see him working on a wall between their villa and the beach. He's shirtless, and wearing an old pair of ripped jeans that she keeps threatening to burn. But now, looking at him, she's glad she didn't. She feels a stirring deep inside her that only Lucas can bring out.

Well, apart from *him*. But that was a different kind of desire. And it came with a heavy tax.

Evil.

And the stink that swamped her senses for hours after. But even so, she could never refuse his advances. Especially after *Unit* missions, when she needed a way to come down from the high of combat. They didn't always return directly to Denmark. It depended how far away they were. Jobs on the European mainland were often in urban areas. They required more planning because of the crowds, so they could sometimes spend weeks preparing a hit, and their escape plan. On those jobs they would often return to Denmark. If the job was in the wilds, or outside of Europe, some of them would take time out to relax.

After the Asian, Latin American and African gigs was when she started falling into the powerful arms of The Dutchman. They would take a villa, never a hotel, and spend a week or so together. She revelled in her proximity to his power. And he to hers. He could be extremely tender, yet he harboured demons, or more specifically, *The Demon*, who, when let loose, would consume everything in its path. She knew she was no angel, but she ticked that off as just being good at her job.

Assassination 101.

But one night on Grand Turk, after their love making in a villa, he had slipped out silently. But not silently enough.

She quickly dressed and followed him from a good distance, as he made his way along the beach. He'd been talking anxiously on the phone earlier, and she had caught snippets of the conversation. It was clear he was discussing something with someone on the island. And Camilla wanted to know who.

She saw him look over his shoulders about three hundred metres ahead, but she was fast and ducked behind a small wall. She watched as he darted to his right, and disappeared. She sprinted forward along the sand, to the point where she lost sight of him, then crouched down and looked up the garden into a beautiful white house.

There were lights on downstairs and she could see a number of people standing and discussing in living room.

They were all looking down at the floor. Camilla snuck along the side of the garden, skirting the dark bushes, knowing that the lights on in the house afforded her some cover. She got as close to the living room as she could before she had to break cover to get a better look.

She crawled behind a low wall, and then slowly raised herself to see what was going on.

She wished she hadn't.

There were six people in the room. Two women and four men, all standing in a circle, holding tumblers of liquor, still looking down. Camilla adjusted her position, trying to avoid creating a shadow from the terrace lights that now fell upon her. As she inched to her right, she stood up, to look through the gap between two of the people.

On the floor was a young man. Or what was left of him. Camilla could make out his face. He couldn't have been more than sixteen. He was still alive because she could see him moving his head from side to side, writhing in agony.

The tape on his mouth prevented any sounds escaping. His arms and legs were spread out, staked to the floor. On his knees, leaning over the boy, was the hunched figure of a tall man in a long black shirt. He was performing a live autopsy, as the other guests stood and admired the macabre activity. A man and a woman were pleasuring themselves as they watched.

Camilla raised her hand to her mouth, trying to keep from vomiting.

She failed, puking over the terrace, moving into the direct light as she did so.

One of the women watching the show caught the movement, and grabbed the arm of the tall man standing next to her. The Dutchman turned and stared through the terrace doors at the disappearing figure that sprinted straight down the garden toward the beach. Camilla had never run so fast, even in combat. She stormed into their villa and threw her clothes into her bag, grabbed the keys to the Jeep, and screamed out of the driveway in search of a boat off the island.

As the wind blew through her hair, she knew she had to get off this tropical paradise. A plane was out of the question, so she floored it in the opposite direction to Grand Turk Airport.

She knew what to do. One thing about Camilla, wherever she was, she always made sure to scope out escape routes. Even when she was on vacation. Call it core skillsets.

An hour later she was ploughing through the surf, directly south, on a stolen motor boat. She knew she didn't have enough fuel to get her to the Dominican Republic, so she did the only thing she could think of. She eased off on the throttle, bringing the boat to a stop. As it bobbed up and down on the tide, she reached into her bag and pulled out her satellite phone.

Then she called Simon. *The Unit*'s logistician magician. The only man she knew could get anything anywhere. Usually involving heavy weaponry.

She was praying he hadn't rotated back to Europe. She knew he had an on-off thing going with Bekka. Which, she told him, was one of the dumbest things he could do.

"You don't get involved with Unit comrades."

"Look who's talking," he'd replied.

They'd all suspected she and the Dutchman were involved. It had made Lærke hate her even more.

She looked up at the clear night, as if searching for the satellite that would connect her with Simon. It kept ringing for a minute. Then he answered.

He sounded tired. She asked him where he was, and he asked what it had to do with her. She told him that she was in deep shit, out on the deep sea, and that she had been compromised. She did not tell him what she had seen. But she told Simon that there was a chance that The Dutchman was coming for her.

Simon didn't say anything for thirty seconds. Then he told her to turn west and head for Cuba. She was to call him in one hour, so he could get a fix on her location.

He knew how to get hold of a seaplane.

Bekka was pissed for about six months after that. The dynamics in *The Unit* changed, and tensions started running high, which made planning difficult, and amped up the mission execution risk.

They managed to screw up one job, which was a protection detail down in Cape Town. They lost their client in a hail of bullets, and had to blast their way out of town with a small army on their tail.

After Grand Turk, The Dutchman didn't say anything unusual to Camilla. He just stared at her with his bright blue eyes. She got the feeling that he enjoyed the fact that she now knew his true nature. And that she would do nothing about it.

One day, she thought, every time she saw him. *One day, I will fucking end your perverse life.* A gust of warm wind wakes Camilla out of her dark memories. She stands up, with dirt on her hands, and looks down to the end of the garden, watching Lucas. He brings a smile to her face. She needed that. She shouts down and asks him if he wants a cold drink. He gives her the thumbs up, and she turns back towards the house to get their lemonades.

Behind her, a few kilometres to the south-east, a small, black Peugeot leaves Fyn, crossing onto the *Storebælt* bridge. At the wheel, a tall middle-aged woman, with scruffy black hair, grips the steering wheel with white knuckles as she passes into the distance, beyond the tranquility of Camilla and Lucas' villa.

East towards Copenhagen.

Late Saturday afternoon, downtown Copenhagen, and everything's a go-go.

The sun's beating down on the capital, fuelling sales of ice cream and cool drinks, as the tourists chill out with the locals. The twin pulses rippling out from *Tivoli Gardens* and Nyhavn, send endless waves of people through the artery known as *Strøget*, on a collision course with outside wine bars and coffee shops at both ends.

Tilda emerges from the Metro station at Kongens Nytorv, wearing a dark baseball cap and wrap-around blue *Oakleys*. She'd dumped her car at the *Marina Hotel* in Vedbæk when she checked in earlier.

It was a good place to hole-up, because it was down the road from Bekka and Simon's villa. She planned to scope it out after dark. She then rode the train to Copenhagen central, and then walked to *Rådhuspladsen* Metro station for the short hop to her final destination. It was mainly for orientation. She wanted to get familiar with the subway system in case she had to make rapid EXFIL.

She adjusts her backpack and pauses in the shade, just outside the *Hotel D'Angleterre*, to get her bearings. A flood of sensations wash over her, and she fights to control the memories and missed opportunities that have defined her last few decades.

She looks up at the glorious hotel, perched within striking distance of Nyhavn. In her role as CEO, she'd had to nimbly sidestep multiple conference appearances in

Denmark over the years. She'd always managed to come up with some vanilla bullshit excuse for not taking up the opportunity of a speaking gig, or meeting investors here. And every time she rejected a request, she'd paid the price for a day of uncomfortable sensations in her belly. She always blew it off as a symptom of the gunshot wound, but deep down she knew it was a craving for her homeland.

She looks directly across the plaza toward Nyhavn, as crowds hustle back and forth. She then turns right, and crosses the road to the far side, choosing to walk down the opposite side of Nyhavn to where all the restaurants are located.

And Quantum Barbs joint.

She employs her best *touristy* look, hunching her shoulders, and taking pulls from a water bottle, as she scans the opposite bank of the canal. The far side is awash with colours, from the brightly coloured buildings, to the thousands of tourists, and the old ships, lovingly adorned with flags. It's a fiesta of fun in the sun, and Tilda gets that familiar uncomfortable sensation that she's not part of it.

She spots Barb's joint about halfway down. It's packed-out with customers decked out on the chairs and tables, and those customers who can't find a seat are sitting on the low wall by the boats, that stretches the full length of the canal.

That low wall...where I met Nikolaj...stop it! She stands in the shadow for a couple of minutes, studying Barb's place and the adjacent cafés. She scans the low walls and tries to spot anything that doesn't fit in.

You mean like me? She muses.

She realises it's impossible to get a fix on anything out of the ordinary with so much going on, and she reminds herself that she's out of practice in the game of surveillance. So she carries on walking east to the bridge, then hangs a left, crossing the canal, and doubling back along the opposite bank, fighting her way through the crowds.

Finally, she reaches Barb's bright yellow building, and she can see that the terrace tables are maxed out. She looks into the restaurant, as waitresses rush in and out with trays filled with wine and iced coffee glasses.

"I've got a table over here for you," comes a voice from behind, causing Tilda to spin on her heels.

She looks down at the short lady with a long black ponytail, and square rimless glasses. "Excuse me?" says Tilda.

"I've been expecting you," says Quantum Barb, gesturing to a small metal table and chair in the far corner of her terrace. Barb strides through the packed terrace and motions for Tilda to sit.

"Have a refreshing drink, and then we'll have a chat upstairs. I just need to help out here a bit. What can I get you?"

"Still water is good, thanks," replies Tilda, still getting over the shock of being expected, and recognised.

She's sizing Barb up through her sunglasses, and has the strange feeling that Barb can see right through her dark lenses.

"Coming right up!" Barb says, spinning, and walking back to the central waitress station to place Tilda's order. She then disappears up the steps, into the building, collecting half a dozen glasses on the way.

What the fuck just happened?, thinks Tilda, scanning her immediate environment. She's trying to get a read on the rest of the customers. Most of them seem like genuine tourists, with a few sprinklings of locals. She does pick out a couple of over-dressed people on the far side of the terrace, and she tags them as possible Quantum Barb clientele.

Her water appears, courtesy of a young Swedish waitress. Tilda thanks her and takes a long gulp, using the upending of the glass to help her pivot her head left and right. Too much foot traffic to spot anything here.

Five minutes later, Barb gestures to her from the waitress station. Tilda gets up and makes her way through the throng of tables, and follows Barb into the building. Barb heads straight up the stairs, climbing three floors to the top of the building, followed by Tilda. She opens a door to a room that looks out across the canal.

Barb says to the two young students sitting in front of a bank of laptops by the wall, "Lisbeth, Gina, can you give us this room for a while. Go grab some dinner and we'll catchup on your progress later."

The one called Gina, swivels on her chair and says in an Icelandic-English accent, "sure Barb, c'mon Lis, I'm starving."

Both of them shut down their screens, get up and walk out, closing the door behind them without looking at Tilda.

Barb says, "those are two of my most promising *CBS* munchkins. They're working on some machine learning algorithms that's gonna turn the corporate world upside down. You might want to consider investing, before they disrupt you," Barb winks, and continues, "you can lose the shades now Tilda. Or should I call you *Lærke*?"

Tilda begins to remove her sunglasses, then pauses when she hears her real name. "*Tilda* is good."

"Of course, it's a wonderful name. And you have built an impressive organisation down there. You've changed a lot since the last time we met. When was that? Late autumn of '94? It's possible my memory is not what it used to be."

"I doubt that," remarks Tilda, continuing straight to the point, "how is it possible you know so much about me, when no one else does?"

"My darling, it's my job to know everything. Before your, how should I put it, *accident*, your reputation in the market preceded you. Fortunately for you, there was not so much imagery around when you were in your killing prime. You have indeed, made some interesting cosmetic choices, which to a layman's eyes have transformed you into a completely different person. But may I make a couple of suggestions?"

Tilda, stunned by the arrogance of the café owner, purses her lips and opens her hands, "be my guest."

"Well, for starters, your walk is a dead giveaway. You have a gait that is as identifiable as a fingerprint. I watched you at Davos walk onto a stage for a panel discussion. When I saw that, I was quite worried about your safety. I wondered, if you hadn't become too relaxed about your new identity. Of course, I am in the business of spotting discrepancies–"

Tilda goes to object, but Barb holds her hands up defensively, "–don't get me wrong, I'm not calling you a discrepancy! Anyway, we aren't here to discuss your image. Why don't you give me The Professor's laptop so I can take a look at it."

Tilda is stunned again, and stares down into Barb's eyes as she stands there in her waitress outfit, with her hands on her hips. Her mind is racing.

How the fu...

Barb can see Tilda's tongue-tied, and says, "listen, you're confused, I get it. Just give me the laptop and I'll take a look at it over night. Come back for breakfast tomorrow at about ten."

Tilda swings the backpack off and pulls out The Professor's laptop, handing it over to Barb, who then opens the door and gestures for Tilda to walk out.

"There's one other thing you can help me with," says Tilda.

"Name it."

Tilda shows Barb a photo of Nikolaj on her smartphone and says, "how can I find him?"

"Well, that's not difficult. He's on TV and a bunch of podcasts every week. I'll text you his home address."

"You don't have my phone number," counters Tilda.

"Sure I do," says Barb, motioning toward the door. She walks ahead of Barb, down the three flights of stairs, and emerges onto the steps into the sunshine. She turns round to say something to Barb, but she's gone over to the bar and is loading up a tray full of iced lattes.

Tilda walks down the steps, through the tables, and out of Barb's fenced-off terrace. She stands there, as tourists walk back and forth around her, looking back at the yellow building, and puts on her sunglasses and thinks, *what the fuck just happened? I just handed over the laptop to someone who knows who I am!*

She reorientates, then heads east, crossing *Kongens Nytorv*, and the long walk down *Strøget* towards the central train station, where she'll hop a ride back to Vedbæk.

The four-Merc convoy, with Danish registration plates, speeds across the *Øresund* bridge towards Copenhagen.

They cruise westwards into the late Saturday afternoon sun, before being swallowed up by the sea as they enter the tunnel section. They emerge back into the sunlight onto the

Danish section of the E20, at the edge of Kastrup airport runway, and head toward the city. One Merc peels off and heads toward *Den Blå Planet*, tracking the coastline towards its destination at the *Marriott*. Two of the other Mercs split off and fan out across the city, towards their hotel destinations at the *Radisson Blu* and the *Admiral*.

The final one tracks north towards its assigned post at the hotel in Skodsborg.

Their instructions are clear:

Find the assassin formerly known as Lærke, and terminate. Standby to neutralise the former operatives located in Vedbæk, but only after receiving direct instructions from D. Maintain a surveillance posture for now.

It's Saturday evening, so Bekka and Simon are in the entertainment business.

Usually, it's the highlight of the week, as they glam-up for their visitors, whose names are strategically pulled from the list of Copenhagen's glitterati. It's often an eclectic affair, with a combo of finance gurus, politicians, TV personalities and the occasional footballer. They'd carefully crafted their network over the years, cross-leveraging each other's connections, and complimenting each other's abilities to charm the pants off anyone they thought could be useful to advancing their personal riches.

Thus, this Vedbæk address was the place to be seen at. Once a year, minimum. The summer gigs were the best, as they could spill out into the back garden, bringing in more power couples, and cutting more deals.

Unfortunately, tonights planned bash was going off the rails, on account of the tension flowing between the hosts. The last couple of days had freaked both of them out.

Bekka was handling it better than Simon. Well, she always did. She had to give him a couple of bollockings to get him focused. This morning he had suggested that they cancel tonight's event, but Bekka went ballistic, so he backed off.

To top it off, Simon got wind that the fucking journalist, Nikolaj, was going to be profiling VC's in his Saturday evening TV slot. And he knew he would be referenced, although he thought he'd probably pacified the guy over their lunch at *Address* a couple of days ago.

Bekka wasn't so sure. She didn't tend to hide behind hope, like her *Anglo* husband. She knew a setup when she saw one. She had verbally beaten the crap out of Simon when he told her about the lunch meeting. He was such a fool to have offered it. You give a predator a taste of blood, they come back for more etc.

So tonight you could cut the atmosphere in the house with a knife. Simon felt like he was in that *Goodfellas* movie, rushing all over the place, fixing the wine and catering, and checking social media. Meanwhile, Bekka handled the rest of the jobs.

And the kids of course. They'd managed to offload them onto her sister over Saturday night, but they had a few scares over the last twenty-four hours in the house.

It had to do with guns. A lot of them. Since the text from The Professor, and Camilla's visit, they'd amped up their personal protection, from a few kitchen knives, to an arsenal of handguns, and one semi-automatic rifle. The problem was storage. Specifically, hiding them out of sight of the kids. Simon got an ass-kicking last night from Bekka after she sat down on the sofa and discovered a SIG P365 sticking into her back from behind a cushion. And the stupid wanker had taken the safety off.

They'd been up all night figuring out how to maintain an air of calm and chic for the guests, yet still be in easy reach of a bit of firepower in case the dinner plans went turbo. They hadn't heard anything from The Dutchman nor Camilla since she'd invaded their perfect lives. However, Bekka had to admit to herself that it was handy having Camilla in the game. Even if she hated her guts. It was possible Camilla might draw Lærke's fire. At least for tonight, so they could hold their dinner party.

As the evening unfolded, the gorgeous and the glorious showed up, jamming up the street, much to the annoyance of the neighbours, who were hosting equally important parties.

Bekka had to admit that Simon was an ace host, and she knew they were a great team. At one point they caught each other's eyes from the opposite ends of the great dinning table, and there was a momentary spark of genuine love that brought smiles to their faces. Then it faded, and the tension of seeing to the needs of their guests, whilst simultaneously watching out for the odd assassination attempt, rose to the surface.

Their state-of-the-art security system was working overtime, but it failed to recognise the black Merc that was parked up on the kerb just out of the camera's range. Nor could it pick up the black Peugeot, that was sitting a hundred metres behind the Merc.

Tilda's pleased when the last of the guests roll out of Bekka and Simon's place. She's been sitting jammed-up in this little car for three hours. She's about twenty-seven years out of practice for stake-outs, and she doesn't miss them. She wouldn't mind relieving herself either, and she curses herself for drinking the full bottle of water.

She pulled up just after dark, when the party was already in full swing. She had driven past earlier, so she had spotted the camera system, so when she returned, she parked about a hundred and fifty metres down the road, to the left of their entrance.

She'd noticed the black Mercedes with tinted windows, when she'd pulled up. It didn't look right to her. It was parked up on the kerb, and she could make out the shape of someone on the drivers side. Her first thought was that Bekka and Simon had called in some extra security, but the Mercedes was parked out of range of the surveillance cameras, and way too far back to help out if anything went down.

Nope, this was another team watching them. Or were they looking for me?

As the last of the guests staggered drunkenly into waiting taxis, Tilda tensed up as she saw the unmistakeable figure of Simon walk out of the electric gates. He looked in both directions, scoping out the scene, but didn't seem to notice either of the vehicles parked further up the road. He turned his back and returned to the house, closing the tall gates behind him.

Tilda flicked the light switch above the rear-view mirror to off, so that when she opened the door, the cabin light would not come on. Then she snuck into the bushes next to her car and relieved herself.

Classy, she thinks. *You're supposed to be a CEO of a German industrial giant. Yeah, well I'm other things too. And even CEO's need to take a leak.*

She emerges from the bush, and opens the back door, taking her baseball cap out of the backpack. She puts it on, and pulls it firmly down over her face. Then she begins walking towards the rear of the Mercedes.

As she squeezes past it on the pathway, she makes an obvious play of looking directly into the drivers window. As she passes, she can see that he looks up at her. She carries on walking till she gets about ten metres before the range of the camera on Bekka and Simon's house.

She takes an exaggerated look towards the house, then she turns and starts walking back towards the Mercedes. She strides quickly toward the drivers side, again making a meal of looking into the car window. The driver looks up at her, although the windows are too tinted for her to make out his features. She carries on until she gets to her Peugeot, then climbs in and turns on the engine, peeling out quickly.

She passes the Mercedes, and then Bekka and Simon's place. In her rear-view mirror, she sees the car lights turn on as the Mercedes pulls out to follow her towards *Strandvejen*.

Gotcha!

"We got company outside, babe," says Simon grabbing the SIG for the drawer where Bekka hid it.

She sprints out of the kitchen carrying her own pistol. "Lærke?" she asks.

"No. Too obvious. A black Merc is parked a couple hundred metres to the left. It's up on the kerb. I think there's another car further up, but it could be just a neighbour's visitor."

"We better do a sweep," says Bekka, rubbing the alcohol mist from her eyes. "I'll go out the back and circle round the side. You go out the front."

Simon doesn't need to be told twice. He goes to the front door, opens it and walks across the forecourt to the white walls that surround their villa. He tucks the SIG into the back of his trousers, and starts to climb the wall, using the rough bricks as foot holds.

He catches sight of Bekka as she emerges from round the side of the house. She shakes her head as he peers over the top of the wall. Just as his head clears it, he sees a small black hatchback pull out further up the road, and drive straight past the house. Almost immediately, the black Merc that he had spotted flips its lights on, and takes off after the first car.

Peugeot. He thinks it was Peugeot. Or maybe a Citroen. He jumps back down, and jogs over to Bekka.

"No signs out back or down the sides. What did you see?"

"Two-car team. I think they must have spotted me because they took off. Could be our Dutch friend is keeping an eye on us."

"Or using us as bait," his wife replies.

Simon nods. "Well, they're gone now. I'll get the camera's adjusted for a wider angle. Let's get back in side," he says, putting his arm round his wife, and kissing the top of her head.

Extreme stress, coupled with considerable alcohol consumption is quite a cocktail, and that night was the first time they had made love in over seven months. But who's counting, thought Bekka, as she lay there listening to Simon's snoring.

Lærke. I know she was out there. Bekka doesn't sleep this night.

She takes him north, dragging him along *Strandvejen*. She figures Helsingør will be a good place to take him out. And also to flush out any other operatives nearby. She knows that he will have checked-in with his team. Maybe even The Dutchman. There's no way he could have recognised her, but they would put two and two together.

Her plan is simple. Get him far from Bekka and Simon's place, interrogate and terminate, then double back to the airport, via the E47, dump the Peugeot and pick up a new rental. Then go check-in to another hotel. She can't go back to the Marina now that she's burnt.

She snakes her way through the villages, northwards. Rungsted, Humlebæk, Snekkersten, maintaining the speed limit, watching to see if the Mercedes is closing its distance. It kept a half a kilometre gap all the way up to Helsingør, which told her that there was no other company to worry about.

She knows the town well. She and Nikolaj used to hang out there a lot, catching the ferry across to Helsingborg in Sweden for weekend getaways. She drives past the ferry terminal on her right, which is now closed, catching a glimpse of the lights across the short strait in Sweden. Then she loops round the ring road, bearing west.

She rounds a corner, loosing sight of the Merc's lights in the rear-view mirror, then she floors the tiny Peugeot, trying to get as much acceleration as possible. She hangs a sharp left, cursing both the acceleration and handling of the car, then takes a sharp right, screeching her tyres, cringing as the noise invades the peaceful, sleeping town. The last thing she wants to do is attract the cops attention.

She takes another left into the car park at the *Sankt Olai Kirke*, then pulls into a space and turns off her engine. She leaps out of the car, leaving her backpack exposed in the back seat, then sprints across to the church, locking the car behind her with the fob.

She sneaks into the shadows of the grand old building, and presses her back against the wall. And waits.

After ten minutes, she's growing impatient. Then, just as she's having second thoughts, a car's headlights come round the corner, exposing her vehicle. She backs off deeper into the darkness, watching as the big Merc pulls up next to the tiny Peugeot.

The door opens, and a man gets out.

Big fucker, she thinks, watching the way he moves for clues. And move he does, like predator. Slowly, carefully and deliberately. He looks into the windows of the Peugeot, then looks up again, scanning three hundred and sixty degrees.

The church is exposed in a square, surrounded on all four sides by buildings. Tilda's watching him, gauging his gaze. When he sweeps it around to the front of the church, she makes a move, casting a shadow that exposes her position. The man catches it, zoning in on her. Tilda scuffles her sneakers, and watches as he reaches behind his back and pulls out a silenced pistol. He looks around again, then begins to jog across the grass toward the church.

Tilda's already moving. She backs up slowly, then spins on her heals and hurries around the rear of the building. She knows where she's heading. Towards the light that would minimise any shadows she casts.

The man reaches the wall of the church and edges up to the corner, extending the pistol in his right hand. He swings it round the corner, seeing nothing. Then he begins to walk the length of the wall, freezing for a second as a car drives past the car park. He waits until it has disappeared, then he sneaks to the next corner, again extending his gun, and peering round.

The blow shatters his windpipe, and is so sudden that his trigger finger sends off a silenced round into the night.

He staggers backwards, dropping the gun, and brings his hands up to his neck, fighting for air.

Tilda stands above him as he slides down the wall, kicking him between his legs. The pain plays havoc with his mind, as he struggles to decide which is worse. Somewhere in his subconscious, he figures that his neck wound is probably mortal. Still, the raging pain from his crotch is too much to bear.

Tilda looks down, muttering, "shit," under her breath, realising that she used way too much force. She'd only meant to disorientate him, but now she could see that her blow was fatal. She's well out of practice.

She kneels in front of him as he gags and squirms. She can see that he has little time left, and there is no way she can get anything out of him. Checking his pockets, she pulls out his wallet and phone, and grabs his keys.

He's staring up into her eyes, helpless, knowing that his whole life had been barrelling towards this sudden death, just across the water from his beloved Sweden.

He's taking too long to go, she thinks, so she gives him another blow, sending him off to meet so many of the other victims from her past. She picks up his discarded pistol, sliding it into her waist, then gets up and looks around to see if anyone is about. Satisfied, she makes her way, cautiously, over to the cars.

She opens up the Merc, using her fleece as a handgrip so as not to leave any prints. There's nothing in there. She locks the car, then gets back into the Peugeot and heads towards the highway, throwing the Merc's key fob out of the window into some bushes.

The Dutchman, who's not Dutch, gets to The Professor's farm on the outskirts of Hinge in the early hours of Sunday.

He cruises into the long driveway, the big tyres on his Beamer making a scrunching sound as they roll over the gravel. He's not worried about the security system, because his operative disabled it earlier. She's still parked just outside the gate.

He pulls up by the old front door, gets out and stretches. This trip took way too long. He could have done it in half the time, but his second stop went off the rails. One of the associates in his satanic club was not satanic enough as it turns out.

During the ceremony, the Frenchman lost his nerve, and ran out of the room. It quickly dampened The Dutchman's desires, and resulted in an early end to the event. The Dutchman washed up after himself, and left the mess to be cleaned up by one of his German operatives. He'd walked outside and found the Frenchman sobbing, and taking long drags from a cigarette as he leant against a wall.

The Dutchman had walked up to him and consoled the man. Then he sliced his throat and gently lowered his body to the ground. He'd walked back inside and indicated to the operative that there was one more task to take care of. The woman, who was on her knees scrubbing blood and faeces off the floor, looked up and nodded, before going back to her task.

Three hours that fucking Frenchman cost me, thinks The Devil, as he walks into the Professor's hallway. He takes a vial of blue *compound* out of his pocket, snaps off the end, and then pours it into both of his eyes. He feels the immediate sensory surge, as the chemicals electrify his synapses, supercharging his awareness levels.

He doesn't think he will find anything of use here. Lærke would have taken it all. But he had an itch he couldn't scratch, and he needed to see The Professor's premises for himself. After all, he had been The Dutchman's first recruit. He was special.

He sees the destruction from the shotgun blast scattered around the floor. The kitchen door is hanging off its hinges, and he rips it off as he enters. He can make out the faint discolouring of blood on the floor.

So this is where it went down, he thinks. She did a poor job of cleaning up, but then again, he has an eye for blood. To the average cop it might have been hard to spot, but a forensic expert would have zoned-in on it in no time.

He wonders what she did with his body. Burnt or buried? Burning attracts too much attention, without the proper facilities. And even then you've got to bury the leftovers. So she definitely dug a hole and dropped him in it.

He wanders out of the kitchen, and along the hall to a back door. He turns his phone's torchlight on and aims it at the floor. Footprints. Big ones. He opens the door and looks out across the back yard that extends into a field. It has a line of trees and bushes skirting the perimeter.

You came in this way, didn't you, you stealthy bitch, he thinks as he looks up at the camera's position above the door. Just above it, behind some guttering, he sees another camera. He reckons The Professor saw her coming. Hence the destruction in the hallway. So she's loosing her edge.

You're not the panther you used to be. He smiles and licks his lips. Then he scans the field. Well, if his old friend is in a hole out there, he's not going to waste time digging him up.

He goes back inside the farmhouse and rummages around downstairs. He can't find any tech, which means Lærke took it. Which could be a big fucking problem. He decides to take a look upstairs and begins to ascend, shinning his torch ahead of him. He gets to the second floor and starts to look into the bedrooms which are just full of junk. This guy really went off the edge, he thinks. There are empty bottles everywhere, and the place smells of rotting.

The Dutchman has always been a pristine devil. He abhorred mess and dirt, and he can't rationalise why a guy with access to tens of millions of Euros in funds would live in a shit hole like this.

Well, he's worm food now. He comes to the end of the landing, and opens the door to the main bedroom. The sheets are all messed up, and there are clothes all over the place. The Dutchman walks in, careful not to disturb anything. He goes to the window and looks out onto the driveway. He can see his operative just outside the gate, slumped against the window in her car. *She will regret that later*, he thinks.

He looks under the bed, and then in the side tables. *Nada*. Then he goes to the wardrobe, checking behind it. He thinks this is a waste of his time, and turns to walk out of the door, but he feels a floorboard give way under his foot, accompanied by a creek. He stops and looks down. He goes back over it, and tests the boards either side. Three of them are loose.

He kneels down, and pulls the mat away, revealing the three boards that have been fastened down with fresh metal screws. He takes the Swiss Army knife out of his back pocket, and selects the screwdriver, then begins to loosen the screws.

It takes him three minutes to get them all out, and when he is finished he levers the boards up. Now he shines the torch into the hole, and he can see a long metal case. He pulls it out and opens it up. Inside, wrapped in a leather cloth, is a freshly minted SIG M400 TREAD SNAKEBITE, and four ammo packs.

How quaint, thinks The Dutchman.

The Professor's obviously been shopping recently, because this is a new model. He wonders if he had other weapons lying around. Or what caused the sudden desire to purchase such a high performance weapon. And how? They didn't exactly get home delivered by Amazon.

Simon? Maybe, although he doubted it. He thinks it may come in handy, so he lays it on the bed and retrieves the spare ammo. As he's reaching for the last magazine, his hand brushes another metal box. It appears to be jammed into the far corner of the hole. He has to extend his long arm all the way into the hole so he can get a hold of it. He grabs the edge and pulls it out, placing it on the bedroom floor. It has a couple metal clips but no lock, so he flips them up, and opens the lid.

In the box is a white sheet of paper, folded in half. He takes it out and unfolds it. There are only two typed words on it.

Fuck you.

The Dutchman springs backwards, driving towards the bedroom door as fast as he can, but the blasts explode out of two opposite walls, blowing him the rest of the way through the door.

8 - ISLAND HOPPING

Oxfordshire, England.

It's way too early for a CORP-ROGUE meet. And on a Sunday! None of the participants are happy. Most figured it could have been done over *Zoom* or *Teams*, but *she* said, "get your arses over here now!"

So the last few hours turned into a climate activists worst nightmare, with private jets booked from across the northern countries, to deliver important-looking people wearing black turtlenecks and other corporate attire, to this most exclusive of Thames Valley addresses.

It's now seven in the morning, and eight limos slink through the high gates of the estate with precision planning. The passengers spill out onto the gravel drive, and are ushered through the large oak door, and into the dinning room.

She sits at the end of the table, chomping on a fat cigar, peering into a tablet through her half-moon steel rimmed glasses. One by one, they filter into the room, assaulted by the heavy smoke, trying not to gag on the fumes.

The doors close behind them, and they take their seats at the table. No coffee, no refreshments. These corporate titans are not used to this kind of treatment. But none object.

They have all felt the whiplash from her tongue in the past. No one wants to set her off. Especially at this time. They're still trying to figure out why they are here. All they know is that when they got the tap, they jumped in the limos that were already waiting for them when they crawled out of bed in the early hours in their home countries. They know the vow they took a long time ago.

When the call comes, they move. *Fast*. For they are part of an exclusive corporate club. A group of seemingly unrelated entities, whose entire existence is predicated on maintaining the equilibrium. For themselves and their seed. They represent the CORP-ROGUE hierarchy.

It's very much an inter-continental show, and this is the European chapter. Of course, they all have global interests, their capabilities and influence ignoring continental boundaries. And now they're staking out everything they can up in space, beyond the *Kármán Line*.

She takes a big tug on her cigar, and blows out a roomful of smoke before dropping it into her coffee cup. Then she peers over the top of her glasses, like a librarian investigating an invasive sound.

The eight in the room sit at attention, sweating under their corporate casual attires. They know she's a stickler for dress code, and none of them want to set her off with a simple mistake, such as wearing anything too grey.

Finally, she says, "do you know why I brought you here at such short notice?"

It was rhetorical, and all remain silent. "Last night, our dear French friend passed away after an unfortunate incident in northern Germany."

The individuals in the room visibly stiffen. No one had noticed that the Frenchman was not present. She continues, "it seems dear Claude's peccadilloes got the better of him, and he was enticed into the embrace of The Dutchman."

She pauses for effect, noting the sharp intake of breath across the room. "Indeed," she says, clarifying their concerns. "The Dutchman landed in Amsterdam a day ago, journeying from his tropical hellhole, apparently on some kind of urgent mission. More on that in a minute.

Unfortunately, for dear Claude, The Dutchman set up one of his macabre soirees, and the light entertainment did not go according to plan. Claude was executed by The Dutchman, and left for one of his operatives to clean up. Fortunately for us, his operative was also mine. It seems the Dutchman was headed into Denmark–"

She looks up in the direction of the only Dane in the room, getting an immediate *oh shit* reaction.

"–on a mission to clean up one of his old messes. Specifically, a rogue assassin from his original *Unit*, who it appears, decided not to die twenty-seven years ago. Indeed, it appears this most entrepreneurial of killers, who managed to remain off the grid for so long, has got the bit between her teeth, and is intent on bringing her former colleagues to account."

She pauses for effect. "I am of course talking about *Lærke*."

Heads drop down, trying not to make eye contact. Very few in the room ever used the services of her. But they all had long memories. And they knew the stories from the whispered conversations in exclusive clubs across the northern lands.

"Unfortunately, for our Dutch fiend, I do not want her terminated. Not yet anyway. I want to find out where she's been, what she knows, and how the hell she managed to stay off the grid for so long. So we shall bring in some external consultants to slow The Dutchman down. Permanently."

She looks up, sensing the concerns. "Yes, yes, I understand the risks. He has leverage on all of you. So we shall tread carefully. But sooner or later he will depart this world for his more familiar subterranean dwelling. And when that happens, we are, how can I put it...*fucked anyway.*"

One of the Brits at the far end of the table makes a coughing sound.

"Well, speak up boy!" she snaps.

"Chairman, if I may enquire–"

"–can you fucking speak English for once!" she yells down the table.

"Well, these external consultants...The Dutchman, his operatives...well they are highly skilled. Who did you have in mind?"

"I'm calling The Norwegian and have him spin-up his Icelandic huntress. She is stealthy and relentless. I am unaware that she has any equal."

The Brit, nervously, goes on, "but The Norwegian won't do business with us. His interests are diametrically opposed to ours."

"Young man, sometimes accommodations must be made to trade with one's competitors. Set up a call with me and him. We can do business where our interests are aligned. That is all."

With that, she looks down at her tablet and fires up another cigar, as the eight guests shuffle out.

Tilda's running late.

She's not used to sleeping in. After she dumped the rental at Kastrup, she went to another agency and picked up another small hatchback, this time a white Golf, with another credit card in a different name. Then she drove north to Lyngby and checked in to her hotel, rolling into bed around three am.

She looks at her watch. *Shit*! It's already nine o'clock. She's supposed to meet Barb at ten. She leaps out of bed, skipping her morning stretching ritual, gets dressed, visits the bathroom, and checks out.

She jumps in her car and then drives directly down to Nyhavn, cursing herself that she didn't make time enough to come in on public transport. Luckily, it being Sunday, she finds a parking space in the street behind Nyhavn. She gets out and makes a wide arc, round the corner of the *Phoenix hotel*, then looping back round to *Kongens Nytorv*, before making a direct line across to Barb's café.

She gets there at ten past ten, and can see that it's still pretty empty. Barb appears at the steps of the café, as if she saw Tilda coming. Well, she probably did. Tilda follows Barb straight up the stairs and into the same room they were in yesterday, and Barb motions for Tilda to sit down.

"Right, let me show you what interesting little gems I found on this," she says, gesturing to the laptop.

Fugloy.

Sigi's sitting, drinking from a big mug of coffee outside her small cottage on the outskirts of Hattarvik. She arrived two nights ago and has been decompressing after two weeks in a hot place where she really shouldn't have been.

Story of my life, she muses as she stares out over the bay. Then her phone rings, and she curses in Icelandic. She looks at the caller ID, and takes the curse back.

"Where are you?" comes the rasping, familiar voice.

"Fugloy. Got in a couple of nights ago," she pauses, waiting for the inevitable request.

"Are you rested up?" "Of course," she lies, swearing under her breath.

"Good. I need you in Denmark in twenty-four hours."

"Are you kidding me? I can't go there!" she says firmly, trying to stay calm.

"You can, and you will. I've fixed transport. Get to Vágar airport. There will be a jet waiting. It'll take you to Kristiansand. From there it's an easy hop over to Jylland."

Sigi sighs. "OK, what's the job?" she asks, looking out on the bay, knowing it's the last time she'll see it for a while.

"I got a call from a lady in England."

"You mean, the *old witch*?"

"Yes. The Chairman herself. It seems our roguish friends in the corporate world need a favour," replies Naddador.

"And you trust her?"

"Of course not, child! But I sense an opportunity for leverage. Call it a longer term play that I have in mind."

"OK. Who's the mark?"

"Well, it's an interesting task. Part protection, and part termination. There will be details waiting for you on the plane. Call me from the car after you get into Århus."

He clicks-off the connection. Sigi gets up and sighs again. She throws the rest of her coffee onto the grass, then goes back into the small cottage to pack.

Jesus, the mainland. She's not too comfortable with this. There are multiple kill orders out on her. Not to mention the odd international arrest warrant. So no way she could get in via Kastrup.

She's packed her stuff into two long bags. One for clothes, and the other for her hunting gear. Then she walks out into the fresh air, takes one last look down into the small village and the bay beyond, then wanders down to her old Forerunner.

He woke up with a devil of a headache.

It took him a few minutes to get his bearings. The last thing he remembered was reading a note. Then nothing. After a couple of hours, he had reacquired his faculties and his operative had filled him in on the details of what happened.

The explosion had woken her from her slumber in the car, just outside the entrance to the farm. She had raced in, with her gun out, and charged up the stairs to where the blast had originated. She found him sprawled on the floor of the landing, covered in debris. He did not appear to have any wounds, but he was out cold.

She managed to drag him down the stairs, and into the back seat of his Beamer. Then she drove a kilometre down the road and parked. She ran back to the farm house and brought her own vehicle to the same location. Then she climbed back into the Beamer and drove him thirty kilometres to the Airbnb where she was holed up.

Now he sits at the kitchen table, alone and nursing a coffee trying to get back the rest of his senses. He assumes that The Professor would not have known who the victim of his elaborate booby trap would be. He probably assumed he would be long dead, so why not take any intruder along with him for the ride.

Charming!

Thirty minutes later, and the Dutchman has showered, shaved and changed clothes. He's still got a bit of a hangover, so he takes another vial of *compound*, emptying it into his eyes, and letting the blue elixir work its temporary magic on his systems.

He'd dismissed his operative, and she had taken a taxi back to Hinge to pick up her own car. She had called to say that the cops and emergency services were crawling all over the farmhouse when she drove past. He acknowledged her work, and told her that she would not be punished for falling asleep at the wheel.

She gulped, audibly, then thanked The Dutchman and hung up.

He walks out of the door, takes a long breath, and looks up at the sun. Then he climbs into the Beamer and pulls out of the small cul-de-sac.

Time to pay Camilla a visit in her little piece of heaven.

"It was surprisingly hard to crack," says Quantum Barb, looking up at Tilda as she opens up The Professor's laptop. "Getting past the password was no problem, but then there was a shit-load of encryption to deal with, as well as a time bomb. Fortunately, one of my munchkins had an Israeli friend and...well, you don't need to know the rest. So now I present to you the fully exposed files of the assassin formally known as The Professor!"

Barb stands up and motions for Tilda to take her seat in front of the laptop.

"I assume you have seen what's on it?" says Tilda looking up at Barb, in her fresh coffee-serving apron.

"Of course! That's my payment, my dear. But my promise to you, is that nothing in there relating to you, will ever see the light of day. It's Quantum Barb's golden guarantee."

"I figured that was the fee," says Tilda, "there must be a ton of data on here. Can you give me any pointers?" she asks, scrolling down the long list of folder icons.

"Well, given your current set of activities, I would suggest looking in the folder labelled **Corp_layer**, and start from there. It's got a lot of data on both The Dutchman's *Unit* ecosystem and his extracurricular activities, some of which I find particularly distasteful. A vulgar man."

"Also, our academic friend appeared to have spent a considerable amount of time mapping the *corporate layer*–"

"What's the *corporate layer*?" interrupts Tilda.

"It's everything my dear. I'm a little surprised you're not part of it. That is, in your position as a leading German industrialist."

Tilda winces, swamped by a deluge of details and responsibilities that she just dumped out of the window when she entered Denmark on this insane revenge mission.

Not insane, my destiny! A burning urge I had to deal with. Or die trying.

Barb coughs, noticing that Tilda's gone off somewhere.

Tilda gets back on track. "What does this *layer* do?"

"It controls everything. Well, everything that's useful. Financial systems, energy exports, research grants, venture flows. They are the continental grease that moves markets. And they basically feed the other two layers."

"What are they?"

"Why, political and military, of course. It's a very symbiotic set of relationships."

"So it's like a big network?" asks Tilda, scanning through sub-folders and bringing up images of compromised individuals and scanned documents."

"More like a hive. And the Queen Bee runs the whole CORP-ROGUE honeypot out of Oxford. She's quite a character. Looks like a librarian, but I'm sure she eats her young. They are probably crapping themselves at this very moment because of you," says Barb, with a mischievous smile.

"Me? Why me?"

"Well, not you directly. They're more worried about The Dutchman, and the fact that he might become more emboldened by any *kompromat* he may acquire from The Professor's unfortunate demise, which was brought about by you. Fortunately, you got this first. That puts you in a unique position to bargain with them."

"Well, I can't stand round here chatting to you all morning, I have a café to run. Oh, but wait, I have one more thing for you. Where did I...ah, here it is."

Barb hands over a scrunched-up Post-it with an address on. "I believe this is the gentleman you were looking for. He's not far away. Actually, I caught him on TV last night, while I was supervising your little digital burglary. He was on another of his single-minded missions to expose the latest industry fraud. I must say that you two have a lot in common! He's single, by the way. Been divorced a couple of times. Anyway, as I was saying...if you don't mind leaving now. Of course, you're welcome to an iced latte downstairs. On the house!"

With that, Quantum Barb opens the door and motions for Tilda to leave. She picks up the laptop and walks to the door, descending the three flights of stairs and exiting into the bright sunshine. Tilda turns and looks up the steps, into Barb's beaming smile.

"Thanks Barb. I owe you."

"No you don't. I got plenty in return. Who knows, perhaps we'll run into each other again." And with that, *Coffee Shop Barb* spins on her heels and goes back in to collect a tray of cappuccinos.

Tilda walks out of the fenced terrace and onto Nyhavn. She looks over at the low wall where she first met Nikolaj. Then she fishes the Post-it out of her pocket, and looks at his address.

Don't do it, she says to herself. *You have more important things to do.*

She turns left and walks to the end, then hangs another left to find her car.

She's got a long day ahead. And business to attend to on Fyn.

The Swedish Unit no longer has a Swedish leader, and the rest of them have been going out of their fucking minds.

Someone cut off the head of the snake in the early hours of the morning up in Helsingør, and the other three have been trying to figure out what to do next. They were handy to have in a jungle gunfight, but tactically they were about as useful as the *Ant Hill Mob* in cities.

Last night, they had sprinted out of their respective hotels, and tore up the E47 at light speed when they got the call from the Swede. He had spotted the target, outside the Vedbæk house, and she was clearly staking the same place out. She had started driving north, up *Strandvejen*, and The Swede was in, quote, stealthy pursuit.

That was the last they heard from him. Eventually, they'd vectored in on his Merc, via its transponder. It was parked outside a big church in Helsingør. Two of them had parked at both ends of the street, and The Brit had walked over to the church to take a look. Two minutes later, the other two operatives in their cars got a text message with a photo of their former Swedish leader, lying round the back of the church.

The Brit typed he had died from a blow to his windpipe. Tension started to rise in the team, and they agreed to haul-ass back to their hotels, and then work out their next steps in the morning. The Brit asked the other two what they should do with the Swede's body, and got a reply from The Norwegian that there would be a ferry to take him home early in the morning.

Now, after having fuelled up on a big breakfast, the three of them decided that they needed to contact The Dutchman, and inform him that their plan had gone down the shitter. The question was, who would draw the short straw.

The Norwegian and The Finn both looked at The Brit and then The Norwegian said, "you're the outlander, and you speak better English than us."

"The fuck I do," countered The Brit.

Just then, The Brit's phone rings. It is The Dutchman. He blanches, then looks up at his comrades and shows them that it's a *FaceTime*.

Bollocks, The Brit thinks, before answering it. He decides to go with nonchalant. "Yes?"

"Yes you managed to fuck up the mission and get your leader killed!" yells The Dutchman into the screen, his eyes burning red.

"Hh...how did you know?"

"It was on the radio you moron. Thanks to you idiots, Helsingør is now assassination central. It's like a fucking Nordic Noir TV show. There's going to be a lot of heat on Sjælland for a couple of days. I want you to listen to me very carefully."

The Brit, his hand shaking, tries to pan his phone back so he can get his two comrades in the *FaceTime*, but they keep shifting out of view.

"I want to see all your faces, so bunch up!" screams The Dutchman, eliciting an immediate bunching response as the three of them cram into view.

"Get back to your hotels. Do not, I repeat, do not go back to Vedbæk. What cars are you driving?"

"Mercedes," replies The Norwegian.

"And I suppose they are all black and top of the line?" asks The Dutchman, sarcastically.

The Brit looks at The Finn, who never says anything as usual, and replies, "yes, they are all high performance, and have tinted windows," confident that his answer will suffice.

"And you think that four black Mercs driving over the bridge and then tearing up and down the E47 in the early morning is stealthy?"

"Well—"

"—It was rhetorical. Lose them, and go rent something that blends in more. And don't use the same cards that you used for the hotels. Now piss off back to your rooms. I have a meeting on Fyn, then I'll be over in the late afternoon to clean up your mess."

He closes the connection, leaving the remaining three non-Swedish members of *The Swedish Unit*, huddled round a blank phone screen.

"Why are you looking at me?" asked the Finn, opening his mouth for the first time this morning.

"You arranged the Mercs, you arsehole," replied The Brit, storming off.

Bekka and Simon have been on cleaning duty all morning. And they're not used to it.

Usually, after one of their parties, they call in the hired help to clean up the mess. But they deemed it too risky. Now was not the time to let strangers in the door. So Bekka did most of the work, while Simon went down to the pier and started washing the boats down.

He was planning on inviting the German industrialist over for a BBQ on Monday night, so he could warm her up, and get a sense of what she was after. He knew Bekka would be a charming hostess, and was often the deal clincher.

He hears Bekka calling him, and he looks up the garden, with the hose hanging limply from his hand.

"You better get up here!"

He drops the hose and turns it off, then sprints up the garden and onto the terrace.

Bekka hands him her phone. On the screen is a short text.

Expect me soon.

"Shit, The Dutchman?" asks Simon, looking at his wife.

"No, it's from Santa you wanker!"

"Well, when is he coming?"

"Are you reading the same fucking message as me? Can you see anything else, apart from expect me soon?"

"Shit."

"Listen, you need to calm down. We can handle him. I'm more worried about Lærke than that satanic bastard. He's not what he used to be," says his wife.

"Nor are we, babe," Simon says, gazing out to sea.

"But we're on home ground. We'll let him think he's mind-fucking us, and relax him. I think it's time you called your old girlfriend. I'll make arrangements to send the kids away for a few days." says Bekka, looking up into her husband's eyes.

He nods, and goes back into the house to call the second most feared assassin in Denmark.

It gets his pulse racing.

Around the time Tilda's heading west across the *Storebælt*, The Dutchman's passing over the *Lillebælt*, heading east on a collision course with Camilla, who's doing the gardening in her villa. Meanwhile, three remaining second-tier hitmen have dumped their Mercs, and have bling'd down to three white Ford Fiestas, and are holed up watching Netflix in their hotel rooms.

Just up the road, in fashionable Vedbæk, two former top assassins are making preparations for the storm that's about to hit them, while cleaning up after last night's party.

And just taking off from the Faroe Islands in a private jet, is Iceland's most feared huntress that no one's ever heard of, and she's on a her way to clean up someone else's mess on Sjælland.

All in all, just another sunny September Sunday on the Danish islands.

Tilda cruises into *Cortex Park*, and it's pretty dead on a Sunday afternoon. Located at the south-east end of Odense, during the week it is a high-tech hive, that straddles the University campus.

It also happens to be where Camilla's robotics company has their HQ, so Tilda's on a scouting mission, sussing out the lay of the land before she makes her approach on Monday.

What she's after is, of course, Camilla's home address. She's not exactly going to book an appointment at HQ, then walk in and park two high powered rounds into Camilla's forehead. Although the thought appeals to her. Nope, she's going to do her at home.

She could have asked Barb for Camilla's address. She could have got it. But Tilda's already too far in Barb's pocket. And besides, she doesn't know which way Barb swings. Assassin-wise.

She parks in a space across the main road, then puts on a new white cap, slings her backpack over her shoulders and crosses the road. She walks across the grass, taking in

Camilla's shiny new HQ out of her peripheral vision. The car park is off to the side of the building which is good, because she intends to tag Camilla's car, and then follow the transponder from a distance. With luck, Camilla's got softer over the years on the surveillance side, so her guard should be down.

Tilda knows she's going to need some time to figure out the approach to Camilla's home. She's hoping it's a house, and not an apartment. Easier kill zone.

The other question that's been nagging Tilda is Camilla's personal status. She'd done her research and discovered there was a husband, but no mention of kids. She'd need to figure out his movements too. Perhaps she'll get lucky. If possible, she wants to deal with Camilla without having the husband get in the middle of it. Not that he could once they start going at each other.

But Tilda has no intention of getting that near to Camilla. Hand-to-hand would be a close call. Especially after all these years. Dead is dead. She's more than happy to use the gun.

She carries on walking through *Cortex Park* and heads towards the University campus, passing the sports track, then taking a wide loop around the grounds. She takes about thirty minutes to get the gist of the environment, including the main drawback. Only one real entrance and exit to the main road.

Then she walks back past Camilla's HQ, on the opposite side of the road, checking security cameras, of which there are a few. She notes the public parking spaces that are adjacent to the robotics company's entrance, and she's already germinating an angle of approach.

She'll park up early here tomorrow with a good view of the comings and goings, and wait till she spots Camilla driving in.

If she comes in, Tilda thinks. If she doesn't then she'll have to find a way of calling the company to fake a meeting with her. Then at least she can find out whether Camilla's even in the country. She may have bolted after receiving The Professor's alarm.

Too many what-ifs to worry about now. Let it play out.

As soon as she sees which car Camilla's driving, then she'll drive in and park as close as possible. She'll get out wearing a business suit and conveniently drop her keys near Camilla's car, then attach the magnetic transponder under a wheel arch.

Sounds simple enough. Too simple. What-if...

She parks her paranoia, and walks back to the car, then pulls out and heads to the hotel in Korup, north-west of Odense.

Camilla walks out of the terrace doors with a tray filled with a pitcher of lemonade and two tall glasses loaded-up with ice. She puts them down on the table overlooking the garden, then picks up the pitcher and pours a couple of glasses for her and Lucas.

Her thoughts have been stampeding out of control ever since she got the call from Simon earlier. As usual, they ended up in an argument, and she knew that she was as much to blame as he was. More so, actually. Their relationship, even after all these years of not seeing each other, was like a tinderbox that required the smallest of sparks to set it off.

Simon tried to rationalise with her that they should put aside their emotional differences and focus on teaming up.

It wasn't just Lærke they had to worry about. Now The Dutchman was in the game, and his solution could involve taking them all out. And there were now families at stake.

Camilla didn't appreciate being lectured on something she had already figured out, and his rationality inflamed her even further. Now, after cutting the call short, she knew that he was right. Simon, Bekka and Camilla were a considerable force to be reckoned with. If only they could get over their petty differences.

Easier said than done, she thinks. But she's resolved to call both Simon and Bekka later this afternoon, and come up with a mutual defence pact.

She picks up the glasses of lemonade and starts to walk down the garden to see how far her husband has got with his new wall project.

Then she stops dead.

Lucas is leaning over the wall, smiling and laughing, talking to a tall older man with long white hair. Camilla can't move. It's like she's sinking into the lush grass. She feels the spray from the water sprinkler as it hits her ankle, and that seems to snap her out of her trance.

The tall man nods towards her, and Lucas turns with a big smile on his face, and waves for her to come down. She has to force herself to move one leg in front of the other.

As she closes the distance on Lucas and The Dutchman, she can begin to make out their banter. Then she hears that roaring laugh that she hadn't heard for over two decades. It makes her bowels shift.

Lucas turns and says to her as she slowly walks up, "Milly, meet one of our new neighbours. He's just moved in up the beach. Willem, this is my wife Camilla."

The Dutchman gives a big smile and says, "so pleased to make your acquaintance, Camilla! Lucas has just been filling me in on the gossip regarding the international community here. I must say, that lemonade looks very appealing."

Camilla robotically hands one to The Dutchman and the other to Lucas.

"Why thank you very much," he says, clinking glasses with Lucas, then raising his to Camilla, but she's in the zone. Her husband doesn't know it but her peripheral vision's working overtime, scanning for danger.

She casually turns and says with a dry voice, "I'll go back up and pour myself a glass."

She can't see any movement up at the house, nor down the sides. She gives the sky a quick glance checking for any drones.

"Why don't we all go up to the terrace, and enjoy a glass together," says Lucas, already heading that way. "Let me just go and clean up a bit. She's had me working like a dog all day on this wall! You two wander up and get acquainted."

The Dutchman lets out another booming laugh, as Lucas jogs back up to the house, drinking from his glass. Camilla watches him disappear into the house, then spins on The Dutchman.

"You have a fucking nerve showing up here," her intense stare burning into his red face.

"Quite a life you have built for yourself. Is he your son? He's sweet. Do you nurse him and drive him to school?"

Camilla ignores the comment and gets into his face, "what do you want?"

"You know exactly what I want. And it's not you. She's coming your way. Either before she's dealt with those two idiots on Sjælland, or after. You are her prize," he replies, breathing his filthy stink into her face.

Camilla doesn't recoil. She doesn't recoil from anything. Though, the foulness brings back an odd familiarity. And she feels a stirring deep inside her. She fights with herself to control her sensations.

The Dutchman senses a change in her. It only lasts a second, but he throws it back at her. "I sense that you haven't quite given up on me. It's been a long time, my dear, but you've never been far from my thoughts. I have watched you evolve into quite the little corporate player over the years. I wonder, have you maintained your more traditional skillsets?"

"Want to find out?"

He laughs, this time it's more of a sneer.

"Are you alone? Or do I have to kill you here in front of them?" she asks, inching closer to his face.

"In your back garden?" he exclaims. "Why how colourful that would be! Actually, yes I'm alone. And I am working my way across this fair land, reintroducing myself to my favourite Unit. The original *Unit*!"

"Get to the point. What do you want? And don't think you're coming up to my house."

"A pragmatic proposition."

"Speak fucking English."

"Lærke's in Denmark. She got The Professor and probably his data, now she's coming for the rest of you."

"She'll come for you too," Camilla says, jabbing her finger into his chest.

"She doesn't know I'm here."

"She will. She will figure that you came over as soon as The Professor's message went out. So you're top of the list."

"We team-up again. I can call in some other operatives as backup."

"I'm surprised you haven't already," she says, staring directly at him.

"Ah, you have! The Swedish crew? I hope not. I've heard they are like a bunch of clowns walking through an egg shop."

"I'm on my way over to see our friends in Sjælland. I'll drop in on them tonight. You take some time to think through my proposition. You can't handle her alone. Not with your sweet young boy around," says The Dutchman, nodding towards the house.

Camilla turns and can see that Lucas has come out on the terrace in a fresh t-shirt, and is motioning to them to come up. She moves in as close as she can, almost touching his face.

"If you touch him, I will carve your heart out and feed it to you."

The Dutchman takes a step back. "I would expect nothing less from you, my dear. Fear not. I am not here for you, or him. This time, anyway. Consider my proposal. I will text you my number. Well, I must go, do give my apologies to your dear young husband!"

He hands her the empty glass, then turns and walks back down the beach. Camilla watches him disappear, then scans three hundred and sixty degrees, again checking for a drone.

Nothing.

Maybe he was telling the truth. She turns and walks back up the garden to Lucas.

"Where did he go?"

"He got a call, and had to run," she replies.

"Well he seemed like a nice old man," says Lucas, filling another glass and handing it to her.

"Actually, I thought he was a bit of an asshole."

Lucas laughs and wraps his arms round her, pulling her close.

"Let's go upstairs," he says.

"A bit later? I've just got something to check," she says, unhooking his arms and walking into the kitchen.

When she gets there she opens the rubbish bin and drops The Dutchman's glass into it. Then she goes to the toilet and vomits.

Tilda pulls up at the *Frederik VI Hotel* and parks round the back.

She'd selected it for a number of reasons. Firstly, because it was a known business conference hotel and would be quiet on a Sunday night. Secondly, it was out of town, but close enough for her mission the next morning.

And finally, it had a restaurant with a good reputation. And she really needed some quality food and time to think over a glass of wine.

She checked in, getting a room at the back, close to the exit nearest to her car. Then she got changed and went for a five kilometre run out of town, along the country lane, doubling back along the same route.

She got back and did her warm down, then showered and spend two hours getting up to speed with her day job. She found it difficult pivoting from the assassin's mindset to that of a corporate CEO, and as soon as she'd fired up her business laptop and phone, she got swamped in a deluge of important requests and adhoc crap that muddied the waters in her mind.

After the first thirty minutes, she figured she had gotten on top of all the pressing issues, only then to have people start reaching out to her, having figured out that she was now contactable. The genie was out of the bottle, and the only way to get it back in was to go dark again.

She gave herself another hour and a half of disciplined focus, then shut off both devices, and walked out into the small courtyard and sat down in a garden seat to enjoy the sun.

Her mind was still buzzing with spreadsheets and organisation changes, risk management profiles and other crap that could easily be handled by her competent leadership team.

The last two years had been a rollercoaster. They staggered through the first year of the pandemic, managing to adapt pretty fast at the corporate level to the home working. But the factories were another thing. They'd been in the middle of a big round of automation at the start of '20. So when they had to send the factory workers home, productivity fell off a cliff with revenues, but so did all of their automation projects.

Gradually, as better insight, protocols and vaccines started rolling out, they'd trickled back in, spinning up the machines, and cherry-picking which automation projects to advance. That's when the first set of supply chain problems began to hit.

As the whole world woke up, demand surged, but the Asian suppliers, themselves hit by COVID, couldn't ramp-up. Chips were the biggest issue. The automotive industry was eating up so much capacity, and her guys were way off the pace.

She fired her Procurement Director for sleeping on the job. Then, in March of '21, they had a big shipment of GPUs on its way over to service one of their biggest production runs since the pandemic struck. Only for their ship to get stuck in a fucking traffic jam at the southern end of the

Suez Canal. They managed to flip it round and it went due south, round the Cape, but it cost her a lot.

That's when she decided to go all-in on the EU's push for technological sovereignty. She'd been in Brussels every week over the summer of '21, working up plans with collaborators, competitors and politicians to put in place the complex investment commitments to wean Europe off Asian electronics.

She closes her eyes, and points her face to the sun, feeling its warmth penetrate her senses. She tries to stop the tug-of-war raging in her mind between her business and her business. It is useless, and she figures she needs something else to calm her mind.

She checks her watch and it's still too early for dinner, so she pulls out her phone and googles Nikolaj. She hasn't done it for a while, and is surprised by the deluge of articles, blogs, imagery and video content. He's become an even more polarising figure, with extremes of fandom and haters, victims and vindicated.

The victims being those unfortunate business and political leaders who had the misfortune to roam into his gunsights. When *Lærke* knew Nikolaj, he was always an idealist who had a new mission every week to pursue. Things tended to happen at a slower pace in those days, though everything's relative if you hadn't yet experienced the digital speed of instant everything.

As Lærke went off on sanctioned killing sprees, Nikolaj killed established careers through obsessive attention to details. He became the goto guy for the major TV channels and serious papers, when corporate behaviour had gone off the rails.

As the internet rocked-up, his business model pivoted to YouTube and podcasts, sugared with lucrative book contracts. He benefited from the fact that the British and American journalistic establishment hung on his every utterance, and his ruggedly handsome Nordic good-looks didn't do any harm either. He was one of those guys who seemed to look better, the more he aged and the more tired he got.

His short snappy pronouncements and retorts could pierce the armour of the most battle-hardened corporate PR-team. *But he does look tired*, thinks Tilda as she scans through a series of videos in Danish, Swedish and English.

She feels a sense of warmth when she listens to him. She's reminded of how he would soothe her by whispering in her ear after their love making, or when he would lay his head on her chest and gently snore, as her mind raged from the contrails of her most recent job with *The Unit*. Of course, he had no idea what she did. She continued to lie about her UN Forces activities, and he seemed satisfied with that. He was after all balancing the twin responsibilities of raising his kid alone and building his journalistic credentials.

But she sensed that he knew there was something more to her, but she appreciated that he did not pursue it.

Thirty minutes later and she's tiring of the negativity that embroils his every activity. One of the reasons why she tried to stay away from the media as much as possible was the lack of real foresight and constructive discussions that took place in the few interactions she'd had. That's why she had Joss. He was far smoother, able to slipstream through the most cynical of interviewers with the drop of a shoulder or the whiplash from his passive-aggressive tongue.

Tilda was too direct. She went for the headshot with every interviewer. It didn't always play well with the board or investors. Not that they could do anything about it. She had the ownership locked up good and proper.

As she gets up to head towards the restaurant, she wonders to herself what an interview between her and Nikolaj would go like.

She begins to fantasise on his opening monologue.

So, we used to be lovers, I was a young, hot-off-the-press journalist, and you were an up and coming international assassin. Then you disappeared and I took a while to get over you. As the years went by, I became successful, but more cynical. And down in Germany you rose from the grave, changed your face and somehow took over one of the largest private industrials in Europe. So, how's it going?

She gets to the restaurant, and discovers she's the only guest. After a quick glance at the menu, she orders the three course set menu, and a glass of Valpolicella and some water.

She sits there, staring out the window at the small courtyard, then she fires up The Professor's laptop, and begins to consume his cavernous vault of intelligence.

Bekka got the notification on her phone from the security system.

The camera on the wall by the front gate had picked up someone loitering directly in front of it. She pulled the phone out of her back pocket, as if she was drawing a pistol.

She knew it would be him, though she'd hoped it wasn't. He was just standing there, staring up at the camera. He hadn't even pressed the buzzer. Bekka could handle most things, but this was the creepiest image she'd ever seen on her phone.

Perhaps it's because he's outside the home of your children, she tells herself. That thought gives way to rage, and she marches off to a chair in the corner, climbs onto it, and pulls down her SIG which was hidden above the bookcase.

She climbs down, checks the phone again. *Now he's smiling*! *Can he see me*? She chides herself for the ridiculous thought.

She wishes Simon was here. He went into town, he claimed, to check on something in the office. She knows he went to the Embassy to reach out to an old mate. Simon liked to call in the artillery early. He didn't fuck about when it came to threats to his family.

He only fucked about when it came to Camilla, she thinks. Then she gets annoyed with herself for such a pointless internal argument. She was trained to focus on the mission. And her mission right now was *The Devil* himself, standing within spitting distance of her children's bedrooms.

She shivers, then checks the pistol, chambering a round. She goes out the front door and across the courtyard to the high metal gates. She can see his tall form between the twisted iron. She walks up to the gate and stands there with the gun hanging from her right hand.

"Good to see you, Rebekka. I see that life has treated you fair. It's a nice dwelling you have made for your two children. It is Cloe and Mark, isn't it?"

That gets her focused. She snaps the gun up and aims it at his head, between the iron bars.

"You threaten my kids. How about I send you on a one way ticket south to meet your maker?"

The Dutchman looks down at her and shakes his head.

"My dear Rebekka. I would never do anything of the sort. I have stayed out of your lives for over two decades.

I'm only here because we have unfinished business that requires our attention."

"We don't need your fucking help. We can handle Lærke."

"It's a sweet thought, but I can read your mind, remember? And you know you are just deceiving yourself. She is not like the rest of us. We were all trained to kill and coerce, but Lærke, well she was, is, a force of nature. After all, she apparently survived. And she killed your friend, The Professor."

"He wasn't my friend," she snaps. "I worked with him twenty-some years ago. That was business. I don't care what happened to him. I just care about my family. And so we are clear, I will do anything to protect them, including taking all of you with me."

"All of us? Including your dear husband, Simon?"

"Including him," Bekka states. "It's a mother thing. You never had one so you'd never get it. Now what the fuck do you want?"

"Where is Simon?" asks The Dutchman, pressing himself against the iron gates, pushing his face through the space.

Bekka takes a step back, reeling from the smell of death that engulfs her. She looks up at him, then jams the gun into his forehead, pushing his head back.

"Simon's not here. Now fuck off. We don't need your help."

"So the Englishman abandons his beloved wife at such a time. I always knew he was a lesser man."

She ignores his comments, knowing that Simon, despite his many drawbacks, is one of the most efficient killers she ever knew. What a strange thought, she thinks. Not exactly an average Vedbæk one.

"You should know that I've called in some help to flush her out. And to protect your young family."

"Who?" she asks, lowering the gun.

"The closest Unit to you," he smiles.

"They are in Copenhagen now."

"Do they all drive black Mercedes?" Bekka sneers, catching The Dutchman off guard momentarily. "And I don't suppose that dead Swede in Helsingør had anything to do with this Unit?" she asks, going for the kill.

"He was part of your protection."

"Seems more like he needed my protection. We know he was here last night. And he tripped Lærke's wire, following her all the way up there to his own death probably. What kind of fucking idiots are you running from your Caribbean lair?"

"There are more coming," he assures her, advancing again towards the gap in the gate."

"Back off, motherfucker," she hisses, raising the gun again. "We will handle her, if Camilla does not deal with her first."

"Ah, yes, dearest Camilla. I ran by her place earlier today. Charming young boy she's living with. Well, I just wanted to reassure you that I'm now here for the protection of you—"

"Fuck off."

"—and your children," he says, nodding towards the house. Bekka advances, and extends her arm through the gate.

The Dutchman, dips his head, looking down at the small fifty-five year-old woman pointing the gun at him. Then he turns and strides back down the road to where his BMW is parked. Bekka watches him climb in and then slowly cruise past, giving her a wave. Then he turns left towards *Strandvejen* and is gone.

Jesus Christ, our whole existence has turned upside down in the space of two days. She sticks the gun into the back of her waist, and pulls out her phone and calls Simon.

"Where are you?"

"Just leaving town, everything OK?"

"No, everything is not fucking OK! We had a visitor. And he still smells of rotting human flesh. Get back here now."

"On my way, babe."

She closes the connection and stands looking left and right up the street.

Lærke. The Dutchman. Another *Unit*. Fucking Camilla. And tomorrow's a school day and a yoga class!

She turns and walks back to the house, hoping that her husband gets back soon.

Simon was just coming out of a meeting with an old mate in a coffee shop, not far from the British embassy, when he got Bekka's call.

He wasn't going to fuck about crawling up the coast road on a hot Sunday afternoon, so he floors it up the E47 on impulse power, then gets off at Nærum, cutting through the forest, then turning left when he hits the sea, flying through Skodsborg all the way home.

His mind is racing. He knew he would kill The Dutchman if he saw him. He didn't care if he might be useful in flushing out Lærke. There's evil which is all around, then there is this fucker. And he reeks of it.

There's no way he's coming close to the kids. He makes a call to Bekka's sister to check on the kids. She asks why both he and Bekka keep calling. He pretends they just got mixed up, then hangs up as he screeches into their courtyard.

He sees his wife come out of the front door, pressing the app on her phone to shut the gates as his bumper clears them. He gets out and walks to the rear of the car, opening it, and pulling out a long sports bag.

"We don't need any more artillery, babe," Bekka says, as she walks to the gate and looks up and down the road again.

"You can never have too much artillery," says Simon in a matter of fact way.

He walks up to her, drops the bag on the ground, then wraps his arms round her. He feels the gun tucked into the back of her pants, and gets strangely reassured. And turned on.

She looks up into his eyes, making him simultaneously melt and harden at the same time. He releases her and picks up the heavy bag then follows her into the house.

Nothing like Sunday afternoon sex to take the edge off the stresses of being a couple of Denmark-based suburban former assassins, he thinks.

Over dinner for the next three hours, Tilda consumes everything that scrolls across her eyes, as she goes through the motions of eating her meal. Finally, the waiter has to apologise that they are closing the restaurant, but that she's welcome to sit there.

She thanks him, then signs her bill, and goes to the room and continues to gorge on the unbelievable treasure trove of information. The Professor, as it turns out, has been a very busy boy over the last fifteen years.

It appears that he planned to publish his research, as he had systematically ordered all of his findings. Clearly it wasn't complete, but Tilda thought if it ever leaked out then it would make the *Panama Papers* look like news of a speeding ticket.

She read on, late into the night, as the converging stories of CORP-ROGUE and The Harbour unfolded before her eyes.

Camilla disappeared from the house shortly after the Dutchman had wandered up the beach. She went to the garage, got in her Lotus Elise, and blasted off south with her hair blowing over her face. It was her typical way of letting off steam, so Lucas wasn't initially bothered by it.

She had looked irritated in the kitchen, and he knew when to let her be. But three hours later she still hadn't returned, or answered his calls. He figured she had just gone to the office and didn't want to be disturbed. He knew he had no reason to be concerned because his wife could certainly look after herself.

How little did he know.

She had filled up the tank, then headed south along the coast, skirting beautiful villages, until she got to Svendborg. Then she worked her way across a couple of bridges, making her way to Langeland. She finally came to a stop in Ristinge, and pulled up near the beach to stretch her legs.

She sat down there for a while, and listened to the torrent of thoughts raging through her mind, as the soft breeze blew her hair across her face.

How could her life unravel so quickly? She'd spent twenty-some years burying the past, and finding purpose, not to mention love, and in the process discovering that there was more to her than the ice cold, cynical killer.

Although, she acknowledged that her former self was never far away. Just simmering under the surface of her perfectly constructed life. Lucas had changed her outlook on life, and she knew that she had a responsibility to protect him from her past.

The question was, what to do now? It wasn't like she could just disappear. Well, certainly she could do that. Funds were not a problem. But that would require dismantling her whole life. And could Lucas handle that? How would he react when she told him the insane story of who she really was, and how they were both caught in the crosshairs of some lethal people.

It sounded absurd. Almost as absurd as her fantasy that it would all just work itself out. No, there was a reckoning coming. The problem was knowing where and when it would come? She had to expect Lærke anytime, and that thought, sitting on the beach way down in the south of Denmark, made her reach for her phone in a panic.

She called Lucas to let him know that she had gone to the office to handle some stuff, and he seemed satisfied. But she was more relieved to know that he was OK.

She stood up and looked south-west across the sea towards northern Germany, letting the wind blow the cobwebs out of her head. It helped momentarily, then they came creeping back.

She got back in the Lotus and headed back up to Svendborg, stopping off to get a snack and put more gas in the tank after realising how hard she had been driving it, throwing it in and out of bends like a go-kart.

She decided not to head directly home, even though the night was closing in. It was warm, and she was shielded by the noisy cocoon of the British sports car. She worked her way through the farms and villages of western Fyn, north until she got to Bogense. Then she made another pitstop to relieve herself and stretch her legs. She pinged Lucas to say she would not be much longer, then she started to head back via Odense.

She knew that she was not alone in facing the danger known as Lærke, but partnering up with Bekka and Simon bought its own set of risks. Then there was The Dutchman who had to be factored in, even after they had dealt with Lærke.

If they could.

And what of the other operatives that he had called up. The whole thing could escalate out of control. And while all this was going on, she still had a company to run.

And Lucas.

Fuck.!

Well, swearing helps, she thinks as she bombs through Korup, past the Frederik VI hotel, heading for Odense, and then on to the house, and her young husband.

Sunday fades into Monday across the Kingdom of Denmark. Another balmy September week of sunny weather is predicted from Jylland, across Fyn and onto Sjælland, but it's forecasted to cool off towards the end as Autumn starts to rear its head.

In the early hours of Monday morning, the Icelandic huntress known as Sigi, is heading south on the E45 in her dark blue Range Rover.

She looks around the plush cabin, missing her shitty old Forerunner, and all the sounds and creaks from the hammerings she has given it over the years. In another age, when she lived in Iceland, she hurled over the tundra in the highest Forerunner in the country. The wheels were gigantic, and the sound from her engine was like the rumblings of one of the great volcanos.

Alas, she had to run away from that, and so much more, as a result of the career path she had chosen. She missed her country of birth, and her daughter who now lived with her...Sister.

That thought sends a shiver of resentment down her spine. Her sister getting to raise her own child.

Well, you abandoned her, says Sigi to herself.

She silences herself, and goes back to pondering her mission. Sigi's still not comfortable about being back on mainland Europe. It doesn't help that she refuses to transform herself to create some form of camouflage from the authorities increasingly sophisticated digital surveillance capabilities. That's why she always comes in private and via regional airports. Sometimes they're just huts with grass landing strips. She's never had a problem with customs. Cash is king, and it greases the rails with the locals most of the time.

She always wore her hair long, and with the same dark red colouring that she'd had since a teenager. It fell over one side of her face, covering up the deep scar that she refused to get fixed.

Naddador had chided her many a time to have it taken care of, but she refused. She wore it as a proud battle wound, and reminder of someone special she had on her kill list. After she settled that score, then maybe she'd get it dealt with.

Maybe not.

The other problem for Sigi in terms of blending in, was that she didn't. She ran close to two metres. Her hulking frame was not an accident of birth, but rather a twenty-five year process of extreme sports and combat training, enhanced over the years by *compound* abuse.

She did not think of it as abuse, and neither did her *father*, Naddador, who provided her with the purest of the blue elixir. She managed her addiction more as a prescription, carefully balanced with her diet and exercise regimen.

She also refused to ingest the *compound* through her eyes, unlike others, including her *father*. While the route through the eyes was the fastest trip to its synaptic destination, over time it destroyed the vision. And she needed her eyes. She could already observe the effect it was having on Naddador.

So she injected it, carefully, and regularly. As a consequence, her physique had transformed beyond all expectations, matched only by her sharpness of mind, and her focus on whatever task Naddador had set for her.

Most of the time he left her to her own devices. She had a profitable gunrunning enterprise going, which she had franchised out to one of her trusted Lieutenants. She spent a lot of time hopping between Africa, South and Central America, and the South Pacific islands, but whenever she got any downtime, she would head back to Fugloy, or visit Naddador in his Norwegian valley lair.

She read up on the mission parameters on the hop over from Vágar to Norway. She still could not figure out why Naddador wanted to do business with the entity, known in intelligence circles as CORP-ROGUE. She thought they were jackals of the worst kind. Purely into subversion for money.

Sigi was different. She believed in something. And his name was *Naddador*.

She had called him again from the jet, and his explanation that it was part of a longer play did little to assuage her concerns. Still, she would follow his instructions to her grave.

Her target seemed like a simple enough task, complicated only by the fact that she didn't know where he was, or how protected he would be. Oh, and it would be in the middle of a fucking urban jungle somewhere around the Danish capital.

So it's gonna be a night time job, she says to herself. The details on this Dutchman are scant, but disturbing. She's dealt with some unsavoury characters in the past, and despatched many more to their graves, but this whole business of devilry and murdering of young innocents, attributed to him makes her stomach turn. And it motivates her. She will enjoy this one. She's still not sure why he has been targeted for termination. She needs to figure that out.

Sigi never does anything without being given a good reason to do so. She reaches behind to grab the coffee flask from her bag, and catches a glimpse of the small arsenal she brought with her.

A pistol, a long rifle, and a KA-BAR hunting knife. And her favourite *Atlatl*. What the fuck did I bring that for? It's not like she's in the Costa Rican jungle. This is *hygge* land! But she couldn't help herself.

Well, never can be too tooled-up, she thinks, as she takes a swig of coffee. She needs the KA-BAR, though. Naddador told her to bring back The Dutchman's head if possible.

Apparently, he promised The Greenlander one for his collection.

9 - COLLISION

Dawn. Rindal, western Norway.

He sits on the terrace at his lair overlooking the small town, cooling down after his daily astanga punishment, and now he picks up the steaming mug of coffee and takes a sip.

He closes his eyes and tilts his head up into the early morning sun. He feels its warmth soothing his damaged retinae, imagining that they are being repaired, as he baths in the star's mystical rays.

Then the moment is lost, and the black dogs appear, scattering his serenity across the furthest reaches of his brain matter. After the hounds comes the bitterness, characterised by the endless conversation that plays out in his head every morning.

Why can't you stop? Every night you say you will, yet come the morning you kneel at the blue alter and enslave yourself for another day.

But then he cracks open another vial of *compound*, emptying it into both his eyes, and feels the instant fizzing behind his eyeballs, followed by the supercharging of his synapses. Then comes the electric surge shooting down his spine, filling his legs and loins with the familiar power.

He stands up, looking down at the vial, now drained of the blue elixir. His puny thoughts banished for another day, replaced with the rejuvenated mental and physical capabilities needed to advance his many schemes.

Naddador is a lair animal. In fact he has many lairs, scattered across the Nordic region. He feels most comfortable in the mountains and deep valleys. He has lived for much of the last few years above this beautiful town, with its lush green fields. It's close enough to the fjords, which guard the access to the vast Norwegian Sea, and several times a week he ventures forth to one of his many boats to escape the land.

He is half-Norwegian and half-Icelandic, and he considers himself all Viking. Not just in the modern, trendy sense of the word. He yearns for the harsh life that his ancestors must have experienced, enduring unimaginable pain and suffering to eke out lives, sustain families and trade with other peoples.

Sometimes, when he has taken *compound* at night, while standing naked and painted and gazing up at the stars in the clear sky, he has touched the ancient ones and lived their saga's.

This morning he has no time for such escapism. His mind is fully focused on figuring out how to capitalise on the opportunity afforded to him by that *Old Crow* sitting on her perch down in Oxford. His organisation has been chipping away at hers for the best part of ten years.

He had originally created *The Harbour* as a refuge for unconventional talent which could be applied in unique ways. Specifically, coercion, outright robbery, and of course murder. He'd built up a cellular structure with him in the centre pulling the strings, with a few trusted Lieutenants who handled all of his interests.

Of all of them, Sigi was the only one he fully trusted. Her devotion to him was like that of a daughter to a father, and he repaid her with a loyalty and a love so fierce that it even scared him.

He did not unleash her on the world easily, and he knew she was not happy with this Danish task that he had dropped on her a day ago. She was running multiple enterprises in the hot places, and he knew she had deserved the long planned rest at her cabin on Fugloy.

Yet this opportunity to penetrate the operations of CORP-ROGUE was too good to be true. He had actually considered that the whole thing was a plot by the *Old Crow* to lure his operatives into a trap.

But then he discounted it, for it was too simplistic an answer. And he knew of this Dutchman. He ran the assassination department for this most global of subversive enterprises. His *Units* had run amok for the last two decades, creating mayhem for the highest bidder.

Naddador was no angel. He had his own set of assets helping to remove human obstacles from global challenges. Yet he always held himself to a higher set of principles. Money was a useful byproduct of subversion, but it could not be the endgame.

And then there were the stories of the foul devilry that this Dutch demon engaged in. The stories had been verified, and Naddador had long ago yearned for the opportunity to wipe his seed from the planet. But he had not proceeded for fear of stoking serious repercussions from CORP-ROGUE's hierarchy.

CORP-ROGUE. *Jesus*!

In reality they were just a bunch of limp corporate business leaders who were born into positions of wealth, and used their organisational charts and offshore funds to try and cling on to some far-fetched notion of running a global order.

And now it appears there is a chink in their armour. When the *Old Crow* reached out to him on Saturday, he was surprised, yet intrigued. Their *zoom* meeting was cordial, especially considering they had each been trying to kill one another for the best part of a decade.

She got straight to the point, which Naddador appreciated. A wraith out of their past had arisen in their mist, killing one of The Dutchman's original *Unit* members.

This man was known as The Professor. Unfortunately for The Dutchman, and for CORP-ROGUE, The Professor had been rather meticulous in his academic research. Specifically, he had the gen on all of The Dutchman's operations, and many of those operations could be tied back to CORP-ROGUE activities.

"In other words, you are fucked," Naddador had said into the screen, looking for any reaction from the woman who looked like a Librarian.

"More like we are partially fucked. And I want to de-fuck it before it goes any further."

She went on to tell him that the Dutchman had got on a plane from his Anguilla hideaway to come over to Denmark and hunt down the Professor's killer.

Naddador had asked why she thought the killer would even still be in Denmark, and she replied that this wraith was part of his original *Unit*, and that she had her own set of motivations.

"Surely, she could be handled by any one of your other *Units*," he had asked.

The *Old Crow* went silent, took her glasses off and let them hang on the chain round her neck. "You don't handle this woman," she had said.

Naddador had asked her why come to him for help. He searched her eyes, as she replaced her glasses, and lit a cigar, blowing the smoke into the camera.

The Dutchman stopped off on his way to Denmark, for a little light entertainment, she said. Things got out of control. An innocent was sacrificed.

He had nodded, and said that he understood The Dutchman was a vile creature, but that still didn't explain why she was asking for his help.

She said that there was another involved in the event. A Frenchman. And he was special. He was part of her management team. The Dutchman killed him, and that was not sanctioned. In fact it broke their most sacred protocol. Over a minor infraction.

He then asked the *Old Crow* what was in it for him. She said that he would get the satisfaction of removing The Dutchman, who had, by the way tasked several *Units* to take out Naddador in the past. He said that he was well aware of this, and had sent their heads back to her return-to-sender.

The *Old Crow* confirmed that she had received them and was mildly amused.

He then asked about this wraith.

The *Old Crow* asked that she be returned to her, personally. When Naddador asked for any information on this wraith, she just gave him a name.

Lærke.

Monday morning and everyone's on the run.

Simon's suddenly decided that today's the day to restart his morning jog. Bekka tried to talk him out of it, saying he should ease into it. But he wants to scout the road. As soon as he started out he realised how out of condition he is. And skipping the proper stretching was a big mistake.

Downtown, three killers who drive three white Ford Fiestas, are pounding the streets. They're not struggling because they're in tiptop condition. They're an odd bunch, made up of a Brit who over-communicates, a Finn who never communicates, and a Norwegian who's somewhere in the middle. They're all trying hard not to think about their breakfast meeting with *The Devil* himself.

On a nearby island to the west, two of the most singled minded killers that ever graced these shores are taking their pre-breakfast runs.

Not together, of course.

The CEO/killer called Camilla is closing in on the final stages of her pummelling run, with a sprint to her house.

Meanwhile, a bit further north on the garden island of Fyn, the CEO/killer known alternately as Tilda/Lærke, is returning back towards her hotel breakfast, thinking about all the ways her perfect plan can get fucked up.

Tilda fucked up.

She knew she shouldn't have taken breakfast at the hotel. But she also knows that she doesn't function well without one. Especially after a power run. So now she's pulling into the car park opposite Camilla's robotics company HQ in *Cortex Park*, and there are already three Mercs and a couple of Beamers in the lot.

Dammit.

So now she's trying to figure out which one is Camilla's. She's only got one magnetic transponder, and even if she had more, she's hardly gonna chase multiple cars all over Fyn. So, now how the hell does she figure out Camilla's car?

Fuck it.

She calls Quantum Barb. Barb calls her back fifteen minutes later. It's the black Merc in the AMG glamour package.

Of course it is, thinks Tilda. As if you need that in Denmark! Then she reminds herself that she cruises round Munich in a Bentley. *Well that's different*, she argues with herself.

So now the next problem is that Camilla's AMG is parked closest to the reception. She scans the building and can see that there are offices above the entrance.

Could that be her office? A distinct possibility. She spots a spare parking slot three up from Camilla's Merc. She starts her engine and drives across the road into the company's entrance, and then pulls up next to one of the Beamers.

She gets out, wearing a business suit and thick black rimmed glasses, and grabs the empty briefcase that she bought on Saturday, and begins to walk towards reception.

Just before she gets to the rear of Camilla's Merc, she drops her keys on the floor and bends down to pick them up. She slips the small magnetic transponder under the rear wheel arch, picking up her keys in a single, smooth move.

She pops her keys into her empty briefcase, and proceeds to walk over to the reception.

And into the lions mouth, she thinks.

She's sweating now, running multiple threat scenarios in her mind, as the distance to the reception reduces. The biggest threat being, of course, that Camilla happens to be walking through reception.

Put it out of your mind. What would she do? Nothing. Yeah, but she would know you're here, dummy.

She chides herself again for walking toward the building. *But what was the alternative? To drive into the car park, crawl under the Merc, then drive out again?* She's already on the security cameras, so she has to make the visit look authentic.

The glass doors to the reception slide open, and she strides in, feeling the sweat trickle down her back. It's a minimalist design with lots of white and black, with uncomfortable looking expensive chairs.

Not like my shop down in Bavaria, she muses.

She approaches the receptionist and then goes through her story, apologising, but she's lost and her GPS is not working, and could she get directions to the University. The receptionist smiles and tells her that she's really close, then points the way. Tilda thanks the man, then turns and walks back out, trying not to walk too fast or too slow.

She gets to her car and climbs in, then looks up at the office windows above reception. She can't see anything through the reflection from the light. She starts the engine, and pulls out of the car park and back onto the main road, heading towards the university, before looping back to the hotel to get changed out of the monkey suit.

Camilla's on a *Teams* with Simon and she's trying to remain calm. She's hurling questions at him, peering into the camera, hanging on his every word. He's not in the mood for her bullshit either.

No, he hasn't heard from The Dutchman since he showed up yesterday to intimidate Bekka. No, Bekka hasn't heard anything either. She would have called. Yes, I will contact you immediately. No, of course we haven't seen Lærke. She won't exactly fucking announce herself. Have you? No, I'm not one of your fucking underlings. We will be in touch if we hear anything.

He cuts the connection on his laptop. Camilla slams down the screen and curses a little too loud, causing her Executive Assistant to look through the glass. Camila gets up and starts pacing the room. Her brain is running all the angles.

Now The Dutchman is here, the question is how to leverage him, and get him and his operatives in between

Lærke and her. She knows she has to drag Lærke away from Fyn.

She's more worried about Lucas than herself.

She'll kill anyone to protect him.

She walks back round to her laptop and opens up the screen again and checks her calendar for the day. There's no way she can focus today, so she walks over to the door and calls to her assistant, telling her to cancel all her meetings for the rest of the day.

The EA asks about the Americans who she's due to have a Teams with later. She says that she'll still take it later, but from home.

She walks back to the desk, sits down and starts closing out the immediate tasks she was working on. She doesn't notice the tall woman walk out of her building across to the car park below her office, and climb into a white Golf and pull out.

"You pissed in the punchbowl, my Dutch friend," states the Chairman, peering into the camera.

The Dutchman's leaning back in his chair, half staring out of the window of his *Marriott* suite, as a yellow ferry cruises by.

"Did you hear what I said?" she snaps.

He turns nonchalantly, back to the screen. "I heard you," he feigns, casually. In his mind though, his feet are paddling like a duck's underwater. He half thought that he would get away with the small indiscretion of removing the Frenchman from his obligations towards the living. Now he curses himself for thinking he could get away with it. The only reason, he thinks, that he's still alive is that the Frenchman was a party to his own perverse extra-curricular activities.

There's no way she could afford to let that get out. The Dutchman knew that was his leverage over the old witch.

"Look, I made a mistake. I cleaned it up. He had it coming, and couldn't be trusted. I made an instant decision. OK, so it was a bit rash. But now it's done. Let's move on," he says leaning back.

She leans into the camera and thunders, "you don't decide when to remove a member of CORP-ROGUE! It's a council decision, and I reside over the fucking council!"

He does not respond. He knows the old witch. It's best to let her vent. Soon she'll be off to ball someone else out.

"So what now?" he asks, trying to sound as casual as possible.

"You're in Denmark to clean up an old mess. So clean it up. But I want you out of Europe and back over in your tropical hole by the end of the week. What's the status on the assassin known as Lærke?"

"She took out The Professor—"

"—yes, that's old news. As is the fact that she took his laptop. And that is my main concern. I couldn't give a fuck about your *Unit*, or this so called *Lærke*. You are to retrieve that data. Do you understand?"

"Of course, it's my primary mission," he replies. *Thanks for stating the obvious, you old witch. One day I will kneel over you and...*

"Pay attention!" she snaps. "I am tasking another *Unit* to come out there—"

"—hold on! I have more than enough capabilities out here to deal with this!" he yells into the camera.

"You mean those clowns who drove over the bridge? You've already lost the leader. I'm sending over my own insurance policy. You need more eyes on the ground, and we need to flush Lærke out. You can't possibly monitor everything on Fyn and Sjælland."

Shit, she really does know everything, thinks The Dutchman.

"Which Unit are you tasking?"

She leans back, taking a sip of brandy from a big tumbler. "You don't need to know that."

"I certainly do! I run all *Unit* operations."

She thinks, his voice is starting to squeal, like a little pig. *Good. Good.* "Not as of this moment. I have personally authorised the activation of external advisors in the area. They are enroute and will be on standby."

"OK, where do I meet them?"

"You don't," she says, casually waving cigar smoke away from her big hair.

"I'll keep them in a holding pattern until I deem they are necessary."

Jesus, she's now monitoring me. His fury's building and he fights to stay calm. Just end this call, then figure it out.

Breathe.

"OK–"

"OK, what?" she snaps.

"OK, I accept your offer of help."

"You accept? You have no fucking choice. Now get out there and find that laptop," she says, leaning in and filling the screen with her scowling features.

The screen goes blank, and The Dutchman, swivels on his chair, gazing out onto the river.

Another Unit. Fuck. More like an assassination squad. And I'm the mark.

She leans back in her heavy, dark brown leather chair, and takes another pull on the cigar.

All this nonsense for a laptop. She's only mildly concerned. The resources she's put into the theatre can handle it.

Of course she didn't tell The Dutchman about her deal with Naddador. He would have bolted back across the Atlantic. She sees this as a great opportunity to rid the world of this pain in her ass for so many years.

And his vile habit.

She thinks of dear Claude. *How could he have travelled so far from the path? Well, each to his or her own.*

Her mind shifts to Naddador. He's become bolder with his ambitions. This *Harbour* he has created, *what an absurd name*! She needs to penetrate it. And the best way to do that is to bring him in closer. Get him on the hook by offering him some bait.

The Chairman knows that he probably suspects this is a trap. Well, she's fine with that. It's a global dance between two subversive organisations. She knows he will deploy his best resource to take out The Dutchman.

That means the Icelandic huntress. Her reputation is fearsome. The Chairman envies not having her in her own operational sphere of influence. She's like a hypersonic missile. She locks on, can evade, then reacquire the target.

And she is relentless.

She leans forward to her desk, and places a fat finger wrapped with three big stones onto a buzzer.

"Well, send him in!" Then she leans back and waits for the snivelling politician to crawl in on his knees, begging for her to extricate him from his latest self-inflicted sexual disaster.

Oh my, leverage, leverage, leverage. And it's still only Monday morning.

It's a Copenhagen brunch, and these three look like a really shady crew.

They ordered early, and that was a mistake, because when The Dutchman arrives he's not in the mood for an omelette. The Finn has half a flødebolle hanging out of his mouth, and the other two are tucking into big breakfasts.

"We're here to make a plan, not eat, you morons," The Dutchman fumes.

They put down their forks, and the Finn tries to swallow the giant chocolate ball. The Dutchman looks into all of their eyes, ratcheting up their tension levels.

He focuses on The Brit and says, "You, get yourself over the bridge to Fyn, and sit on Camilla."

"You mean that bridge over there?" asks the Brit, gesturing over his shoulder.

"No you fucking idiot. That one goes to Sweden. That's where you just came from. The one over the *Storebælt*. Fyn's to the west of Copenhagen. Try *Google Maps*."

Then he looks at the Finn who's still struggling to swallow the chocolate ball. "You, I want you to sit on Vedbæk, do you understand me?"

He gets a half gesture from the Finn, and banks that as an *affirmative*.

Then he turns to the Norwegian. "And you, I want you to watch this guy. He's famous here. Some kind of big shot journalist."

"Why him?" asks the Norwegian, staring longingly at the remains of his omelette.

"Because twenty-seven years ago, he was the lover of Lærke."

"That's a bit of a reach," exclaims The Brit.

The Dutchman spins on him and spits, "are you questioning my methods?"

"N...no, of course not," he says, looking down.

"So now that's clear, all of you watch out for any other operatives in the area."

"You mean another *Unit*'s been tasked on this?" asks The Norwegian.

"Apparently, yes. But not by me. Oxford think they need some kind of insurance policy. Probably in case you clowns fuck things up again."

"We won't, we assure you," says The Brit, grovelling.

"Why are you still here. Get moving. You can get food on the way. I will check in with all of you later."

They all get up in unison, looking at their unfinished breakfasts, and make their way out of the café to their cars.

The Dutchman looks down at the omelettes, then catches the waitresses attention, and orders his breakfast.

He's trying to figure out which *Unit* the old witch has tasked. He knows they probably have a kill order out on him, but only after he retrieves The Professor's laptop. That means he's probably safe as long as he doesn't have it.

Well, safe from them. But then there's Lærke to worry about. And Camilla, Bekka and Simon.

No. He knows they need him until they kill Lærke.

If we kill her. We'll get her, he thinks. *Otherwise it's gonna be a short week for all of us.*

As subversive organisations with a plan for global domination go, CORP-ROGUE had the advantage of several hundred years of CV experience.

They'd spun-up over tea and biscuits in *ye olde English coffee house* around the time that the pirates transitioned their business models to Joint Stock Companies. Of course, it was not whole organisations that were subversive. It was a select few individuals, born into the right schooling system, and nurtured up fast tracks into positions of influence.

They started off with a good old fashioned blood oath, slicing their palms then shaking hands, but that went out of fashion after a spate of infections dwindled their numbers.

Now, membership of this elite, virtual organisation was guaranteed through mutual destruction pacts. In corporate circles this was known as *leverage*. In ordinary English it was known as *blackmail*, a distasteful word that was consigned to the buzzword bin circa the nineties.

After the phenomenon known as the internet unleashed whole new platforms for the propagation of influence and the movement of goods, services and finances, CORP-ROGUE became even more globalised.

Some felt it was becoming too big and hard to manage.

Translation, it was becoming impossible to keep secret.

Yet still, its hierarchy continued to push for the expansion of new members from burgeoning new industries. Over the centuries, CORP-ROGUE had been the undisputed market leader in subversive influence.

However, in the second decade of the twenty-first century, rumours began to spread of a disruptor, who had began to chip away at its traditional business model.

Word first reached Oxford of the entity known as *The Harbour* in 2014. Information was scant, but disturbing, as this new *startup* was apparently parked right on their backdoor.

In the Nordic region.

Fragmented information was pieced together, and it was determined that it was unlike CORP-ROGUE because it was controlled by one central character, who had a strange name. Well, strange if you were an Anglo-Saxon.

The name was Naddador.

As rumours fed rumours, he achieved unicorn status in a very short time. It was said that he was a throw-back to the Viking sagas of old, and that he was as ruthless as he was smart. It was said that he was capable of violence and tenderness in equal measures.

The business-led CORP-ROGUE management could not make sense of either of these attributes, having spent most of their days constrained by white collars and knotted ties, issuing orders for others to execute their dirty work.

The Harbour was also said to differentiate itself in that it was not into power for the sake of power. It apparently had a mission which was based on technological innovation, specifically in the energy sector. Naddador, it was said, was like his ancient viking ancestors, focused on harnessing the wind, waves and sun to accelerate a sustainable future.

This *mission statement* was anathema to CORP-ROGUE, which was more focused on the next quarterly report. Word started to seep back to Oxford, through its European franchises, that *The Harbour* was buying up early stage technology companies focused on renewable energy, satellite and quantum computing.

It was rumoured that it had also started seeding northern universities with research grants, hidden under blankets of shell companies, across these converging technological shifts.

CORP-ROGUE's top management struggled to get a grip of the threat of Naddador and his *Harbour* outfit. They adopted their traditional corporate reaction, which was to assume it was direct competition to their own subversive activities. What they failed to appreciate was that Naddador was actually trying to drive a transformational shift in harnessing sustainable technologies.

However, CORP-ROGUE were right about one thing. Naddador made full use of all of the weapons in his arsenal, in order to advance his interests. First and foremost was his Field Services Team.

It was led by the most feared huntress in the modern era that no one had ever heard of.

Her name is Sigi, and now she sits on the mat in her *Airbnb* in Snekkersten, a few klicks north of Vedbæk, performing her daily exercises.

She's in a holding pattern, waiting for news on The Dutchman. She'll *zoom* into a conference with Naddador later in the morning, where he will provide her with The Dutchman's latest known whereabouts.

You see the problem with CORP-ROGUE is its organisation chart. It's very leaky.

And Naddador has a Trojan Horse. A couple, actually.

Tilda's back at the Frederik VI clearing the backlog of tasks spiralling out of Bavaria.

She even took a couple of *zooms*, but left the camera off. Just before noon she gets a strange ping.

Camilla's transponder just went active. She shuts down her business laptop and fires up the app. She can see the Mercedes is on the move, just exiting *Cortex Park*. She sits on the edge of her bed, and watches as it hops on the E20, tracking toward the east coast. Some twenty minutes later Camilla has come to a permanent stop.

Tilda decides to wait a while to see if Camilla settles in. She goes to get some lunch, not taking her eye off the red dot on the map. At the restaurant table she opens up *Google Earth* and zooms in on the location. It's a big villa backing onto the beach by the *Storebælt*.

Jesus, I drove right past her twice when I went to see Barb! And murdered that Swedish operative up in Helsingør, she reminds herself.

Oh yeah, there was that too.

Focus!

Camilla's villa looks like a plush joint. She can make out the parking garage behind the gate. It also has walls down both sides, affording privacy from the neighbours.

Good.

She goes out to sea, then pans back around to check the wall that skirts the beach.

Looks quite low.

The road on which the house is located disappears off into a forest, so maybe there's a place to pitch up. But now she's working attack trajectories. She assumes Camilla's place is tooled-up with a lot of surveillance tech, and Tilda knows she needs to get a closer look.

Enter the drone.

The problem with that is, of course, flight permission rules. And the fact that drones are noisy and everyone can spot them. So she's not going to put it in the air. She just needs to get a sneak peak at the rear of Camilla's place.

So she'll park herself further up the beach, then use her phone to control the drone as it skims along the beach.

Real low.

Then she'll lift it up when she gets to the rear of Camilla's place, and take a looksy.

Seems simple enough. What could possibly go wrong? Apart from other people, and the fact that she's trying to spy on one of the most accomplished killers ever to have graced these shores. Not that it's a big market here. But apart from all these variables, it's a simple enough job.

Right!

She checks the charge on the drone, and downloads the latest updates for its app controller, then she packs it all up, gets in her car, and heads east a few kilometres towards Hans Christian Andersen airport.

There's a lot of fields around there. She'll play around and get a feel for the drone's phone controller, then head south.

On a collision course.

Camilla's upstairs in her study, looking out over the *Storebælt*.

It was the view that nailed the deal when they bought this house. Well, when she bought the house. But she bought it for them as a wedding present.

Lucas took to it with a passion that can only be found in engineers or artists. It was a bit of a fixer-upper, and she was maxed out on the acquisition trail. Within eight weeks of moving in the, place was transformed.

And she loved waking up in it, and especially loved coming back to him. He was the only person she ever knew who could make her forget everything. Even herself.

She found a new depth inside herself, that at first scared her, because it threatened to crack the titanium armour she had built for self-preservation. But he broke through it, not deliberately, it was just that he was so kind and caring. She learned to embrace it, and it was certainly noted by her inner circle, and the employees in general. She became more approachable, and as a result gained more trust and deeper insights from her team. Although, she still maintained the steel spine needed to drive the business hard.

She's never been back here during a working day at this time, and she finds it strangely liberating. The double doors to the upstairs balcony are open and the warm wind is providing her with nature's air con.

She doesn't expect Lucas home till after six, so she may hit the gym before. She gets back into business mode, thinking about getting those fucking Americans onside.

She'd balled her team out about the speed of progress. She scans a bunch of *Teams* chats, flipping between finance, sales and R&D, accumulating progress, and firing back support, or requests for more data, but she's struggling to focus. She keeps replaying the calls she made to those fools on Sjælland from her car.

Simon seemed calmer, and she had a long discussion with him about possible vulnerabilities, and how he had paid a visit to an old supplier and fortified the house with more guns and ammo.

Camilla hadn't needed to do that. She had weapons in easy reach. Once, when Lucas had found a handgun, it had freaked him out, but Camilla blew it off with an explanation about a crazy former boyfriend who had made her life hell.

He seemed to buy it. Luckily, he didn't find the other three.

Next she called Bekka, although she'd hung her finger over the dial button for thirty seconds before committing.

That conversation lasted for two syllables. *Incompetent bitch*, she thought, after Bekka cut the connection.

She had one of those memory mind-fucks about Simon for about two seconds. Something about a boat in Belize.

Then she was back to thinking about The Dutchman. He'd called her a couple of times, but she hadn't answered. She'd known it was him because he followed up with texts demanding she call him to checking in.

Check in!

Go fuck yourself, you satanic creep!

She knew she'd have to call him soon though. He had access to assets he could put into play, far more effectively than she could.

She gets up and walks to the balcony and looks out across the sea. Then she grabs the phone and calls him.

The Brit was in a foul mood.

Not only had he been sent off on a wild goose chase onto another island, but he was also crawling along in a white Ford Fiesta, thanks to The Dutchman's overreaction to their original choice of high performance Mercs.

If that wasn't bad enough, the E20 westwards out of Copenhagen was backed up, because of traffic and road works. His only light moment came when approaching the highway construction and reading the sign that said...

Fart Kontrol.

Once clear of the roadworks, the E20 again turns into a race track, with even the lowest powered cars driving ten centimetres off his rear bumper. This constant highway harassment magnifies his irritation, and he is mightily relieved when he sees the toll booths to the *Great Belt* bridge come into view.

Only for confusion to kick in.

Which of the lanes should he take? With cars and trucks racing past him in a sprint towards the bridge, blaring their horns at his indecisiveness, he panics and almost causes a multi-vehicle pile-up as he swerves into the credit card lane.

The speed calms down across the long bridge, and he looks to the right and watches the slow moving ships, carving their northerly passage towards the *Kattegat*. As he approaches the Funen side, he checks the GPS and gets off at Nyborg, then makes his way ten kilometres north along the coast towards the address that The Dutchman provided him with.

Beach life. And death.

Tilda got off the E20 at Nyborg, then tracked north ten kilometres towards the stationary transponder. She'd driven past Camilla's house, gripping the steering wheel, looking directly ahead. Her wraparounds and baseball cap were her only disguise.

Through her peripheral vision she could not see over the high walls as she drove past. But she could see the red dot on her *iPhone* indicating the car was parked behind them. Her pulse raced and she fought to steady herself.

So here you are, Killer Queen. She'd continued along the road until she came to a small forest, which she had selected as the best place to park. From there, she could walk down to the beach, a few hundred metres north of Camilla's place.

She reckoned there were maybe ten properties between her and the target. *That's a lot of beach. And potentially a lot of people walking along it. Which means the drone's a bit of a risk. Well, fuck it, the whole idea was high risk. Especially the prize at the end of it.*

She'd hoped that doing the surveillance job on a Monday afternoon might mean that the locals were working. But she quickly discounted that fantasy. The COVID pandemic had turned upside down peoples work habits. It was highly likely many of these houses were filled with corporate warriors *zooming* away in their Bermuda shorts, trying to stay awake through endless *Powerpoints*.

Or sunbathing on the beach behind their Funen paradises. *Well, too late to turn back now*. She's committed.

If there's anyone around she'll have to skip the drone, and walk up the beach.

But that is high risk!

She breaks through the trees, and walks out onto the edge of the beach. She looks left and right. To her left she sees a group of people camped out on towels, about three hundred metres away. To the right, no one. Just the long beach, interrupted by sea breaks made of big stones, and a few piers.

Far to the south she can see the E20 as it slipstreams onto the *Storebæltsbroen*, and makes its way toward Sjælland. She walks a little further south, then finds a spot where she has a good view in both directions.

She drops her towel and book, and then takes off her backpack and puts it on the sand. She sits down on the towel and starts rubbing tanning oil into her legs, arms, shoulders and face, then opens up the backpack and takes out the drone.

She checks again in both directions and is satisfied the coast is clear. The drone is a go, but one thing she'd discovered during her trial run an hour ago, was the glare from the sun on the *iPhone's* screen.

She'd rolled up at a field about a kilometre from the *HCA drone test centre*. She'd figured that a flying a drone near a drone testing centre would not arose too much suspicion.

And she only needed to have it up for a couple of minutes as she familiarised herself with the app's controls. She quickly found out that the screen was hard to read under the intense sun.

And that's a big fucking problem when you're supposed to be in control of a robot spying on an assassin. So she would have to make sure the sun was not shining onto the screen when she sent the drone skimming along the sand.

One more thing to worry about.

She takes out the drone and unfolds its arms and propellors. Then she fires up the app and turns on the drone. She pairs the drone with the phone and gets the usual warning messages about flight paths and no-fly zones, which she ignores.

She checks the battery. It's got twenty-seven minutes. She figures she'll only need about five.

Looking up and down the beach again and seeing it's all clear, she places the drone at the edge of the towel, then drags her finger down the screen to turn on the motors. It chimes and then the four propellors begin to furiously spin.

The noise makes her pulse race again, and she nervously looks round.

No one in sight.

She slowly engages the controls and lifts the drone half a metre off the sand. No time to waste, so she sends it whizzing south down the beach towards its destination. From her position, she can make out the building where Camilla lives.

Where Camilla lives!

She peers into the *iPhone's* screen watching the journey of the drone through its front-facing camera. She's steering it left and right over the sea breaks, keeping as low as possible, but not too low as to risk grounding it.

Finally, it reaches the rear of the neighbour's house, and she eases off the power. The drone slows, almost to a stop, then she adjusts its course and pilots it over the bushes skirting the beach, towards the walls guarding the back yards.

She's now lost sight of the drone, so she's going purely by the phone's screen. She looks over her shoulder again.

The people haven't moved.

She looks back down to the screen and glides the drone slowly towards the back of Camilla's property.

A black shape races past Tilda out of nowhere, spraying sand all over her.

She drops the phone, and scrambles to pick it up, even as she hears the proximity warning beeping.

She grabs it and peers into the screen. The drone's collision avoidance software prevented it from hitting the wall.

Jesus!

She looks up and sees a big hound disappearing down the beach in the direction of Camilla's house.

And her drone.

A woman jogs past in a red and white striped shirt and cutoff jeans, all smiles, and nods to Tilda, who forces a wave and half a smile back.

Her mind's racing. Too many variables to process. She needs to get a peek into Camilla's back yard, but that dog's closing in.

And the woman. Where does she live? If she decides to cut between the trees to the houses then Tilda's game is up.

She edges the drone back into position, then slowly raises it to the top of the wall. She looks up and sees the dog disappear down the path towards Camilla's place, followed by the woman.

Fuck!

Out of time. She lifts the drone and flips on the video and scans as much of Camilla's back yard as possible. She's not paying any attention to the details of the house because she'll review the video later.

Then movement directly in front of the drone. Up on the balcony.

Tilda zooms in, and sees a tall woman with headphones on, talking animatedly, pacing up and down.

Camilla!

Tilda slides the app to full zoom, checking the recording, then zooms back out, and does a sweep of the sides of the garden. Then she drops it below the level of the wall, and flies it forward, looking for a gap between the bushes, and back to the safety of the beach.

The drone reaches a path, and she banks it hard left and then low onto the beach. She turns the camera so it's facing her, then races it back up to her position, landing it on the edge of her towel.

She can feel herself sweating as she shuts the motors down, quickly folding its arms and placing it in her backpack. She pulls out a bottle of water and takes a big chug. Then she sits there, trying to slow her pulse.

The last time she saw her was also on a beach. As she was bleeding out, twenty-seven years ago.

She sits for another five minutes, re-orientating herself, then stands up, gathers her towel, book and backpack, and heads back to her car.

Tilda takes the memory card out of the drone and plugs it into the adaptor, then connects it to her *iPhone*, and begins to import the video file. She fast forwards to the point where the drone has raised itself above Camilla's rear wall, then begins to review the footage.

Both sides of the house are fenced in by walls, and she sees no easy access from the neighbour's properties. She then freezes the video. Camilla's unmistakable frame fills the small screen, as Tilda zooms in. Camilla is pacing left and right, speaking into the microphone in her headphones, oblivious to the flying robot that is spying on her from the beach.

Tilda freezes the video, and sits there for an eternity, staring.

She's interrupted by the harsh tapping on her side window.

She drops the phone and looks round to see a pistol with a long silencer pointing at her head.

Camilla rips her headphones off and throws them back into the room.

Fucking asshole, she thinks.

She grips the balcony and looks out across the sea, trying to calm down. The Americans have just done a one-eighty, and dropped her R&D plans in the shit.

She's got a back-up plan. She always does. But she hates using them, because no one ever pulls out of a deal with her. She puts the Yank on her list for a future reckoning, and starts thinking about her next moves.

She looks down the garden towards the wall that Lucas has almost finished. She sees one of her neighbours walk past, and can see her big black dog doing zigzags between the beach and the back path, chasing sticks.

Camilla's never spoken to the lady, but she thinks she would like her. There's something optimistic looking about her, and she always waves.

She waves up at Camilla, who waves back, then goes into her study and looks at the *Teams* chats scrolling down her screen.

I need to get out of here.

She checks her watch. Still time to hit the gym before Lucas gets home. She pings him a message to say that she'll be back around six, then goes to the bedroom to get changed and pack her gym kit. She's walking out the door when she gets a response from Lucas, who says he'll come back early and finish the wall. He suggests they barbecue.

That brings a smile to her face, and she goes out the door and gets in her AMG. The funding hassles are a distant memory.

Fire hydrant.

That's what the man with the gun reminds Tilda of.

He has no neck. It's like his big bald head just merges with his shoulders. And he's solid.

Maybe a bit too solid, she thinks. *Certainly he moves like a pro*. And he backed well away from her as she climbed out of her car.

"Turn around and face the trees."

British.

Tilda turns slowly away from the car.

"On your knees, now!"

She follows his instructions and kneels down on the dirt path. He walks round to face her, pointing the gun at her head. He pulls out his phone and takes a couple of photos of her. Then he walks round to her back, and presses the muzzle against her head.

This is not an execution, Lærke tells Tilda.

He would have taken the photos after he'd finished me.

She feels the gun barrel moving against the back of her head, and figures that he's probably working his phone.

Sending the photos to someone. Or all of them.

Noise.

Panting.

A rush of black darts across Tilda's far right peripheral vision.

The man snaps his head around, as the dog rushes between him and Tilda's car.

Now!

Tilda channels *Lærke*.

She's more efficient.

More brutal.

She grabs the thick stick that she's been eyeing ever since he got her on her knees.

In a flash, she whips round, and smashes the stick across the man's kneecap.

The stick disintegrates, but so does the man's knee. He howls in pain, as the dog runs off into the distance.

She stands up and walks the two paces to the man, who is lying prone on the ground. Then she kicks him twice in the balls. Then a third time.

He releases the grip on the gun, howling again.

Jesus, shut up, Tilda thinks.

She's already thinking about the dog's owner. *How the hell will she explain this?* And she doesn't want to have to silence her.

Tilda doesn't kill innocents.

Nor does Lærke.

Not anymore.

She picks up the pistol and puts it against the mans temple, then pulls the trigger.

Twice.

Two short *pffts* signal the end of the man's existence, as his brain matter blows out the other side, onto the fertile forest floor.

Tilda throws the gun into her open door, then takes his phone and unlocks it with his face. She picks up the mans feet, and begins to drag him into the bushes. He's heavy work, even for her, but she emerges after a minute, having pulled him as far as possible into the dense forest.

She goes back over to where she executed him, picks up some dirt and leaves and covers up the blood and matter. She double-checks that she didn't drop anything, then climbs into the car and slowly pulls out of the woods so as not to leave tracks.

The Dutchman knows the Brit is dead.
Three calls. No answer.
The Brit always answers.
He dials the Brit a final time. Zip.
So Lærke's on Fyn. No question.
Then he calls Camilla. She hasn't answered any of his calls since he saw her yesterday. He understands. But her arrogance will cause the death of her lovely young boy.

Lærke doesn't leave witnesses. And there's a good chance dear Lucas could be used as leverage against Camilla. And she will need it.

In his mind, Lærke vs Camilla is too close to call. Especially now they've piled on another twenty-seven years. All those years ago, hand-to-hand, he probably would have gone with Lærke. Which is why Camilla shot her cold.

She probably knew it too. "Fifty-fifty", he says out loud, as he dials Camilla a final time.

No answer again. *Damm her. I'll catch up with her much later*, he muses to his satanic self. He's running out of operatives. His Swedish Unit is cut down to fifty percent efficiency.

He calls Tallinn and spins-up his *Baltic Unit*. The only one within striking distance.

If Lærke does get past Camilla, then she'll head straight for Bekka and Simon.

The Baltic Unit and the remainder of The Swedish Unit give him six considerable assets on Sjælland. Plus Bekka and Simon.

And me.

Can he trust Bekka and Simon? *Of course not.* But they have two kids.

So The Devil has leverage.

The gym was packed and her irritation levels were going off the scale.

Too many assholes having conversations while hogging the benches, or taking calls while they rested on a machine she needed.

She thought about actually killing one guy with a man bun who was doing emails. So she bailed out after ten minutes and went for a run instead. She ran ten kilometres, looping back to the fitness club, where she took a shower.

The run helped, and as she headed home, all her problems had been temporarily blown away by the exertion. And the thought of falling into Lucas' arms tonight.

She smiles as she waits for the electric gates to open, then she pulls into the drive, parking behind Lucas' Toyota.

She laughs to herself. She's been trying to get him to replace it for a long time, but every time he just says, "it's just a temporary skin to get me from A to B."

She gets out, carrying her backpack to the house and opens the front door. She feels the sea breeze blowing through the house from the open terrace doors, and she can see him working at his laptop outside.

"Hej, be right there!" she says, and goes into the kitchen.

She drinks a big glass of water, then takes the bottle of *Hendricks* gin out of the freezer. She pours two generous doses, adds the tonic, ice and some lemon slices, then places them on a silver tray and walks out to the terrace.

"Jesus, what a day," she says as she sets the tray down on the table.

"How was–" She looks up at Lucas. His hands and feet are tied to the legs and arms of the metal chair with silver industrial tape. Another piece of tape is stretched across his mouth, silencing him.

Camilla looks into his wild eyes and staggers backward, triggering her senses, drawing her attention to the tall figure standing by the wall, in a shooter's stance.

She doesn't recognise the woman, although she knows who she is. Well, actually, she does recognise her. She's seen her somewhere before.

On TV or some conference?

Whatever, she knows it's Lærke, and it makes her blood boil.

Then she remembers Lucas.

He looks up at her with his wild confused eyes, trying to mumble through the tape. Camilla looks away from him, then over to face Lærke's gaze. She's running an inventory of the killer facing her. Her former colleague.

Whom she murdered on a Minorcan beach.

"You've changed a bit," says Camilla breaking the silence. "Although, you're still too thin. It must have been expensive and painful."

"Somewhat."

"Good."

"You haven't. You're still a murderous cunt," comes the response from behind the gun's silencer.

Camilla, smirks. "OK, so what now?" she asks, trying to remain calm, and loosing that battle.

Lærke notices her balling her fists. "Now I kill you. After I execute your sweet husband in front of you."

Sigi's been scoping out the region.

She drove north, round the coast to Hornbæk and grabbed a bite to eat. She doesn't do well in holding patterns.

Especially in Europe.

Where she's wanted, pretty much everywhere.

It's not that she's worried. Sigi doesn't do worry. Especially when she's loaded up on compound. She doesn't actually need that either. Not in daylight, anyway. But it soothes her irritation.

Fucking baby-sitting mission. It wouldn't be so bad if she just got the order to take out The Dutchman and his crew.

Now she's on her way back to her digs in Snekkersten, passing through Hellebæk, when she gets a ping.

She picks up her phone. The message is succinct:

OK on Dutch and Friends. No for the locals. Details to follow.

Naddador.

Sigi puts down the phone and smirks.

She's back in business. She'll hit the *Airbnb* and go through the latest intel. Then make her preparations, execute her missions, then get the hell off this island.

If she can wipe them all out within three days, then she could be back on Fugloy in her cottage for the weekend.

The fallout from the TV semi-hit job that Nikolaj did on Simon at the weekend was not too bad.

Thinks Simon.

His wife knows better.

Bekka had tried to tell him multiple times on Sunday, and this morning, that it was a ruse to flush out some more sources. Many of their friends had already gone strangely radio silent. Their in-crowd were like a bunch of meerkats, constantly watching out for opportunity, but as importantly, danger in the form of the wrong kind of exposure.

So now their in-crowd was out-crowding them.

Simon, despite Bekka's protestations, decided to test the water and arrange another lavish dinner party at their place this coming Saturday.

No one responded.

That means they're all going to be glued to their screens, and have no intention of being seen chez Simon & Bekka.

"What the hell have you gotten us into?" Bekka yells at Simon.

"What the hell d'you think pays for this address?" he responds.

"And who the hell d'you think runs it?" she counters.

This is going nowhere, and they both come to their senses, managing to park their egos in neutral.

"OK, so what do we do about it?" he implores his wife.

"I say we split. Head south. Take the oxygen out of everything. Let him run his fucking exposé. Within six months it'll have blown over, and it'll just be one of those old stories that no one gives a shit about anymore. You can certainly run your business from France. Everyone's gone hybrid now anyway. I'll hand over the studio, so no problems there."

Bekka looks out across the water towards Sweden.

"What about the kids? We can't just pull them out of school."

"We can easily get them into the international school. Remember, we got offered those places a couple of years ago. And money talks down there," she says.

"There's one thing you haven't thought about," Simon says, coming up behind his wife and wrapping his arms around her.

"You mean Lærke. Sure I have. Would we be running from some temporary news story just to put ourselves in her gunsights down there? So up here we have Camilla–"

"–and The Dutchman and his unit–"

"–yes and them. So we have numbers on our side here. But I got a feeling that he will just use us to flush out Lærke, then clean up old business by taking us out," says Bekka, unwrapping his arms and walking to the window.

The evening shadows are beginning to stretch across their back yard, and Bekka shivers, then turns around to face her husband.

"We go south. Before Saturday. We have more space down there. You can call upon some extra firepower if we need it. Up here we're constrained by the tightness of our fucking social network, not to mention this urban jungle."

Simon nods. It's the only choice. He's partially relieved that his wife made the decision for him. He knew she would. She always does.

"I'll start making our plans. You handle the kids."

"Now that's a surprise," says Bekka, walking past him to call her sister.

"You may as well take your cap and sunglasses off," says Camilla, trying to sound calm, edging towards the large Lucifer barbecue.

"And you may as well stay away from the grill. If you want your toy boy to see tomorrow," says Lærke, aiming the gun at Lucas's chest.

Camilla stops dead and glares at Lærke. Then she looks down into Lucas's wide eyes. She stares back at him coldly, unable to summon the words or expression to assuage his fear and confusion. Instead her anger continues to redline, and she fights to remain defiant.

"So you're going to kill me here, then what? There's half a dozen assets scattered across Fyn and Sjælland looking for you!" she says, sneering.

Lærke removes her sunglasses, placing them on top of her cap.

Beautiful eyes, thinks Camilla.

"You mean like the Brit in the forest just up from here?" she says, nodding to the left.

A flicker of confusion flashes across Camilla's face, and Lærke picks up on it.

"Ah, so you didn't know about him. I assume he was courtesy of your old Dutch lover. Keeping an eye on you. Unfortunately, it didn't work out for him. Get on your knees."

Lucas tries to shout but the tape turns it into a mumble. He starts to rock back and forth on the chair, his eyes bulging, jumping from his wife to the woman standing across from them with the gun.

Camilla looks down at him and tries to smile. She places her hand on his shoulder and squeezes as he continues his useless attempts to wrestle free of the silver bonds.

"I said on your knees," repeats Lærke, bringing Camilla's attention back from her husband to her executioner.

Camilla takes her hand off of Lucas, then lowers herself to her knees.

"Hands behind your head," commands Lærke.

"You're enjoying this, aren't you?" says Camilla looking up into the strange face that's staring coldly back down at her.

"It's not about enjoyment, Camilla. It's about wiping out your existence. You're a particularly cruel bitch who always thrived on murder."

"That's rich coming from you, Lærke," sneers Camilla, scowling at the gun.

Lucas freezes his movements.

He stares up at Lærke, then back at Camilla, whose mind is trying to make sense of her husband's change of behaviour, even as she faces her own imminent death.

She looks up from her kneeling position to her husband and says, "dearest Lucas. Know that everything we had together was real. This is nothing. She will not hurt you."

Lærke takes a step back.

What did Camilla call him?

Lucas!

No. No. No. It's not possible.

She stares into the wide eyes of the young man that she tied to the chair. A glimmer of familiarity.

No. It can't be.

Lucas's eyes are wide and boring into Lærke's.

Shit!

Lærke's mind is racing. She makes a decision to separate them. If it really is *Nikolaj's Lucas*, then she will not let him watch the execution of his...wife!

Jesus, the thought of that turns her stomach.

Images flash across her mind.

Of carefree times with Nikolaj and his young son. This man. Lucas.

She's made a decision. She'll leave him out on the terrace, and finish Camilla inside the house.

She breaks her stare with him and walks toward the kneeling assassin.

The intense pain follows the impact of the bullet as it blows through the right side of Lærke's midriff.

She staggers backward, clutching the wound with her left hand, and simultaneously sweeping her gun hand round, looking for the shooter.

Camilla doesn't need an invitation. She's already leapt to her feet, and kicks over Lucas, who is sat prone in the chair, to get him out of harms way.

Harms way, she thinks. *There's a fucking gun battle on my terrace*!

She moves fast. Not for Lærke, but instead she leaps through the terrace doors, making for the GLOCK that's waiting for a rainy day, parked behind a couple of books on Danish philosophers on the shelf.

As she moves, she catches sight of red and white at the bottom of the garden, just by the beach wall that Lucas was building. She swipes it from her mind, intent only on neutralising Lærke.

She reaches the bookshelf and rips out the books, sending *Søren Kierkegaard* flying across the room and through the glass coffee table. She grabs the GLOCK and a spare clip, and flips off the safety.

She knows it's loaded. What's the point of one that's not?

Then she slams herself against the wall and tries to peer round to get an angle on Lærke.

She sees her legs stretched out, blood seeping onto the expensive stone terrace. Camilla raises her gun, extending her arm slowly and aims at Lærke's leg.

She applies pressure on the trigger. Then another shot rings out, followed by a muffled sound.

Camilla looks directly ahead and sees Lucas writhing in agony, unable to detach himself from the chair, as the blood from the bullet's impact drains out of his leg.

Artery, thinks Camilla. *I need to get to him or he'll bleed out.*

More silenced shots spray the ground around Lucas, causing Camilla to duck down as they ricochet into the back room.

Then more shots.

But not from the same weapon.

This one is firing back down the garden toward the unknown assailant near the beach wall.

Lærke!

Camilla lunges out of the terrace mimicking Lærke, blasting down toward the woman in the red and white stripped shirt.

That can't be my neighbour with the dog, she thinks as she dives for cover, ejecting the empty clip and slamming in the other one. She reaches up to the table and pulls off the cloth, then crawls over to Lucas. She rips off the tape from his legs and then wraps the cloth around his thigh, just above the wound. Next she tears off the straps on his wrists, and eases her husband out of the chair and onto the floor, behind the low wall filled with flower pots.

She's vaguely aware of the sounds of suppressed gunfire over her shoulder. She looks into Lucas' eyes and can see they are drifting towards unconsciousness. She clasps both her hands on his cheeks and forces him to wake up.

"Stay with me baby, stay with me! I'll be right back!"

She takes another pull on the cloth tourniquet, ties it off, then gently lays down his leg. Then she refocuses on the more urgent task at hand.

She picks up the gun, and spins round to face Lærke, who is propped up against the wall of the house, blasting down range. Then her ammo clip runs out and she releases it, jamming in another.

Camilla looks over at Lærke, who returns her stare.

No time for her now, thinks Camilla. *Lucas is all that matters.*

She checks the mag, then slams it back in the GLOCK Then she raises her head over the low wall, just as the potted flowers explode above her. In her peripheral vision she sees Lærke send another volley down the garden.

Jesus Christ, bitch! Can't you fucking hit her?

Then Camilla sees that Lærke's in trouble. She's bleeding heavily, and it's affecting her aim.

Camilla's not conflicted. She knows that Lærke's got the woman's attention. When then next volley of silenced projectiles impacts the wall next to Lærke's position, Camilla raises herself, and sends the whole clip down to the bottom of the garden.

She sees her neighbour in the red and white shirt get blown against the beach wall, then she ducks back down.

Two rounds left. She looks over to Lucas, then across to Lærke. Both are loosing consciousness.

Again she peers over the low wall, but this time she can see her neighbour is sprawled out on the grass by the wheelbarrow that Lucas had been using for his cement. She gets to her feet, then slowly begins to walk to the bottom to check on the assailant.

She doesn't make it.

Three bullets rip through her back, then a fourth blows through the back of her head.

Camilla doesn't feel the pain. But she does feel curiously calm. Somehow she senses that all her systems are shutting down, yet she feels strangely warm and peaceful.

She senses Lucas, her husband, the man who brought her in from the darkness. She lives through a lifetime of their wonderful memories together in the instant it takes for her life-force to extinguish itself.

Then Camilla collapses dead on her perfectly manicured grass, as the water sprinkler soaks her bloody back.

The assassin who came through the house and exited the terrace doors, didn't do his homework.

He was so focused on neutralising Camilla, that he failed to observe the other target who was propped up against the wall of the house.

Lærke had watched her nemesis get blown away in the garden. Then she looked up at the man, and emptied her last three rounds into his side.

10 - DEATH BY POWERPOINT

All hell broke out on Fyn.

The garden of Denmark was reeling from the gun battle that had taken place on the back yard of a high-end villa just up the coast from Nyborg. These things just didn't happen in Denmark. And especially not on Fyn.

The cops arrived first, alerted by the neighbours who'd heard gunfire in the early evening of Monday. The ambulance services were on the scene not long after. Three bodies were found. One male and two female. A fourth man, believed to be one of the owners of the house, was on life support as a result of a gunshot wound to the leg.

He had been airlifted by chopper to the Rigshospitalet in downtown Copenhagen because the nature of his wound required a specialist team of surgeons. And because his father had insisted on it. And his father was not someone to debate. He was an esteemed TV journalist and revered podcaster, and he used his considerable leverage to bring his son back to the capital fast.

The helicopter had landed on the pad on the roof of the hospital, and surgeons had worked for five hours to save his leg. The young man, believed to be in his early thirties, was now said to be in a critical condition and heavily sedated.

The other owner of the house was a woman, believed to be the wife of the injured man. She had apparently been shot in the back and was found face down on the back garden. There was a gun in her hand, and preliminary reports were that it had been discharged.

The other woman found dead at the scene was discovered near the wall that separated the property from the beach. She was apparently a neighbour from a few houses up, and had only moved into the rented accommodation a month ago. She was also found to be brandishing a firearm which had also been fired.

Closer to the house, a man was found lying dead on the terrace, next to the wounded house owner. The dead man had been shot several times in the right side of his chest. He was also found to be carrying a weapon.

Just to the right of him, a pool of blood was found, together with bloody foot prints, and the police had informed the press that they were searching for a fifth individual.

A day later, it was still unclear as to who shot who, and what the motives for this violent gun battle that has traumatised this once peaceful corner of Denmark. The following day, it was announced that the female owner of the house was the successful CEO of one of the largest robotics companies in northern Europe. Speculation then turned to industrial espionage conspiracy theories, as her company was also engaged in military contracts.

The police's progress was not helped by the fact that the house's security cameras had been disabled. But the carnage was not limited to this single back garden. In what police believed to be a related incident, a second dead man was discovered a few hundred metres along the coast.

His body had been found when two walkers saw a large black hound biting into a man's leg that was half hidden in some bushes in a small wooded area. On closer inspection, the locals were shocked to see that the man had been shot in the head. The police later verified that two bullets had actually been fired into his brain.

In another ironic twist, the dog detective that had been credited with discovering the man's body, was also said to belong to one of the women found dead in the back garden just down the beach.

This spate of attacks devastated the local community, and turned the island into a cordoned off zone as the cops tried to track down the missing person and owner of the blood that had been left at the scene.

As they worked through the forensics to try and explain the sequence of events, the international press descended on the idyllic island, turning the place into a zoo. Then, someone made the connection between the gun battle and a recent killing outside a church in Helsingør a couple of nights back.

The Dutchman doesn't do fear.

At least not in his own mind, although he's great at externalising it. In fact he's thrived on putting the fear of the *Dark Lord* into many of his adversaries over the past thirty years.

But now he's nervous, and the needle's moving towards fear. The news of the carnage hit the airwaves late on Monday. By Tuesday lunch it had gone global, with every TV network and *YouTuber* with a newscasting side gig trying to out-speculate everyone else. That was par for the course. Then on Tuesday afternoon, he was the news.

Someone had released *his* photo to the police, who then presented it at a news conference, as a person of interest in the events that unfolded on Fyn. It was a picture from about ten years ago, and he had to admit to himself that he looked pretty good.

Then the reality of the fear combined with the anger kicked in. He knew instinctively that it was the *old witch* in Oxford who had authorised it. CORP-ROGUE had decided to cut the cord on him, and he could not blame them. Still, he was now in the cross-hairs and he had to assume that there was a *Unit* tasked with taking him out.

His only remaining assets in Denmark were The Finn and The Norwegian, but he wasn't confident in their allegiance to him. The *Baltic Unit* that he had tasked had gone dark, and not responded to any of his messages. Thus he assumes his whole *Unit* network is now compromised.

Years of painstaking planning, development and machinations, all down the toilet in twenty-four hours. He knows he needs to get out of Denmark. The question is how?

Airports, ferries and roads are a no go. The police have put checkpoints on all the bridges leading to Sweden, Fyn and Jylland. He thinks his best chance is getting hold of a small boat, and making his way south to Germany. Once he's on the mainland then he can easily disappear.

His paradise in Anguilla must now be considered to be compromised, so he's banking on Africa. Or maybe Central America. To travel though, he needs to change his appearance, so the first thing he does when his face goes viral is to cut off his lush, silver hair, then shave it down to the stubble. Then he dyes his silver eyebrows darker, and starts to work on a beard. Which will take a while.

Meanwhile, he's got one ace up his sleeve. If he can get The Professor's laptop, which he assumes is full of all kinds of *kompromat*, then maybe he can use it to lever his way back into the *old witch*'s favours. It's a big *if* though.

Because first he needs to find Lærke. Then he needs to kill her.

Easier said than done.

He knows she was behind the events at Camilla's place, although he's still not quite sure how it all played out. For starters, *who was the female neighbour with the gun*?

Clearly, someone was well ahead of the game, having planted her there a month ago, according to the police report.

Then there was the other man who had been shot on the terrace. *Was he part of the same crew as the neighbour?* He certainly wasn't from one of The Dutchman's *Units*.

His Brit operative was obviously the one that had been discovered by the dog in the bushes. *Now that had to have been Lærke's work. A double tap to the temple. Very efficient.*

He looks at his freshly shaved head in the mirror, admiring his work. It works with the shape of his skull. He knows what he's going to do now. There's only one place Lærke will go, now that Camilla is out of the game.

Bekka and Simon.

Tilda had eased herself up painfully from the stone floor after killing the man who came through the terrace doors.

She checked the side of her stomach and could tell that she had just been winged. The bullet had gone straight through her side, making a bloody mess, but nothing that couldn't be patched up.

She hobbled over to Lucas who lay on his back, and checked his pulse. It was weak, and she reached down to tighten the tourniquet. Then she took some water from the jug on the table, wetted a cloth and wiped his face.

His eyes fluttered open and he looked up into her eyes. She could see the confusion on his face, but she had no time to explain anything to him. Far in the distance she heard sirens, and she knew that was her signal to move fast.

She kissed Lucas on the forehead, then stood up and jogged down the side wall towards the beach. She knew it was a risk, but less so than exiting from the front. Her car was parked about five hundred metres south, and she needed to be in it and out of the area by the time the cops showed up.

When she arrived back at the hotel in Korup, she entered through the rear door and made her way to her room, clutching her side. She congratulated herself on not checking out earlier, although she'd considered it.

Now she set about cleaning her wound, dousing it with alcohol. Then she consumed more of the cheap whiskey herself as she prepared herself to sew up the hole. She'd done it before, many years ago, but that was on someone else. The angle of the exit wound made it difficult for her to finish off the rear set of stitches.

And there was the added problem that the booze was starting to seriously interfere with her surgery skills. Still, she finished it off and inspected it after again cleansing it. It wasn't gonna win any crochet awards, but she figured it would hold, depending on how she treated her body.

And therein lay the problem.

She still had Bekka and Simon to visit.

And that Dutch bastard, if he was still here.

He's still here, she thinks, as she sticks a big plaster over the stitched wound. Then she goes back to the bedroom with a couple of towels, lays them on the bed, and falls into a deep sleep.

Marriages marinated in murder are surprisingly resilient.

At least thats what Bekka thinks, as she watches her husband pace frantically around the living room, in front of the morning TV showing the latest images from the events on Fyn from last night. Lots of stock footage of red and white police tape stretched across roads, roadblocks on bridges, and reporters with big furry microphones trying to out-analyse each other.

Bekka knows that they've got a strong marriage, and that will get them through this.

If they live through it.

She's well aware of Simon's *shenanigans* over the years, but she knows she's no angel.

There have been a couple.

More like four.

One was a year after Cloe was born. She was bored and he was AWOL, even when he was still in the house. After that she traded affairs in a war of attrition with him, until each caught the other out. Then they both fessed up to all of their extracurricular activities.

Over a barbecue and shots.

It was a strangely liberating experience. The sex that night relit a candle that lasted a few more years. But then she slipped up again. Some tomcat she ran into at the Skodsborg gym. It didn't last long, and she did actually feel guilty.

Until she got word on the Copenhagen drums that Simon had done the same.

So they had another fessing up session. The sex wasn't quite so good that time. But it was adequate. For the last two years, she's known he's been faithful. Well, she's sure she knows. He's easy to read, and she has some of the best intel sources on Sjælland. So things are copacetic. Until now.

Fucking Lærke.

Why did you come back from the dead? Because she wasn't dead, you idiot.

For the last week she's only been focused on one thing. Protecting the children. She would sacrifice Simon, herself, and anyone else in a heartbeat. She thinks it might come to that. Especially as now it's not just Lærke.

Bekka's intuitive enough to know that The Dutchman will wipe them out if Lærke doesn't. That's why they need to run.

The news about Camilla's unfortunate death accelerated their plans. Bekka's had an internal dialogue going with herself ever since they heard the news. On the one hand it couldn't have happened to a more deserving bitch. On the other hand, Camilla was a useful tool.

If it was up to Bekka they would have been gone yesterday. But Simon's got some things to close out tonight in person. Some fucking German industrialist he needs to meet. He told Bekka that he could retire on this deal.

What a wanker, she thinks. He cleared seventeen million on the last deal. Euros, not Kroner. She told him that was retirement money, but he didn't buy it. He said the taxman/woman/person/entity snorted up over half to fund fresh road markings.

She snaps out of her thoughts and says to her pacing husband, "put your phone down and talk to me."

He looks down at his wife, perched on the sofa, searching for reassurance, then looks back at his phone.

"Sit down!" she demands.

He jumps out of it and throws the phone onto the coffee table, then drops himself into the overstuffed chair opposite her.

"We need to split now, babe," says Bekka in a calm voice. We'll take my car, and I'd prefer to be mobile rather than constrained by airline schedules."

"I told you, I need to take this meet. It's at five this afternoon. We can either go later this evening, or early tomorrow morning."

"What's the big deal? It's just another fucking speculative meet."

"No, she wants to buy-in with her corporate innovation fund. We've been discussing upwards of half a bil. I have to take it. The follow-up stuff I can do from France."

He looks into her eyes, pleading. She knows he's going to take the meet whether she agrees or not. So she nods then says, "OK. We go first thing in the morning. We'll pick up the kids on the way tomorrow. I'll pack their stuff."

"Cloe will freak," says Simon.

"She will, but you'll buy her off with something, as you always do."

Ouch! He winces, knowing that it's got an element of truth. Or more like a huge chunk of truth. He swallows his retort, knowing she has him, and now is not the time to get into one with her.

"OK, tomorrow morning it is. I'll get my stuff together later. I need to get to the office and start working up my pitch."

"Sure," she waves him away. "Go make your fucking pitch to the bitch."

"English babe."

"I said fine, I'll see you later." She gets up and walks into the kitchen to start working her phone.

Tilda wakes up and she thinks she's Lærke.

On account of the aching pain in the side of her stomach. It takes thirty seconds to fully exhume herself from her deep sleep. She reflexively touches her old wound, then realises that it is the *old wound*!

So there's a new one!

She checks it and can see that the plaster has held, but blood has seeped through, and onto the towels. She gets up slowly, testing her movements, surprised to find that the ache recedes when she moves.

She carefully strips-off the plaster and inspects her needlework, and is not impressed. Still, it held, apart from the bit of seepage. She goes back into the small room and grabs the last small bottle of whiskey and starts to dab the tender wound. Then she applies another plaster, and does some stretching, testing the limits of her mobility.

It doesn't occur to her to check the time until after she's finished. Then she discovers it's gone ten.

"Verdamt!"

She's missed breakfast, and she's famished. She carefully showers, then dresses in her black business suit. Only then does she fire up her *iPhone* and begin surfing for news. And she's all over it.

Well, not her, but the fallout from the gun battle at Camilla's place.

Camilla! Good riddance, Tilda thinks. Then she remembers how Camilla was running down the garden, blasting away at the woman by the wall.

The dog woman. How the hell did she fit into all of this? She was very good. Tilda recalls her bouncing past her when she was directing the drone from the beach.

Who sent her? Tilda takes a wild guess, and it comes up orange. Tilda's under no illusions that Camilla was trying to save her. She was in maximum protection mode. Tilda/Lærke had seen Camilla charge into a hail of bullets once before.

Call it some twenty-eight years ago. Not a scratch that time. This time she got scratched.

Out.

Why did she do it? Not for Tilda, thats for sure. She looks down at her feet.

Jesus, Lucas!

It was all coming back now. Camilla was protecting Lucas. And Lucas was her husband!

How the fuck did that happen? Well it happened, get over it.

Now she switches to Lucas. She remembers he was in a bad way. The news did not name him as the dead man.

Lucas. Lucas!

Nikolaj!

Christ. Not now.

She forces herself back into information gathering mode. The events were prime time across all the European papers and social channels. She scanned the German ones, more out of habit than anything else. No new details had been published. But there was one suspect.

The Dutchman's face filled the screen of one of her regular daily subscriptions.

What the hell? He wasn't even there! Someone must want him off the grid. Seems no one's looking for a tall woman in a white cap with sunglasses and messy black hair. So maybe she caught a break.

Next she fishes out her business phone and fires it up.

Instant digital mayhem appears as over thirty messages pop up. She forces herself to ignore them, and fires up her *Outlook* calendar.

The meeting's locked in for five pm tonight.

His office is located along Bredgade in Copenhagen. She goes to the website and gets familiar with it. Then she fires up *Google Earth* and orientates herself with the surrounding access roads and paths. She shuts off her business phone and checks herself in the mirror.

Check those dark rings. And your hair looks like shit. I'll go with the wild look for him.

Then I'll kill him.
And then I'll go find his wife.

After packing her bags, she takes them out of the rear exit of the hotel to the car, and loads them into the trunk. Then she wanders around the carpark to the front of the hotel, back into reception, and checks out.

When she gets back into her car, the bullet wound flares up, causing her to wince. She takes a painkiller and washes it down with water, and then pulls out of the carpark towards Odense, and her next mission.

To get breakfast.

Sigi thought she caught a break.

The mayhem across on Fyn flashed up on her phone, and she immediately hoped her mission would be aborted.

She called Naddador and he was pissed. She knew the tone of his voice. He was tapering down off of a *compound* hit, and now was not the time to bother him with irrelevant requests.

Sigi didn't consider this irrelevant. And besides she knew he would never stay mad at her for long. She was, after all, his *daughter*.

Of sorts.

Not biological, but in every other way.

So Sigi's hoping that Naddador pulls the ripcord and bails her out of Denmark. Except he doesn't. He tells her to stand by, and await further instructions.

Now Sigi's pissed because she reckoned she could have been back in her cabin on Fugloy in twenty four hours. So she waits.

And then earlier this morning she gets the ping.

Stay and close the deal.

What fucking deal, she asks herself.

She opens up her laptop and accesses her secure cloud storage, and can see that a new file has been deposited. She opens it up and can see a bunch of photo's and last known GPS locations.

This is not Naddador's work, she thinks. *Must come from the client. More like competitor*, she muses. CORP-ROGUE!

She consumes all of the intel, then deletes the file, and goes for a power run. And when Sigi runs, she powers.

Especially after a vial of *compound*. She's back after a ten kilo, and heads to the shower after stretching out. Her brain's still fizzing from the *hit* and the juice pumping through her system from the run.

She checks the map and zones in on the Vedbæk address. Then she zooms her *Google Earth* over to the two hotels where the Finnish and Norwegian assets were staying.

And Finally to The Dutchman's last known location.

If they're still on the island, then they'll have to make their moves today. Or more likely tonight. So she'll hangout in Snekkersten until late afternoon, then cruise down towards Vedbæk, grabbing a bite to eat at a local joint.

Her plan is set, there's just one unknown.

The assassin known as *Lærke*.

She doesn't know where she is, or what she looks like.

What seems certain is that she was involved in the termination of some of the assets yesterday evening on the other island.

The only thing she knows for sure is that this woman is driven. And what drives her, is to wipe out the last remaining members of her old *Unit*.

Jesus, talk about holding a grudge, thinks Sigi. She then reminds herself of the multiple grudges that she still carries around, like a second skin.

She casts aside the useless thoughts and picks up her *Atlatl*, and begins to inspect it for cracks, lovingly applying a soft cloth to the carbon fibre frame.

He watched their patterns for the last two days.
He hadn't yet decided which one he would take. Both would be preferable, although it would be harder to manage.
But he would settle for one of them.
All he needed was one. Leverage first. Pleasure second.
He stares through the windscreen as they get out of the car. Then he takes a sip from the coffee cup. The aromas rising from the steaming drink mixing with the foul odour of rotting flesh emanating from his glands.
He checks the rear-view mirror again, satisfied with his new skinhead look. As the woman drives off, he pulls away from the school and heads back into town to make his final plans.
He knows it will be a long day. Come darkness, he will be on a boat heading for the German coast.
Perhaps he would have young company for the trip. He licks his lips again.

By lunch on Tuesday the cops still don't have anything to go on.
Apart from three bodies in a back garden, another found up the road in a bush by a dog, and a mysterious pool of blood that's missing an owner.
Oh, and the other owner of the villa, who for the last twelve hours has been falling in and out of consciousness.
Which is where his father comes in.
Nikolaj.

Who's parked next to Lucas' bed at *Rigshospitalet*. The cops are there too, and they want to interview Lucas.

Nikolaj's told them to go fuck themselves.

In English.

So they've de-camped from the hospital to try and figure out the puzzle of why so many armed people went turbo at a beach house in *hyggeland*. Most of the ballistics have come back, and they've started to piece together a story for their bosses. And for the media who pile more pressure on their bosses.

Apparently, the owner of the house, the renowned CEO of a big robotics company, had gone nuts and shot one of her neighbours, who also happened to be carrying a gun.

Then the CEO was shot in the back by the neighbour's husband, who had come through the house, apparently to rescue his wife. At least this was the working theory on Tuesday afternoon.

But that still didn't explain why so many people in a quiet road along the *Storebælt* were packing so much heat in the first place.

And then there was the bush-dog-man with the double tap.

And finally the missing person, minus a pool of blood.

It was beginning to look like one of those Nordic noir TV shows. The latest theory of *who killed who* had leaked to the press. As had the fact that the sole survivor had been tied up.

The *Armchair Generals* in the studios went into speculative overdrive when it was discovered that the young man was the son of Nikolaj. Nikolaj's phone started ringing, all the time. In the end he turned it off. Then they started calling the hospital and asking to be patched through to Nikolaj. When a nurse approached him, he told her to tell them to go fuck themselves. Again, in English.

His ex-wife turned up later in the afternoon, armed with a new husband and a shitty attitude. After trying to explain the condition of their son to her, she balled him out, screaming *how could he let this happen to her boy?*

Nikolaj told her to go fuck herself. And the trophy husband.

This time in Danish. He was a Spaniard.

They left the hospital to get some rest from all the stress.

Throughout the afternoon, Nikolaj sat by his boy and clasped his hand. He could not make sense of any of this, despite the emerging pieces of information that were flooding in. The conspiracy theorists were having a field day, trading speculations about secret assassination squads that had been living in Denmark undercover for years. When Nikolaj heard that one, he again turned his phone off.

So now he sits and waits for his boy to wake up.

Powerpoint assassin.

Simon's banging away on his *MacBook*, going full-auto on fonts and graphics that slide, spin and disappear. He'd tasked his team a week ago with producing a *comprehensive* deck that he would use to woo the German investor.

The first problem was that Simon only reviewed their presentation thirty minutes ago, and the second problem was that it was comprehensively incomprehensible. In other words, it was crap.

So he's furiously reworking it, expanding the original eighty-five slides to a blockbuster one hundred and twenty-seven. Not counting backup slides.

His assistant pokes her head through the door of the conference room and says that his guest has arrived downstairs. He nods without looking up, and scrolls up to slide seventy-six to adjust the width on a couple of organisation chart boxes.

He hasn't noticed the five missed calls from Bekka on his silent phone.

She drives into the parking garage opposite the *Odd Fellow Palæet*, then exits on foot, turning left and striding toward *Bredgade*. She crosses the road, passing the *Phoenix Hotel*, heading south.

She knows where she's going because she had scoped out his office on the Saturday when she met Quantum Barb. It was an old townhouse building, a hundred metres past the *Phoenix*.

She gets to the front door and scans the buzzers with various names. There are a number of companies located in this building. Mainly consultancies and lawyers. Prime real estate with a prime price tag. She presses the buzzer for his company, and after ten seconds a woman's voice comes through the intercom.

Tilda explains who she is, and that she has a meeting scheduled for five. The lady buzzes her through, and Tilda opens the old door, then walks through the courtyard towards Simon's office.

She looks up at the high walls, all pale yellow and well maintained, with a lot of vegetation draped down the sides.

It's strangely silent and serene, almost like being in a cathedral, with hardly any noise from the rush hour traffic streaming past outside.

She gets to the door and it buzzes open. She looks up to the security camera above the door and reflexively adjusts her sunglasses, then walks into the building just as a lady comes down the stairs.

"Welcome, he's waiting upstairs on the second floor in the conference room at the far end. I'm sorry, but I am late to pick up my kids," she says as she rushes past.

"Absolutely no problem at all," says Tilda, watching the woman exit the building and run out of the courtyard. Tilda stands there and composes herself in the small mirror.

She's lost the wig. Now she's back to her old look.

Well, not quite, she thinks. She adjusts the harsh cut of her blonde hair, then she starts to climb the narrow stairs, finally reaching the second floor.

She comes to a long corridor, lined with various abstracts and small offices. She can see him sitting at a conference table at the end of the floor, his head buried in his computer. She begins to walk down the corridor, as the sounds of her high heels echo off the walls.

She'd considered the dangers of the *stilettos*. They weren't exactly designed for combat. But she knew she needed to look the part getting in and close to him. She also knew now that she was exposed. The security camera picked her up, and those images were probably in a cloud.

Well, she didn't expect to be going back to Munich anyway. One way or another, her corporate life was dead. That's why she'd made succession plans, sealed and held by her lawyer in case the whole trip went to shit.

As she passes each office, she glances in, noting that they are all empty.

Well it's five, hot and a Nyhavn beer is calling. Good, she thinks.

He looks up, alerted by the sound of her approach. He waves at her, and then goes back to tapping.

Arrogant prick, Tilda thinks.

She's been more used to executives coming in to meet her!

She passes the final office before the conference room. Empty. So no one's on this floor. No cameras either.

As she walks through the conference room door, she removes her sunglasses. Simon gets up and smiles his strangely familiar plastic smile, and begins to walk around the conference room table.

Tilda's running an inventory. On him, the room, and the visibility from the buildings across the courtyard into the conference room.

He has changed, and he hasn't, she thinks. *He still moves like a tank. Subtlety was never his forte. He always used to pull his shoulders back, like he was on some fucking parade ground.* Now that stance only exaggerates his belly. Which is flopping over his belt.

But she can see he's still stacked. And lethal. You never loose those skills sets. They just slow down a bit. She should know.

He strides up to her and extends his hand. She meets his eyes, and grasps his clammy hand firmly.

"I'm so pleased to meet you in person. I can't shake the feeling that we've met somewhere in person. Have we?"

"Yes," replies Tilda.

Lucas looks up into the harsh light, blinking to focus his eyes.

His throat has never felt so dry. He looks down the bed and can see his leg is heavily bandaged. He tries to move his hand, and then realises someone's holding it.

He turns his head to the right and can see his father slumped in the small chair. Lucas tries to uncouple his hand so that he can hoist himself up, and the movement startles Nikolaj out of his sleep.

A big smile spreads across his face as he looks at his boy. Then he rubs his eyes and leans over the bed.

"How you feeling?"

"Where am I?" asks Lucas, looking around the room, his eyes beginning to close again.

"*Rigshospitalet*. You had a big operation last night. You've been sedated since then."

"Copenhagen? Wait, where's Milly?"

Nikolaj looks down at the floor. He'd been dreading this question ever since he got to the hospital. He looks up and sees that his son is about to drift off again. Then he mumbles one word.

"Lærke."

Bekka's usually the calm one.

If Simon doesn't answer his phone...well that's often par for the course. She knows he's busy, or out schmoozing clients. But this time it's different. This time she can't get hold of her sister.

And the kids aren't answering the mobiles.

And Bekka doesn't need any more clues to know that there's danger close.

Bekka was *The Unit*'s radar.

After she called the school was when she knew for sure. They told her the kids were picked up by their *uncle*.

She runs to the living room, climbs on a chair and grabs the pistol that's lodged behind some books. She checks the magazine and loads one in the pipe. Then she stuffs it in her waist, grabs her keys and runs out of the door.

Screaming out of their driveway, she dials Simon again.

"Pick up!" she yells.

Voicemail.

She cancels it and calls her sister again.

Voicemail.

She turns right onto *Strandvejen*, and floors it north towards Humlebæk, and her sisters house.

"Was it Davos?"

Tilda forces a smile, and affects a strong German English accent. "Possibly. I have been there a couple of times before the pandemic."

"Indeed! Well that must be it. Are you alone? I was expecting your team."

"I prefer to take care of this alone. It's a sensitive activity, as I'm sure you will agree," she says, looking through the windows, searching for any movement in the office across the courtyard.

He brings her attention back. "Can I get you some coffee, or tea?"

"Water will suffice, thank you."

"Then water it shall be," he says, overdoing the host bit, leaning over the table to grab the decanter of water. He picks up a glass, wrapping his damp hand around the rim of it.

He's still a peasant, she thinks.

Then he begins to pour. "Please, take a seat. My team has prepared a comprehensive overview of the market opportunity for you, so I will take you through it now."

"That won't be necessary," Tilda says, causing Simon to look up from the table, surprised.

"Well, I assumed you would want to–"

The long blade shears through the left side of his belly.

She grabs his broad shoulder and pulls him towards her, driving the knife deeper into him, causing him to drop the glass.

The crystal shatters on the wooden floor, echoing down the hallway of the old building. The shock in his eyes instantly shifts to self-preservation as his brain registers the pain engulfing his body. His muscle memory kicks in, even as she twists the knife inside him, attempting to maximise the damage and incapacitate him as fast as possible.

She's not fast enough. He grabs her wrist and attempts to pull the knife out, but her iron grip has too much leverage on it.

She twists again, slicing it through his intestines. He howls, then pulls his head back and attempts to slam it into hers. She sees it coming, and ducks as his head glances off her temple.

It's enough to destabilise her, and she instantly regrets the shoes. Her right heel slips on the spilled water, and he senses an opportunity. His left knee comes up, smashing into her side, sending her sprawling over the table, pulling the knife out as she falls.

He collapses onto the side of the table as the blood fountains out of the gaping wound. He scrambles, clutching his belly at the same time as looking for a weapon. He grabs the screen of the laptop and smashes it into her shoulders.

It has little effect, and bounces off her and onto the table. She gets to her feet and backs off a metre. She can see he's mortally wounded.

He knows it too.

She kicks off her shoes, then lunges at him, causing him to stagger to the right. He's fighting a loosing battle to hold in his guts, and he begins lashing out wildly, yelling at the top of his voice.

She grabs the water decanter off the table and hurls it into his face, shattering it. His hands come up to his face, releasing more blood from his open stomach.

Now she closes in on him, whipping out her leg and slamming it into his groin, then spinning round his body, slumped over the table. In one whirling movement, she brings the blade up behind his neck, then drives it into him.

He arches his back, unable to separate the pain from the different zones in his body. He twists his head, trying to look at her, then she grabs his shoulders, flipping him over onto his back on the beautiful wooden conference table.

He stares up at her, helpless and raging. He tries to speak, but her thrust to the back of his neck has paralysed him.

He begins to hallucinate, as images of Bekka and Cloe and Marky merge with memories of a murder he helped commit on a Minorcan beach.

He can't process how this has become his reality.

He is not a victim! He can't be dying!

He's not yet, and Lærke, standing over him, watching the confusion in his eyes, leans closer into his face. She can hear the husky breathing as he fights vainly to live.

She brings the thin blade up in front of his eyes, then says to him, "say hello to your wife."

She slashes the knife across his throat, pulling back to avoid the blood as it splatters across the shattered laptop's screen, dripping down the edges of the Powerpoint.

He's exhausted.

He'd been at his son's side since he came out of the operation. He knew he needed to go home and get freshened up. The surgeon had told him that Lucas was stabilising, and he would continue to drift in and out of consciousness. He recommended that Nikolaj come back in the morning. Nikolaj told him he would be back in two hours.

His ex-wife had not been back since, which basically summed up her relationship with reality, thought Nikolaj.

He kissed his son on the forehead, then grabbed his jacket and exited the building to find his bike. The ride to his place in Frederiksberg would give him some much needed respite from the worry for his son's well being. And to help him try to make sense of the events that had almost buried his boy.

Nikolaj and Lucas had now become the story. His phone had been going crazy for the last twelve hours, and he'd turned off all the social media notifications. He needed to get out ahead of it, but he had no idea where to start.

Bekka screeches into her sister's driveway and jumps out of the Cayenne, leaving the door ajar.

She bangs on the door but doesn't hear a response. Then she remembers she's got a spare key, so she fishes it out, unlocks the door, and charges inside. It's silent in the single story cottage, but the alarm is off. She can also smell something's off in the house. Like a rotting smell. Old garbage maybe.

She hurries down the hall to the kitchen, yelling, but there's no response. The kitchen looks like a bomb site. Dishes lay smashed on the floor, mixed in with cutlery. The wooden kitchen table is hanging on three legs, and the floor by the back door is covered with shattered glass.

She reaches round and pulls the pistol out of her waistband, then edges back out into the hall. One by one, she kicks in the doors, extending her aim as she sweeps each room.

Finally, she comes to the master bedroom. Her sister's room. It's slightly ajar. Again the smell.

What the hell is it? She takes a step back, then kicks in the door, scanning the room with her gun.

Her sister is lying on the floor. She has a cloth in her mouth, and her hands and feet are tied with plastic strips. Blood is seeping from her eyebrow as she stares up, wild-eyed at Bekka.

Bekka doesn't react. She freezes, then she checks the wardrobe and the door to the ensuite, as her sister looks up at her pleadingly.

Satisfied that she's not bait, Bekka kneels down and cradles Anna's head, pulling the cloth out of her mouth. Anna gasps, panic invading her speech, even as Bekka begins to slice through the plastic ties on her limbs with her knife.

"They...they came. This man. This awful man. The s... the smell. He–"

"–where are Cloe and Marky?" says Bekka, wiping the blood off her sisters head.

"I couldn't stop him. It was...there were three of them. So big...he. His smell...I–"

"–I know, I know. Now listen to me very carefully. Did you see them come in cars?"

"Nnn..no. They were in the house when we got back. The other two grabbed the children. I couldn't stop them. He...that man. He pressed me to the floor and got on me... his smell."

"What did he say...focus Anna! Did he say anything?"

"He...he said something strange. He just said tell her to bring me Lærke."

Bekka helps her sister sit up against the bed. Then says, "listen, I need to go find them. Your head is OK. Can you stand?"

"Yes, I think so. But Bekka, what are you doing with a gun?"

"I can't explain it now. But I have to move fast if I am to get them back."

"Where is Simon?"

Bekka looks away, "I don't know."

"Does this have something to do with his work?"

"Yes possibly. Look, I need to go. Wait five minutes and then call the police. Don't tell them I was here."

"But why not? What are you into? And the gun?"

"Just promise me Anna. Not a word on me!"

Bekka helps her sister onto the bed, then fetches her a glass of water. She kisses her on the cheek, then rushes back out to her Porsche. She guns the engine, just as her phone rings.

Caller ID blocked.

She answers it, pressing herself back in the seat.

"How's your sister?" hisses the voice.

"You bastard. I will tear your body limb from limb!"

"Quieten yourself, child. You are in no position to make such vain promises. Do you want to see your children alive again."

"Where are they?" she screams.

"Well they are perfectly safe, of course. My two associates are taking very good care of them. Now, let me explain how you and your idiot husband can begin to piece your materialistic lives back together again."

Bekka sits there, breathing heavily, fighting back the tears and the rage.

"Are you listening?" he whispers.

"I'm here," she manages to respond.

"Bring me Lærke. And the Professor's laptop."

"How the fuck am I going to get that? I don't even know where she is!"

"Well she's close that's for sure. She made such a mess yesterday evening, that she's now on a clock. So she will come to you. And your husband. That is, if she hasn't already visited him."

Bekka's silent.

Christ, Simon. No!

The Dutchman interrupts the pause. "Ah, so you haven't heard from him. Well, then it seems you have a job to do on your own."

"You bastard, I coming to–"

"*Silence!*" he screams. "You will receive precise instructions later this evening. If you want to see your offspring again, you will follow them to the letter. Meantime, I suggest you make yourself busy. Bring me Lærke."

The phone goes dead. Bekka stares out of the windscreen. Then she begins to sob uncontrollably.

Sigi watched out of the rear window of the dark blue Range Rover, parked one hundred metres past the house in Humlebæk.

She had tracked the target from her house, although that had not been easy. The Porsche had been driving north at high speed, and the last thing Sigi wanted was to attract attention. So she'd hung back, and caught a break. The Cayenne had got stuck behind Strandvejen traffic. She caught sight of it as it turned off into the town, again slowing, which allowed her to follow at a safe distance to the final destination.

She had driven past the house, catching a glimpse of the woman bracing the front door with a pistol in her hand. Sigi continued to the end of the road, then pulled up on the side.

Five minutes later, the woman came storming out of the house, jumped in the car and fired up the engine. But she didn't pull out. She was talking animatedly with someone on the phone. Then she tore out of the driveway.

Sigi flipped the Range Rover around, and tried to catchup with the Porsche as it turned right, this time heading south. In the distance she heard the wailing of sirens.

Blood work.

More specifically, the frantic scrubbing of Simon's blood from her formerly pristine white blouse.

She pulled his body from the conference room table, onto the floor. The mahogany wood had acquired a darker hue from his mortal wound.

She checked the windows and could not see any movements across the courtyard. She stood there for thirty seconds, breathing heavily, trying to compose herself. Her blouse was soaked red, and her hands were streaked with his blood.

She turned and looked down the hallway, listening for any sounds.

Nothing.

Next she padded painfully down the hall, looking for the bathroom. She found it halfway down, and walked in to face the bloody mess that she had made of herself. She put her foot onto the sink and pulled out the splinter from the broken glass, flushing it down the hole.

Now she removes her black jacket and red-stained shirt and went to work on it, just managing to make it worse by spreading the stain across a wider area. She squeezes the remainder of the water out of it, and puts the damp blouse back on. Replacing her jacket, she closes it, snapping all of the buttons as high as possible. There was a slight pink stain above her breast, but most of the mess was hidden. It should get her to the car.

Exiting the bathroom, she goes back to the conference room to survey her destructive attack. She searches through his pockets, removing his wallet, and picking his phone off the table, unlocking it with his lifeless face. She leaves the laptop on the table.

A noise echoes down the hallway. The sound of a door banging. It seems to come from downstairs. Then the sound of a vacuum cleaner.

Time to move. No time to clean up this scene.

And anyway, where would she start?

She grabs her shoes, wiping off the blood on the side of Simon's trousers, puts her sunglasses back on, and walks quietly down the hallway.

She gets to the stairs, and can hear the sound of the cleaner hoovering on the floor below. Taking advantage of this, she comes down the stairs fast, and bumps into the other cleaner.

They both apologise to each other, and Tilda walks round her, exiting the building, under the security camera.

She knows she's blown. Both from the camera and the cleaner. Her only hope is to get to the car, and get out of Copenhagen as fast as possible.

She needs a place to clean up. She knows she complicated things by not using the gun. But she needed to look in his eyes as she plunged the blade into him. She chides herself for letting her ego get the better of her.

But where to go now? It wouldn't be long before the cleaner discovered Simon's body. Once the police arrived, the first thing they'd do would be to pull down the security footage from the cloud. Then they would sweep the local area, which would include cars in and out of the area.

She had no hotel, and she didn't know anyone she could trust in the city.

Well except one person. And she had been responsible for putting his son into hospital.

11 - CHARLOTTENLUND

The conference room killer hit the news around seven on Tuesday evening.

The cleaners had followed their regular operational pattern, starting on the lower floors, then working their way up. The team leader had gotten to the second floor and had begun hoovering the long, narrow corridor, ducking in and out of the small offices.

Then he spotted something unusual at the end. A man was lying on the floor of the conference room. The cleaner dropped the hose and ran to the meeting room, where he found a man lying in a pool of blood.

He tried to shout to his colleague, but he had left the vacuum cleaner running, so his screams were drowned out. There was blood everywhere, and broken glass on the floor near the man's body. His lifeless eyes staring up into the ceiling, unable to communicate the last things he saw.

So what did the cleaner do? Well, he did the most obvious thing that anyone in his situation would do.

He took a bunch of photos and uploaded them to his *Instagram* account.

Only then did he think about running back and getting his colleague, who happened to be the brains of the operation, and she called the police.

When the cops arrived, they fanned out inside the building, and across the courtyard, checking out the adjacent offices. More cops and investigators arrived over the next hour, jamming up *Bredgade*. The media only got wind of it via the viral posts, and then they turned up, creating even more disruption.

The police began interviewing witnesses, and the first interviewees were also the best sources of clues. One of the cleaners had bumped into a tall, blonde woman who was rushing out of the building around five-thirty. The cops quickly reconciled this with the security footage of the woman entering and exiting the premises.

The executive's assistant had also been contacted, and she had confirmed that she was the last person to leave the office except for the boss. She also identified the woman of the same description, entering the building.

She also happened to have a name, as she had made the calendar reservation. The victim had been quickly identified as a British venture capitalist who ran a boutique shop, and was known as being one of the most successful investors in the Nordic region. His name had not been released to the public, pending notification to his family.

However, the media had managed to blast the name of the company across the air and net waves. The cops quickly discovered that the name of the last meeting in the man's calendar was a German industrialist.

On *googling* her, they got a close match with the woman picked up by the cameras, although her face had been covered by huge Italian shades. Someone tipped off the press with the name of the woman, and all of a sudden Tilda's viral, with images and videos of her at speaking gigs orbiting the world, as the main suspect in the Copenhagen conference room massacre.

Meanwhile, buried deep in the raging news cycle that has gripped Denmark's attention for the last twenty-four hours, was a small item about a break-in that had been discovered in a farm just outside the village of Hinge, Jylland.

Apparently, the farm owner was a renowned Professor from a local university. He had not shown up for classes for several days. Eventually, someone took interest and asked the local police to check out his place.

They discovered a scene of destruction, with windows blown out and walls blown in. Blood stains had been found on the kitchen floor, and there was evidence of shotgun blasts, and an explosion upstairs. Usually, this would have warranted a TV special. But it was pushed well down the ratings by the happenings on Fyn and Sjælland.

No one had yet made any connections.

By now Tilda's lost the blonde look and is sporting her shaggy black wig again.

She'd hurried awkwardly back to the parking garage and grabbed her bag out of the trunk. It was dark and cool in there, and few cars remained as the hot business day was coming to an end.

She checked for cameras, and couldn't see any within sight of her car. Then she climbed in and managed to struggle out of her in and managed to struggle out of her suit and blouse, tossing them into the back. Then she pulled on her cargo pants and a dark blue t-shirt. She kicked off the high heels, and replaced them with black sneakers. Finally, she replaced the Italian sunglasses with the *Oakleys*.

Transformation complete, she started the car and exited the facility.

It was much later that an eagle-eyed junior police officer spotted a strange occurrence on the parking garage's security cameras. A black Peugeot which was driven in by a blonde woman fitting the suspect's description, was recorded driving out an hour later, this time with a dark-haired woman at the wheel.

Unfortunately for Bekka, she's trending on Instagram. Not that she was surfing at this moment.

She'd sped back to the house from her sister's and was frantically running round collecting up as much firepower, cash and passports as she could find.

Then her phone lit up.

Half of her friends who had not responded to her after the Nikolaj exposé at the weekend, were suddenly pinging and calling her, swamping her with crying emojis.

OMG!
I'm so sorry!
Are you OK?
Poor Simon!
Will you still run yoga classes this week?

It went on.

She had no idea what they were talking about. So she called Embeth.

And Embeth tells her to not look at Instagram.

Bekka looks at Instagram.

Then she drops the phone and screams.

The *Baltic Unit* dropped off The Dutchman's radar twenty-four hours ago, after he had asked them for help. They were still en route to Denmark, but they had a new mission.

The Dutchman and his crew.

Oxford had re-tasked the *Unit*, compensating them with a bucketful of digital coin, to take out their former leader.

They were an entrepreneurial bunch, with diverse holdings, up and down the Baltic states, which soaked up their ill-gotten gains from their days jobs as international assassins for hire.

Officially they were composed of the standard *Unit* size of four, but the Latvian got COVID for the second time and bailed out.

The two Estonian's had raced through Latvia, picking up their Lithuanian colleague, then sped through the *Suwalki gap* and proceeded straight across Poland into Germany, before grabbing the ferry at Rostock bound for Gedser in Denmark.

It was a roundabout way of getting into Denmark, but they needed their *tools* which couldn't be checked-in for the simple one and a half hour flight to Copenhagen. So by the time they pulled up, it was Tuesday night and they were tired, hungry and pissed-off from each other's company. The coin at the end of the mission was the only thing that kept them focused.

The GPS tracking data that Oxford had provided to them from the remainder of the *Swedish Unit*'s smartphones had worked out. And that's how they had snuck up on The Dutchman and his Norwegian and Finnish sidekicks. They were parked up on the side of the road, just across from *Amager Strandpark*.

The *Baltic Unit* had pinpointed the signals to a black Ford Transit van, and a 7-Series Beamer. They drove past the vehicles and then pitched up in a parking space a few hundred metres north. They dare not get out of their own vehicle as they were well known to the other *Unit*, having partnered-up with them on a couple of occasions, neither of which had worked out well.

Most of the *Units* were constantly competing with each other, and that's how The Dutchman had designed the system. But sometimes he had been forced to combine teams, when an extraordinary amount of firepower was required. Hence, the Baltic team had no qualms about taking out their competitors.

What was unclear was what The Dutchman and his *Unit* were up to. Oxford had provided little insight, apart from their location trackers and instructions to eliminate them.

So they hadn't yet worked out their plan of engagement, and so they decided to play the waiting game and let The Dutchman make his next move.

Nikolaj took a detour on his way back. He needed some air so he biked to the lakes, then rode south along the western bank until he got to the *Peblinge Sø*.

There he found an empty bench and sat down. He stared across the water to the far side, aimlessly watching joggers go by. The wailing sound of sirens to the east focused his attention. There was obviously something big going down, as an ambulance raced over the bridge just to his left, from the hospital that his son was recovering in.

He brought his attention back to Lucas, and the last thing he said.

Lærke.

What did that mean? He couldn't be talking about his Lærke. Unless he was hallucinating.

His.

You mean some woman you dated over twenty years ago. Who left on another one of her foreign NGO assignments one night after a dinner at our favourite restaurant. And disappeared forever.

You mean that woman?

He'd searched for her for over a year. Used every journalistic contact and trick he could muster.

Nothing.

There was zero record of her even existing. And he couldn't turn up any alias.

During that time, his heart fluctuated between devastation and anger. Devastation that she was the woman that he was planning to ask to marry and be the new mother to his son, and anger, because she had abandoned him.

If she had. Perhaps she'd been killed.

But he had no way of knowing either way.

After nine months he began to tire of the search, but Lucas asked him every day when she was coming back, and he did not have a good answer for the inevitable follow-up questions that would arise if he told his boy she had disappeared.

So he continued with the facade of the search for another five months. Eventually, he found comfort in the arms of another, and the threads of memories he clung to began to wither.

In parallel, Lucas's daily focus on football began to distract him from the regular questioning. Lærke vanished into the past, only surfacing occasionally as he reached the bottom of a bottle of scotch on lonely Friday evenings. And there were a few of those.

He was definitely hallucinating, Nikolaj says to himself again.

He checks his watch and then gets up, climbs on his bike, and sets off for his apartment.

He locks his bike in the courtyard and then enters the building, skipping the elevator and climbing to the fourth floor.

By the time he gets to his front door, he's sweating from the ride through the hot Copenhagen evening, and the climb up the stairs. He curses his fitness again as he unlocks the door and enters his spacious apartment.

He'd picked it up a few years ago as a bargain, courtesy of a divorcing couple who were engaged in internecine financial warfare. He'd spent a small fortune re-doing it, painting over all the red and black shit they had left, softening the space with soothing greys and creams.

He kicks off his shoes, and walks into the kitchen to get some water. He fills up a pint glass from the cold tap, then takes a chug on it.

He's turning round, drinking it to the bottom, when he comes face-to-face with a tall woman, standing in the corner of the living room.

The Dutchman climbs out of his Beamer and walks up behind the black Ford Transit.

It's a balmy evening, and the long stretches of beach and grass at the *Amager Strandpark* are packed. Kite surfers fly past, catching the evening breeze, and rollerbladers swoop in and out of the pedestrian traffic.

He looks through the tinted rear windows of the van, satisfied that he can't see anything, then walks up to the passenger side door, massaging his freshly shaved scalp, still getting used to the exposure to the elements.

The passenger side door opens, and the Norwegian climbs out. He stares at The Dutchman, taken aback by the new look.

The Dutchman ignores him and says, "are they under control?"

"The boy was playing up. We had to gag him. But they are comfortable enough I suppose, given their fragile circumstances."

"And they have water? Make sure they have water," insists the bald man.

"They do. What is the plan? We cannot wait here for much longer. We will begin to attract attention."

"We're moving in fifteen minutes. North."

"How far?" asks the Norwegian.

"Charlottenlund. You will follow me. That's where we'll meet the Vedbæk woman."

"Did you hear about her–"

"–Yes, you fool. It's been all over the news. So Lærke's close. Bekka is the last, and she will not wait around for long. So it's a leverage game. We have her offspring, and Lærke needs to move fast before Bekka leaves the country, once she has secured her kids. I'm banking that Lærke already has eyes on her target. Prepare to move, and stay a couple of cars behind me," he says, turning back to his Beamer, looking around as he wanders back.

A hundred metres ahead, one of the Estonians looks back and watches the exchange between the newly shaved Dutchman and the Norwegian.

He sees the Norwegian climb back into the van, then turns to his two colleagues and says, "they're moving soon."

Bekka's staring out across the calm sea. Her mind is a raging storm.

The cops have just left. They'd spent two hours there. First breaking the news that she already knew, together with the rest of Copenhagen, then questioning her like she was some kind of fucking suspect. And all the while in the back of her mind, all she could think of were her children.

The cops had asked where they were, and she replied that her sister had picked them up. What else could she say? She just hoped the bluff would pay off, and they would not follow-up.

They seemed pretty anxious to leave, and when they did she immediately called her sister. Anna was still freaked out by the kidnapping earlier. Her guilt was consuming her, and Bekka had to spend five minutes calming her down to ensure she would not go to the police.

Jesus, I just lost my husband and my kids. And she's in a state!

She knows Lærke will come for her soon, and she's on a knife-edge. If Lærke kills her, then her kids are dead.

No question.

She doesn't even want to contemplate their fate at the hands of that fiend.

If she kills Lærke, which in her opinion, she stands a one out of three chance, then she's going against The Dutchman's instructions to bring her to him.

And how the fuck would that work anyway? How exactly would she bring Lærke to him? Certainly not voluntarily.

Jesus, Simon gone. I need you my sweet, flawed Englishman. You are a bastard for leaving us.

She snatches at the phone as it rings.

No caller ID.

"Yes?"

"Be on the road running parallel to *Charlottenlund Slot* at twenty-two hundred. Park on the coast road and cross the road, walking towards the castle. When you are parallel with it, stop and await further instructions."

"Wait, my kids! Are they–"

"–That depends on you," he hisses. "For now they are secure. Be there, and bring her, and the laptop."

He cuts the connection and she stares down at the phone, heartbroken.

Then she gets up, walks across the living room and grabs her GLOCK from its hiding place.

Come to me Lærke, you heartless bitch.

"Sit down, Nikolaj," Lærke says, motioning to the sofa.

"In my own house! Well thanks a lot!"

He's trying to remain calm, but his voice squeaked up a note. His mind is running in multiple directions at the same time. Intuitively he knows who she is, but he doesn't recognise her, or her voice.

In the back of his mind is the last word that his son whispered earlier.

Lærke, but he still can't rationalise her presence.

"Who are you, and how did you get in here?" he says, remaining standing.

"Well, getting in here was not a problem. Call it skill sets that I acquired a long time ago. As to who I am, you know the answer to that."

She turns and glances out of the building, staring across the city.

"It's been a while since I've been back. It all seems strangely familiar, and yet so alien. And you," she says turning back to face him, "you have, and haven't changed."

"What did you do to my son?"

"It wasn't me. He was an unfortunate...*bystander*."

"He wasn't a *bystander*!" Nikolaj says, moving towards her, balling his fists.

"The cops said he had been restrained. Something about being taped to a chair!"

"Well, yes that was unfortunate, but you see I needed him to get to *her*. I never meant to hurt him. I didn't even know it was him!"

"So you didn't shoot him?"

"No, someone else did."

"Who?"

"I wish I knew."

"Who are you, Lærke?"

"Not the same one that loved you in another age."

"Why did you leave?"

"I didn't leave. I just didn't come back."

He smirks, "there's a difference?"

"There is when you are shot and left for dead on a beach," she says.

"Apparently you didn't die. So where did you go? And how did you change yourself so much?"

"Eventually, Germany. And it was an expensive, painful process. But I had no choice. It was for my own safety. And yours and Lucas'."

"Don't mention his name, you almost got him killed."

"I'm sorry Niki."

He goes to respond, but her use of his nickname, and her tone catches him. He walks over to the sofa and sits down, rubbing his face and head, as if it will help him process the situation.

He looks up and she's staring down at him. "You are bleeding from your side."

She looks down and curses, tenderly touching the stain appearing through her t-shirt.

He gets up quickly and walks to the kitchen, startling her and causing her to take a step back.

"Easy there. We need to clean you up."

He comes back with a damp cloth and a first aid kit, and motions for her to sit down.

She tries to stare him down, then backs off and sits on the chair.

"Lift up your t-shirt," he says, looking into her eyes. She carefully pulls the t-shirt away from the leaking plaster, allowing him to peel it off.

"Jesus. Is that a bullet hole?"

"Just a nick. It went straight through. There's no major damage. Just clean it up and put on one of those fresh plasters."

"Who *are* you?" he asks, as he goes to work, dabbing away the blood. "And why were you at Lucas' house?"

"His wife. Camilla. She and I go way back."

"In what way? Ah, sorry about that," he says as she winces.

"We used to work together. When you and me were together," she says, looking down at him as he finishes cleaning the wound.

He looks up into her eyes, searching for some familiarity. But this woman is so unrecognisable. Yet they are having this conversation as if they know each other.

"I know," she says, reading his mind. "It's too weird. How do you think I feel, looking down at the man I loved and lost so many years ago."

He applies the plaster, then presses it gently onto her muscled stomach, keeping his hand on it a little too long. Then he pulls it away and stands up.

She replaces her stained t-shirt over it, and gets up. "Thank you."

"I need to understand this. This...this whole thing. Your disappearance, where you went all those years...and what Lucas has to do with anything."

"Of course, I understand. How is he doing?"

"He's stable and recovering," Nikolaj says, staring directly into her eyes.

"Thank god for that. Go and get me a drink. Then I'll tell you a story."

The BMW pulls up on the right side of the road, just before the *Café Jorden Rundt*.

The black Ford Transit swoops into the last remaining space just behind, pissing off the driver of a Mercedes that was trying to reverse in. It speeds off, blaring its horn and extending a middle finger from the drivers side window.

The Dutchman gets out of the Beamer and walks back towards the Transit. The walkway is still buzzing with cyclists, pedestrians and rollerbladers, and he curses himself for selecting this location. Still, he knows it will quieten down with the approaching darkness. And besides, he has escape options here. North, south, west on the road.

And access to his small motor boat that he has secured just up the road at Skovshoved Havn.

He slides open the side door and climbs in, looking down at the two petrified kids.

Bekka isn't expecting a knock at her front door.

She figured Lærke would attack through the rear doors, or one of the side windows. She had been patrolling her house, clutching her phone in one hand, and the GLOCK in the other.

She's just coming down the stairs for the umpteenth time, when she hears the knocking. She immediately tenses, bringing up the gun and aiming it at the big oak door.

She can see a large figure, distorted, through the frosted glass pane.

It's too broad to be Lærke, she thinks. *And it's taller. Very tall.*

She creeps down the remaining steps, gun hand extended, and pads to the door. Could be the cops again, so she tucks the gun into the back of her pants, latches the door chain, then slowly opens the heavy door until the chain goes taut.

She peers up into the eyes of the tallest woman she's ever seen. Her dark red hair is hanging over the right side of her face, and Bekka can make out the end of a thick scar.

"Who are you, and what do you want?"

"You and your children are in great danger. You need to let me in," comes the reply.

Bekka is trying to process the accent.

What is that? It sounds Nordic, or is it Scottish. No, Icelandic!

"I asked who the fuck are you?" repeats Bekka, pulling the GLOCK from her waist and sticking it through the gap in the door.

"You won't need that," comes the reply. "At least not for me." The woman doesn't even flinch, ignoring the gun barrel, and continuing to stare down into Bekka's defiant eyes.

"I can see you need more convincing. So be it. I have orders to protect you, and that extends towards your children as well. I am after the person you probably know as *The Dutchman*. And any of his acolytes. There is another. A former colleague of yours. The assassin known as *Lærke*. I am to retrieve her. It is my understanding that she is responsible for the death of your husband."

Bekka looks down at the floor, as Sigi continues. "My commiserations. She also terminated your two other former associates. It is clear that she will come for you. She will not succeed. I will restrain her. But you will not kill her. I will assist you in reacquiring your offspring, then you will execute your plans and leave this country. I recommend your planned destination in the south of France. It is the optimal location for you to remain."

"What...how do you know all of this? Who the fuck are you? Who talks like this?"

But Bekka's rational brain is already processing what she heard. This woman could clearly blow through her door, and the gun seems to act as no deterrent.

She feels herself subconsciously unlatching the chain, and opening the door, gesturing for the giant Icelander to enter.

"You are wise," she says, as she strides into Bekka's hallway, replacing her own pistol into a pocket in her cargo pants.

"My name is Sigi. We will now make preparations."

Lærke closes The Professor's laptop.

Nikolaj leans back into the sofa and rubs his eyes. After a minute he says, "I can't process all of this."

"I understand. It's inconceivable. Yet it's all true."

"There are just too many layers for me to make sense of," he says, staring out the window across the darkening Copenhagen skyline.

"Just focus on the personal element. I don't expect you to sympathise with my motives, but I want you to try and understand them. And I plead with you that Lucas' involvement in all this is a tragic, unfortunate coincidence."

He looks into Lærke's eyes, searching for some physical recognition.

"I think I understand. But what will you do now? And what of me and Lucas?"

Lærke looks down at the floor. "Well, I can't go back to Germany. I'm the news after the incident at Simon's office."

"Incident?"

"Yeah, sorry, I forgot how clinical I sound. Anyway, I'm blown. But I still have two people to take care of. And they're close."

"Bekka, and this Dutch guy," Nikolaj affirms.

Lærke nods, gets up and walks to the huge window.

"Have you thought about the fact that you will orphan her kids?" Niki asks, getting up and walking over to her.

"Yes. But I try to compartmentalise it. It's something they taught us early on."

"Does it work?" he asks.

"Never. It just dulls the thoughts a bit."

"You said that Bekka had tried to save you on the Minorcan beach. And that she had been the one you were the closest to," he asks, looking into her eyes, searching for some semblance of humanity.

"Yes. But she didn't try hard enough."

"You're too cold, Lærke. There's more inside you than this hatred. I know you. Even if you think I don't know you."

She pauses, staring across the rooftops, running her finger across her sensitive fresh wound.

"Even if I let her go, there's still The Dutchman. He needs to die."

"But how will you find him?" says Niki.

"Through Bekka. He wants to use her as bait to get me. So I'll let that play out."

She snaps out of her gaze. "I need a car. I dumped my rental, and the cops are looking for it."

"Where are you going?"

"Vedbæk. To talk to Bekka."

"Talk?" asks Niki, looking into her eyes.

"Yes, if that's possible. I just made her a widow after all. Her husband was a bastard, but he was also the father of her kids. And they'd been together a long time. So it could go either way. But I need to try."

She turns to face her former lover. "You are a persuasive man," she says, leaning forward and kissing him lightly on the lips.

Niki's heart melts as he feels the feathered touch of her tongue as she glides it along his lips, just like she did so many times in another age. He closes his eyes, and feels himself floating willing it to never stop. Then it stops as she pulls back.

"I'm sorry Niki. I shouldn't have."

"I'm glad you did," he says, looking into her sad face. Then they both look at the floor, suddenly lost for words.

"You need a car. Take mine. It is parked in a garage just down the road. I haven't used it for weeks. I just get about on the bike."

"Are you sure? I don't want to get you into trouble."

"I'll give you my mobile number. Just leave the keys on the wheel wherever you dump it and send me the location. No one need ever know."

"You should have been a spy, Niki," she says, smiling for the first time and stroking his cheek with her hand.

"Well I'm a TV journalist, as you know!" he laughs.

"Close enough!" she leans forward and kisses his cheek. "I need to go."

"Let me get the keys." He walks over and grabs the key fob and tells her where she can find the car.

"What do I do with this laptop?" Niki asks.

"Keep it safe. Only one other person knows exactly what's on it," says Lærke, collecting up her backpack and gun.

"Who's that?"

"A café owner in Nyhavn."

Niki looks at her confused.

"Don't worry. Just keep it safe. She walks up to him and wraps her arms round his shoulders, pulling him close.

"You take care of yourself. And give my love to Lucas. Tell him that I'm sorry. You can decide if you tell him anymore details about Camilla. I understand if you don't."

She kisses him on the lips, then walks out the apartment door, leaving Niki standing there, dazed and confused.

The Dutchman runs across the highway to the *Café Jorden Rundt*, sitting on the small island between the roads, narrowly avoiding the battered old Saab as it charges north. The woman driving with the white cap pulled down over her face has to swerve to avoid him.

He walks into the café and orders a double espresso. The waitress explains that they will be closing at nine, and he nods at her. He takes the coffee out to the terrace and finds a table where he can observe all directions, as well as the black Transit.

He checks his watch, then opens up his phone and sends Bekka a text reminding her to be at the location in one hour. He figures she'll be early. She may already be here, scoping out all the angles. He doesn't think she will have any other assets in play. She hasn't had enough time to plan anything. Lærke saw to that.

He checks his watch again, swigs down the espresso, then gets up and walks back across the road to the van.

Lærke is a panther. Stealth was always her forte. So was speed, and a quick death usually guaranteed for her prey. She knew it, and it enabled her to stay calm in the most tense encounters.

But now she feels herself slammed into the side of Bekka's house. Her face pressed against the white wall, hardly able to breathe, as the iron grip squeezes her neck. Her right arm is pinned up behind her back, sending sharp pain signals into her brain.

Then she hears a voice from another time.

"Let her go."

Lærke feels the relaxing of the grip on her neck and arm, but it doesn't fully let go. She twists her head to try and get a look at her attacker, and finds herself looking up into the lifeless eyes of the biggest woman she's ever seen. Her red hair is falling onto Lærke's face, and she can feel the woman's minty breath on her check.

The woman releases Lærke, shoving her into the wall, as she backs off a metre. Lærke spins, and comes face to face with two GLOCKs. One from her attacker, and the other from a short, athletic woman whom she hasn't seen in twenty-seven years.

"Walk," commands the tall woman with an Icelandic lilt.

Lærke looks at Bekka, who nods and nudges her gun towards the rear of the house. Lærke doesn't need to be told twice. She's already run the numbers, and knows she stands no chance in close quarters with these two. She's still trying to process the strength of the stranger. *And where the fuck did she come from*?

Lærke walks round to the back garden, and is prodded in her back with a gun towards the open terrace doors. She walks into the plush room and turns round to face them as Bekka comes through the double doors, closing them behind her.

"Sit," states the stranger.

Lærke sits down into the armchair, places her hands on the rests, and only then realises that her gun was taken from her waist outside.

"Who's this?" asks Lærke, nodding towards the giant Icelander.

"A friend of mine," replies Bekka.

"I should kill you now."

"Yes you should. In fact I'm surprised you haven't. I assume that by bringing me in here, you think we have something to discuss," replies Lærke, defiantly.

Bekka sits down on the sofa opposite her, while the Icelander remains standing, pointing her gun down at Lærke.

"I will kill you for Simon. But right now, let's just say I need you. That Dutch bastard has my children. For all I know he has an army over here. I need your help."

"You need my help. Like I needed your help on that beach a quarter of a century ago."

"I'm not going to indulge you in this right now. We can deal with the past after I get them back. Right now I need you. And I believe we would both benefit from removing The Dutchman from the planet."

"That we agree on. But who is she?" asks Lærke, looking up at Sigi.

"Like I said, she's with me. With us, if you're in."

"You may call me Sigi," says Sigi, walking to the front window and checking the perimeter.

Lærke looks down at the floor. Then re-engages.

"OK. What's the plan?"

Bekka leans over the coffee table and hands Lærke her phone, showing the instructions from The Dutchman.

Lærke looks up from the phone, "and the plan is?"

"The plan is the three of us kill all of them."

Leverage makes men overconfident. Which makes them vulnerable. And the problem with leverage is once you've used it, then you've lost it.

The Dutchman, of course, is no stranger to leverage. He's levered his way up via decades of diabolical machinations. Of the countless politicians and business leaders who had visited his island paradise, excited by their unquenchable thirst for the vile pleasures he could provide, he was always amazed how easy it was to gain advantages over these great titans of power.

Over the years, he had become too relaxed about his ability to shape and shift complex political and financial policies and investments, through his subversion, and the extended reach of his *Units*.

But now, as he strolls around the sand-coloured driveway of the *Charlottenlund Slot*, his senses are on edge, and he feels an unfamiliar ache in his gut that has not visited him in over twenty years.

Perhaps it's my public unmasking, he thinks to himself, as he scans the trees either side of the dark castle.

No, it's her. Or more specifically, them. If somehow Bekka has managed to bring Lærke to him, then it's possible they made a temporary devils bargain. And that concerns him.

Still he has his own operatives in play. Well, the only two remaining. The Finn deployed from the van to the other side of the road, and went deep into the forest with the two children in his clutches. His Norwegian is somewhere on his perimeter, tracking him, and scanning for danger.

Three against two, he thinks. *Correction, three against one plus Lærke.*

If she comes.

She'll come.

But he has the leverage.

The kids.

And that gives him confidence.

He reminds himself to find out what happened to the *Baltic Unit* after they dropped off his radar. No one does that to him. He will extract their hearts after he has finished his business in Denmark.

He walks through a break in the trees, exiting onto the road junction just across from the great house. He sees a small figure standing on the other side of the road, and he can make out Bekka's form in the darkness.

He scans left and right along the road, then begins to walk across to the other side. Once there, he turns to face her. She is standing twenty metres away on the quiet road, her hands empty, staring him down. The Dutchman begins to walk towards her, then stops when he's ten metres away.

"Where is she?" he asks Bekka.

"Behind you, bastard," comes the whisper from just inside the tree line.

He turns slowly, and can make out the shape of a stranger, pressed against a tree, aiming a pistol at him.

"My, how you've changed, my child," he says, smiling at Lærke as she emerges from the shadow.

He feels another gun in his side as Bekka comes up behind him.

"Where are my kids, you fucker?"

"I'm impressed. How is it that you two came to such an arrangement?"

"It's temporary," comes the voice of Lærke. "We have a common purpose–"

"–for now," continues Bekka prodding him hard. "Now where are they?"

The Dutchman looks down at the small woman, into her determined eyes. He smiles again, although he's beginning to register the rumblings of a panic. He nods in the direction of the forest.

"In there. One hundred metres. With one of my associates."

Bekka looks behind him at Lærke. She doesn't need to be told. She backs slowly into the dark forest just as a small popping sound comes from across the road.

Lærke turns and sees Bekka on the ground, clutching at the back of her leg. She sees movement to her left as The Dutchman makes a break for it into the trees. Lærke aims her weapon across the road, trying to figure out where the shot came from.

Another pop.

This one blows out some bark from the tree just above Lærke's eye. She spins back behind the tree and wipes the splinters from her forehead.

Two more pops.

Then a scream.

Lærke slowly pokes her head round the other side of the big tree.

Bekka's been hit again. Looks like the same leg. She knows what he is doing. But she won't bite. Bekka will just have to suck it up.

Another shot. But this one's different. It's not silenced. It comes from further down the road.

Lærke sees a figure fall next to the trees across the road.

Someone else is in play here, she thinks, scanning for where the new shot came from.

Nothing, just silence and the distant hum from the coast road as it snakes its way north.

Lærke leaps out of her cover, half expecting to be cut down. She can't believe she's doing this for Bekka.

Because she's your friend.

And she's a mother.

And you know she was put in an impossible situation twenty-seven years ago on that Mediterranean beach.

Get over it! The others are gone. Just this Dutch bastard. Then you can build a life.

Another new one.

She sprints over to Bekka who is rolling on the sidewalk. Two bullet wounds in her right thigh. No time. Lærke grabs her arms and drags her into the forest and piles her up against a tree.

She looks into her friend's eyes.

"My...Cloe...Marky–"

"–I'll get them. Take this," she says, pressing the GLOCK into Bekka's bloody hand.

Bekka looks up into Lærke's unrecognisable face as the tears stream down her cheeks.

"I know," says Lærke, as she disappears deep into the Charlottenlund forest.

Assassination central.

A small forest on the Nordic Côte d'Azur.

The two small children huddle together, deep in the forest, against a big tree. The sounds of the wind blowing through the darkened woods adding to their terror.

They look up at the big man standing over them. They have never seen such an imposing figure. He has cropped blonde hair and an expressionless face.

Since they had been kidnapped, they had not heard him say a word, even to acknowledge comments from the other two men. This made him more scary.

The Finn stands there with his gun raised, scanning the forest, listening out for approaching sounds. He cursed The Dutchman for assigning him to guarding the children. He would prefer to be mobile, hunting their prey.

For that is what he is.

A hunter without equal.

The Norwegian would debate that, of course. But the Finn knows it. Since the age of seven he was reared on the eastern border by his father and uncles. Trained how to be patient. How to track, hunt, kill, skin and cook. Knowledge passed down through generations, honed against the elements, tempered in the furnace of wars with eastern invaders, and enhanced with the latest technologies.

At sixteen he killed his first man.

He didn't give it any more thought than if it was a wolf. They had buried the body of the foreign dealer deep in the forests of Kuusamo, not far from the border which he had been frequently crossing.

Welcome to Finland, he thought, as he crept up behind the drug peddler, and sliced his throat.

That was an age ago. Now he stands guard in another much smaller forest.

Forest! Hah, this feels more like a garden.

The Finn thinks he sees a glimmer of light directly ahead of him, and he's confused with himself that he's unable to react.

As the carbon fibre spear slices through his forehead, his brain is racing to catch-up with the fact that he's already dead.

Or he will be in approximately five seconds.

His eyes dance about, desperately searching for an explanation as to why he's pinned to the tree. As his senses dim, his last remaining synapses struggle to visualise the tall form that is walking towards him.

Sigi stands there, looking down at the blonde man whose eyes are rolling. She reaches down and separates him from the tree, then rips the spear out through the back of his head, turning the lights out on this great Nordic hunter.

She kneels down and wipes the blood off the spear, then slides it into the sling over her shoulder with the *atlatl*.

Then she looks down at the kids and brings her forefinger to her lips.

"Ssshhh," she whispers, before disappearing back into the darkness.

He runs in the direction of the Finn and the children, stopping twice to pause and listen for her footsteps.

He saw Bekka go down, but then the gunshot came from across the road.

Who was that?

All he knew was that his Norwegian operative was dead.

He needs to get to the Finn and set him loose. He is the best hunter for these conditions.

The Dutchman knows what he will do with the children. Who knows, he may even keep one of them.

He sprints into the small clearing and can see the children huddled on the ground. But the Finn is not there.

He approaches slowly, circling the clump of trees. Then he stops dead in his tracks. Two big feet are sticking out of a bush, just behind the tree where the kids are sitting.

Verdomd!

He spins round, scanning the forest, then backs up towards the bush. He leans in and turns the Finn's body over, exposing the gaping hole in the middle of his head.

That's no gunshot, he thinks. *What the fuck made that*?

A crack.

The sound of twigs snapping. Then another. He whirls round, swinging up his pistol in the direction of the disturbance.

Too late.

He is blown off his feet as the bullet explodes through his shoulder. He hits the floor and instinctively rolls, trying to reach for the gun with his left hand.

The boot smashes into his face, breaking his nose and bringing him to the verge of unconsciousness. He rolls again, shaking his head and manages to get to his feet. He brings his eyes up, trying to refocus them. And comes face-to-face with Lærke.

She aims the gun at his head, and he smiles at her. Then she adjusts her aim and blows out his right kneecap.

He screams out in agony as he collapses, clutching his knee.

Lærke approaches him, then suddenly becomes aware of the two small pairs of eyes staring up at her in horror.

Well, it's too late to go back now, she thinks, as she stands over The Dutchman and blows out his other knee.

He lets out a loud wail, exhaling decades of violence and evil he had visited on the poor and vulnerable of the world.

Lærke kneels down over him, reeling from the vile stench coming from his mouth and body.

The bullet rips through her back and exits her chest, embedding itself into the face of The Dutchman.

Lærke arches her back and tumbles over onto the soft floor of the forest, her eyes fluttering as she stares into the face of The Devil.

The bullet carved into his cheek, and he lies there, trying to speak as he holds his shattered knees. Then Lærke hears a crackling sound from behind her. She tries to turn her body but the pain is too much.

She can feel herself passing out, and she fights the darkness, as a tall shadow falls over her.

Sigi kneels down and flips Lærke over, inspecting her wound.

"It seems to have missed your heart. But you will not last long."

"Wwhho...what–"

"–There were two others. It seems they were hunting the same targets we were. I took care of them. We need to move you fast. Your friend is OK. I will guide the children to her. The police and emergency services will take care of her. Is there somewhere I can take you?"

Lærke can feel her eyes closing, then a hard slap across her face brings her back.

"Where can I take you?" repeats Sigi.

Lærke reaches into the pocket of her cargo pants and pulls out her phone. She opens it up and pulls up the address of the *Airbnb* in Århus.

"That's a long way," says Sigi. "It's unlikely you will make it. So be it."

Sigi turns to face the prone Dutchman, pulls out her huge hunting knife, and quickly draws it across his throat. Then she reaches down and hauls up Lærke, lifting her into her arms and begins to carry her out of the forest.

She looks over her shoulder at the kids and nods at them to follow.

12 - DARK SUN

Strobing lights breaking the darkness. The soft vibration of a high performance vehicle. Falling in and out of consciousness.

Lærke lies on the back seat of the SUV. Sometimes she thinks she hears Icelandic. Snatches of conversation between the driver known as Sigi, and a man's deep rasping voice coming through the cabin's speaker. Then she passes out again.

The next time she wakes up it is light. She feels constricted. Like something is holding her down. Then the pain comes as she tries to adjust her position on the bed.

She focuses on the room. It seems vaguely familiar. Her senses begin to sharpen and she realises she's back in the *Airbnb* just outside Århus. But her chest feels so tight.

She tries to raise her head up, and can see a thick white bandage wrapped tightly round her body. She turns her head and sees a bottle of water, some pain killers, and two small vials of blue liquid on the bedside table.

She lifts herself up slowly, and leans over to grab the water, chugging it down in great gulps. She takes two attempts to swing her legs over the side of the bed, then looks down at the small note on the table, under the blue vials.

Use these. One a day. S.

Sigi. The giant Icelander.
That's how she got here. But where is she now?

Lærke tries to push herself out of the bed, but falls to her knees. The pain is too intense. She sits on the edge of the bed, catching her breath. She can see a red patch forming in the centre of her chest.

Then she looks at the blue vials on the bedside table.

What are they?

She reaches over and picks one up. It has a snap-off lid, so she pulls it off and then smells the liquid.

No scent.

Nothing to lose.

She knows she going to die soon anyway, so she empties it into her mouth, then collapses back onto the bed.

Wham!

What the fuck was that?

She feels a fizzing behind her eyes, then a charge of electricity shoots down her spine. She sits up in a jerking motion, ignoring the pain from her chest. Then realises there is no pain.

Now her synapses are firing like starbursts. She looks at her fingers and can suddenly feel her touch receptors as the air circulates round them. She tries to stand up and finds it's not a problem. She brings her hand to her chest wound and gently touches it. It feels like a dull pain, but she's mobile.

She picks up her phone and checks the time.

Jesus, it's late in the afternoon.

Then she pulls on her cargo pants and gets a clean shirt out of the suitcase she had left here. She makes a pitstop in the bathroom, and goes into the kitchen to make some coffee.

What am I doing, she thinks. *I need to get out of Denmark.*

She knows this drug, whatever it is, can't last for long. And she's only got one left. After that, then she may as well curl up in a ball and die.

Or turn herself in?

Perhaps they could save her.

Then what? Become a caged animal for the rest of her life. Paying for all the death she had visited on others. No, she will leave, now.

Fifteen minutes later, she's on the road south in her Tesla. She keeps the radio off and passes through Kolding on the E45. She notices that the weather has started to change. Gone is the late summer heatwave, giving way to a cooler brownish afternoon sunshine.

As the Tesla cruises along on *Autopilot*, she begins to notice the trees have started shedding their leaves.

Then she does something strange. She sets the navigation system for Tønder, and sits back as the car pulls off at the next available exit.

It winds its way south-west across the lush Jylland countryside, eventually coming into Tønder as the evening begins to set in. She takes over control of the car, just as a sharp pain hits her in the chest.

Dammit, that didn't last long, she thinks.

She's working on old memories now, driving through the town and heading for the marshes. Eventually, she sees an old landmark she remembers from her last visit here with Niki.

She pulls up onto the side of the small road, and lowers the passenger window. Then she twists her body awkwardly so she's looking out across the marsh.

The pain is getting stronger now, and she can feel the warmth of the blood seeping out of her wound.

Where are you?

There!

It starts with a small disturbance in the marsh. A small flock of birds shoot into the sky. Then more. And more!

Then *whoosh*!

Lærke watches as thousands of starlings begin their dance ritual, swooping across the early evening sky, creating the most amazing shapes. Their balletic flight path seemingly directed by a collective consciousness far beyond any mortal human's understanding.

She looks down at the last blue vial on the passenger seat. The pain is coming on strong now. Then she turns and looks at her strange face in the rear-view mirror.

Hello Lærke.

She smiles at herself.

Yes, this would be a good place to rest.

She picks up the second vial and empties it into her mouth, feeling the immediate impact on her senses.

She looks out across the marsh as vast swirling shapes glide across the skyline in front of her.

Pulling a blanket from the back seat, she wraps it around herself, and snuggles into the seat, and settles down to watch the show.

They found her there the next morning.

Her eyes were open, but she had long since passed away.

She had a faint smile of satisfaction on her lips. The local walkers had contacted the police, and it was quickly established that this was the German woman wanted in connection with the brutal murder of the British Venture Capitalist in his Copenhagen office one day ago.

Little else was released, other than her name.

Tilda.

EPILOGUE

Over the next four weeks, more details emerged about the gruesome spate of killings along the Sjælland coast on that warm, late summer evening.

Bekka had spent the first two weeks recovering in *Rigshospitalet*, ironically, just down the corridor from Lucas, whom she never met.

No connection was ever made by the investigators between the disappearance of The Professor on the farm in Jylland, and the murders on Fyn and in Copenhagen. However, a red thread was partially developed between the murder of the British VC in his Copenhagen office, and the kidnapping of Bekka's children, and her subsequent injuries.

Bekka underwent multiple interrogations at her hospital bedside, even as she underwent additional surgeries on her damaged leg. She made it clear that she had no idea why her husband would be targeted, nor why it would extend to her children.

She claimed that she had been blindfolded, and she had not seen any of her assailants. Fortunately for her, Anna, her sister, maintained her side of the story. Anna brought the children to their mother's bedside every day during her recovery period. After two weeks, Bekka was released from hospital and transferred back to the villa in Vedbæk, where her sister had made sleeping arrangements for her downstairs.

The first thing Bekka did was to put the house on the market. It was sold in two days, at a heavy discount, to a foreign couple who were seemingly oblivious to the shenanigans that had taken place a month prior in this usually idyllic part of the world.

Two months after the incident, Bekka was able to drive, and she packed the kids and their luggage into her *Cayenne* and set off for the south of France.

Despite constant pressure from the invasive press, she remained silent, committed to the protection of her children.

Lucas also made rapid progress on the road to recovery, although his emotional recovery was still a destination far off in the future.

He had lost his beloved wife.

Not only that, but the woman from his youth, whom he had looked up to as a surrogate mother, had exploded back into his life, and was somehow involved with his wife's death.

He could not reconcile those two facts, nor the smears that began to surface on social media about his wife's involvement in international military contracts.

Nikolaj visited his son every day, and eventually helped him back to the big empty house on the Funen coast. The rear terrace had still not been cleaned up, even after two months, and there were bloodstains everywhere.

The cops had trashed the place in their frantic search for more clues, and Lucas just spent half a day sitting on the sofa, staring sadly out of the window towards the *Storebælt*.

For his part, his father offered no new insights to his desperate son. He did not tell him that Lærke had visited him in his apartment on her final night in Copenhagen. What would be the point?

The best Nikolaj hoped for was that he could help his boy eventually move on from this devastating loss, and somehow come out the other end with something worth living for.

Nikolaj, of course, was fighting his own sadness. While he did not recognise her physically, the visit from Lærke that evening had offered him a straw to grasp, however unrealistic and brief it was. When he heard the news reports of the murderous goings on in the forest up the coast, he sat there, dreading the discovery of Lærke's body.

Or even worse, her arrest.

He kept well away from the story, although his media colleagues continued to hound him about progress of his son, and his son's connections to the violent goings on across the water in Fyn.

He told them to go fuck themselves.

In English.

He did not have to wait long for the news he dreaded.

Two days later, reports came in that the police had identified the body of the German industrialist, just outside Tønder, wanted in connection with the murder of the British VC.

No one made the connection to the person formally known as Lærke. Except for Lucas, who saw a photo of her a couple of weeks later. He did not broach the subject with his father. Lucas was a man after his father's own image. And he could see the sadness in his eyes at the arrival, then sudden loss of the woman he had loved.

It became a complicated no-mans zone for them as they sought to rebuild their relationship. Essentially, they avoided any discussion of what happened.

Nikolaj gradually got back into the groove of his weekly journalistic fistfights, although it was noted by many that he had become more serious and cynical. Yet his approval ratings continued to soar, especially with international audiences, who got off on his combative *Viking* communication style when taking on the the fraudsters and charlatans who had the misfortune to come within striking range of his verbal axe.

He had always harboured ambitions to write a novel. One of those Nordic noir jobs that seemed to swamp the airport bookstores. He knew that he sat on a goldmine of information in the form of the battered laptop belonging to The Professor, which he kept hidden in his apartment.

A couple of times he had delved deep into the files, using the passwords that Lærke had left him. He knew he could never use any of it for fear of putting his boy in harms way. But he had the beginnings of a story in his head.

One wintery day, as he sat outside in one of the Nyhavn cafés, under the heated lamps and wrapped in a complimentary blanket, he flipped open his *MacBook* and began typing.

The waitress came over with his big mug of coffee and an open sandwich, placing them on the table. Nikolaj looked up and vaguely recognised her. He thought she was the owner of the place.

"What are you working on?" asked Quantum Barb.

"I'm trying to get started with my first novel," he replied with a wry smile.

"Well, if it's anything like your TV shows, then I'm sure it will be a best seller!" she said.

"You know me?" asked Nikolaj, suddenly surprised.

"Of course! Everyone knows you. I'm sure you have some great information squirrelled away," she said, winking at him, before turning and heading back into the café.

Nikolaj watched her hustle back to her business, smiled to himself, then began attacking his keyboard.

She grips the wheel of the Audi as if she were hanging on for her life. Her white knuckles straining at the force she's applying.

Two hundred metres.

The border is coming up fast.

Twenty seven-years since she last crossed it.

That was going in the opposite direction in a plane. A violent trip.

One hundred metres.

She feels the cold sweat trickle down her back, and she presses herself into her seat, as if to delay the inevitable crossing.

Denmark.

The Chairman sits in her fat leather chair, puffing on a fat cigar. She moves the ice around in her tumbler of whiskey and checks her watch.

Eight-thirty in the morning. She's got a packed day ahead with multiple visits from fawning politicians, most of which need her help to get them off the hook for their latest mishaps. How she bores of these pathetic men, and they are mostly men, who spend their whole lives trying to maintain their position in the pecking order while offering so little service back to their constituents.

Still, leverage is leverage! And she's in it for the long game.

She's reviewing the most recent progress reports from the *Unit* operations. Since the fortunate demise of that vile Dutchman in Denmark some months ago, she had regained control over the assassination business, bringing it closer to the other, less violent, business activities of the CORP-ROUGUE organisation.

She was pleased to see that things were back to normal in the market, especially when it came to sparring with her old nemesis.

The half-Norwegian, half-Icelandic viking known as Naddador.

She knew he was making moves into the energy market across the northern seas. Yet so far, her subversive tentacles had not managed to get a grip on his plans.

Well, she's patient. And like all men, he will make a mistake. Then she will pounce.

She takes another puff, then buzzes her assistant to show in the Minister who had been caught dressing up in the wrong kind of clothes.

Jesus, it's going to be a long day.

The storm rages across the bay on Fugloy, and she watches from her kitchen as the rain lashes down onto the fjord.

She clasps her hot mug of coffee and listens to the crackling from the stone fireplace behind her. She's been here four days and she's expecting his call soon. It excites her, but at the same time she wishes she could just stay here forever. It's the closest she can get to her beloved Iceland.

She knows one day she must return, but not yet. She has much work to perform for her real *father*, Naddador, to bring into fruition his ambitious plans.

She walks to the door and opens it, embracing the howling wind that blasts into her small cottage. She braces her huge frame against the door, and looks down towards the tiny harbour.

For some reason, she thinks of a woman that she briefly knew. A mysterious woman of great strength, whom she had crossed paths with a few months ago.

Sigi raises her coffee mug and salutes the former assassin called Lærke, knowing that someday she will meet her again in the great halls of *Valhalla*.

ABOUT THE AUTHOR

Pat Halford is also the author of the Finnish thriller "North Karelian Boomerang", and the Icelandic thriller, "North to Akureyri". He lives and works in the Nordic region, building R&D technology consortia across corporates, research, startups and universities. He is also an expert at the Singularity Group, and a frequent international conference moderator, and advisor to VCs and startups.

Made in the USA
Columbia, SC
10 March 2024